THE BROKEN BELL

Alan Kennedy

LASSERRADE

Illustrations by John Johnstone

For Elizabeth

CONTENTS

THE BROKEN BELL

CHAPTER I

THE INJURED MAN

YOU could say that their French holiday began one day early in August, although they were certainly not in France at the time; in fact, it was a cloudy day, promising more rain.

The family was having a late breakfast in the cottage by the lake.

Poppy was kneeling on the window seat, pressing her nose against the glass, watching the boats come and go, wondering when Elizabeth would arrive, feeling impatient.

It was two days after the great storm.

*

There were boats everywhere that morning, buzzing about Uncle Albert's battered old trawler, the *Arethusa* – the one place where he could work at his painting in peace.

The plan was for Daddy and the other men to help tow her away from the shore and out of danger.

Mother had been asking whether anyone wanted to finish the very last of the toast when she looked up at the rattle of rain against the window.

"Not more rain surely? There's been enough for a whole year."

Then came Elizabeth's cheery knock on the door and Daddy called out "Hello, hello, come in whoever you are," although he looked as if he knew very well who was there.

Elizabeth stumbled in, bringing a gust of damp air with her, but laughing in spite of everything and shaking raindrops out of her hair. She was still trying to catch her breath after running all the way up the cliff path.

Mother pointed to the teapot with the knife she had used to butter the toast, but Elizabeth shook her head.

"No, thank you very much. I've had lashings and lashings of breakfast already. Uncle said he wanted a decent breakfast

1

because he was feeling thin and some night raiders had eaten everything on board."

She grinned at Poppy. "Yes, I know. He doesn't look all that thin."

"And I don't think we raided him, either," said Ian, "he said it was salvage and Daddy agreed. Anyway if it hadn't been for Laura ..."

He stopped and saw Mother glance across to where Laura was sitting. Perhaps it was best not to talk about that; Laura had done more than any of them to save the boat in the storm. All the same, she had been very frightened.

Elizabeth went to the window and stood looking across the lake, beyond the stranded boat, to the outline of a dark stone tower that seemed to grow out of sandy cliffs stretching into the lake. They heard her murmur to herself.

"You do have a grand view from here ..."

Mother laughed out loud.

"You know, it's not at all hard to read thoughts sometimes."

Poppy looked up.

"It will only be to see what it's like."

She didn't have to explain. After all, they'd been planning it for ages. Everybody knew she was talking about their first expedition to the old tower at the end of the lake. They had camped there for more years than they could remember. But there had been so much rain this year the whole lake was flooded. Perhaps the camp site had been washed away? They simply had to find out.

"Just to reconnoitre," said Stuart, "then, if it's not too bad, we could take the tents and things across tomorrow ..."

He stopped, seeing Daddy's expression change.

"That's alright isn't it?" Elizabeth was nodding, but no one spoke and he went on.

"Anyway, it can't hurt to go and see ... it won't take very long ..."

Mother was looking thoughtful.

"Are you sure? Do you have to go today, in all this rain? It's going to be awfully wet everywhere."

"It's fun in a tent in the rain," said Ian." Then he added, "When we have the tents, that is."

Mother just smiled and started to gather up the teacups.

Daddy stayed sitting quietly in his favourite chair by the window. He was smiling at Elizabeth.

"What interests me is how exactly you aim to get to your precious tower? You can't do it from the road. The causeway is flooded after all this rain. Don't you go trying to sail over that until you know how deep it is. I don't want you losing the bottom of your boat." He looked at Mother.

"I suppose we could spare one or two of them, but I'd be sorry if the whole lot went off to join Davy Jones."

"We wouldn't do that," protested Poppy, "anyway, he wasn't an explorer. We're explorers."

"You're not explorers yet. I still want to know how you'll get there."

"We'll have to climb the cliff path I suppose ... that's the only way ... there's nothing else for it," said Elizabeth, then rushed on, before he could say anything.

"Just Stuart and me first, of course. To check that it's safe. Once we're up there we can solve the causeway problem."

Daddy looked very uncertain.

"Well, at least the rain's stopped. I suppose the weather might hold, but you'll have no sun today. You should just take the one boat for this trip. Which one has the shallowest draft?"

And when Daddy said that, everyone knew he was really saying yes.

*

From then on the morning was rather a muddle. Mother decided Poppy should change her sandals for a pair of Wellingtons. Then there were sandwiches to be made, although no one could make up their mind what they wanted, because no one was really thinking about sandwiches at all.

Then, just when they were nearly ready, Daddy remembered he had to find something they needed on the old boat. So they sat waiting for him as patiently as they could, with Stuart restlessly pacing up and down, looking at his watch and checking the weather through the window.

Daddy came back at last carrying a wooden pulley and wiping his hands on a cloth.

"Well, have you worked out which one it is? Which boat has the shallowest draft?" He smiled at Stuart.

"If you can't say, you're not going."

"It's mine, of course" said Elizabeth. "When *Fairway* has her centreboard up she draws lots less than *Kingfisher*."

So, later than they had expected - and much later than Stuart had hoped – the expedition set out down the cliff path to the lake.

There was no need to launch *Fairway*. With so little beach left after the rains, she was already half afloat. Elizabeth took the helm, with Stuart and Laura side by side amidships and Poppy squeezed before the mast with Ian.

They looked back and waved to Daddy standing at the foot of the cliff, waiting for somebody to come and row him across for his day's work on the *Arethusa*.

There was no wind in the lee of the cliffs and the sails took their time before they stiffened in the breeze and the loaded boat heeled over to meet it. Elizabeth said what they were all thinking.

"It's good to get away from grown-ups." She grinned across at Stuart.

"Even the best ones. Don't worry, they're all like that, you know. Mine are just the same." She held out her hand looking up at the sky.

"I think I felt a spot. We've escaped just in time. I'm not sure the rain will hold off after all."

Laura started to pull out the bag with the waterproofs.

*

It ought to have been easy. After all, Stuart had climbed the steep path up to the camp site lots of times before. Elizabeth brought them as close to the shore as she dared, anxiously scanning along the foot of the cliff until she spotted the flooded remains of the old landing place.

She started to signal to Stuart, but he had already reached down and passed the painter to Ian. Poppy leaned over the side and dipped one hand gingerly into the water.

"It's more of a mud bath than a lake. I wouldn't like to go swimming in this. You can't even see the bottom."

"It's alright," said Elizabeth, "there aren't any rocks here. That's all that matters." She reached across to Ian.

"It's going to be pretty beastly wading through all this stuff. Give me the painter. It's only the two of us going up. You can keep dry."

But she was too late. Ian had already hopped over the side and was standing, shivering slightly, knee-deep in chilly water.

"Gosh, it's deep," said Laura, biting her lip.

"Have you got a good foothold? Mind your step. Don't go and fall over. I think you would have been better taking your sandals off."

Stuart was about to jump overboard. He hesitated a second, looking at Laura. She was anxiously stretching a hand out to Ian. You could never tell with Laura, she looked almost ready to say it was better they came back another day.

He pulled his shoes off as quickly as he could, tied the laces together, and hung them round his neck. Then he was over the side, wading to the bank before Elizabeth had even got her shoes untied.

"What's the rush?" she shouted, "half a second … I have to see to my shoes."

But Stuart was already pulling himself onto the bank, cheerily calling back, "It's alright, I know the way."

She was left hanging over the side of the boat watching his legs disappear up the steep slope between the trees.

*

It was true he was hurrying just a little bit, but he'd climbed up the path to the tower before. It wasn't as if he didn't know the way. Anyway, they had lost so much time already that morning, it was worth pushing on.

He came to a little pool of water on the path and as he tried not to step into it he saw a frog diving down to hide under some leaves. The green sort with long legs. He looked back to see whether Elizabeth was behind, wondering whether the frog would still be there for her to see. It was quite a big one.

As he stepped over the pool he felt his foot sink into soft sand and he grabbed a branch to steady himself. But it wasn't a branch at all; it was just a bit of broken stick that came away in his hand and he found himself tottering back on one leg desperately reaching out to find something else to grab. There was nothing.

He twisted round, caught a curious glimpse of his heels sliding forward, and found himself leaning back into empty space.

For a second, a canopy of leaves went spinning over his head then he hit the path with a thump, skidded on his back for a moment and toppled over the edge into a mass of gorse.

The drop was only a few feet, and it was bad luck he landed so awkwardly on his arm. Otherwise, he didn't hurt at all; it was just that he was hanging upside down, peering out through a tangle of prickly green.

So long as he stayed still and avoided the thorns it was perfectly alright. He felt almost like laughing. But that was before he realised he could not get out on his own. Every effort to right himself brought a jab of pain in his arm.

He heard Elizabeth's shout and had an upside down view of her splashing across towards him. Although it didn't seem very dignified, there was nothing for it but to hang there and wait to be rescued.

*

All that the others heard of the fall was a funny kind of slithering noise and a sharp sound like wood cracking. Then a pair of shoes, still tied together, suddenly splashed into the water next to the boat. At the same time, something heavy fell into a gorse bush at the foot of the cliff.

At first, they thought Stuart had knocked a stone down. But no one could see him at all. He was not on the path anymore. Instead there was a voice, a bit muffled but very like Stuart's, coming out of a bush and saying, "I'm alright … I'm alright … silly really … I slipped …"

Laura squeaked with alarm and jumped up, holding the mast and leaning out as far as she could. A strange tangle of legs was waving out of a gorse bush at the water's edge.

"He's fallen in," said Poppy.

"That's torn it," said Elizabeth, almost to herself, then she shouted, "hang on, Stuart, I'm coming," and jumped feet-first into the water, one shoe on and one shoe off.

She splashed her way to the rescue, leaving the others bouncing about as *Fairway* lurched from side to side.

Laura screamed, "Is he alright?" She was looking round frantically.

"I can see a shoe," said Poppy.

She leaned over and grabbed something floating in the water and pulled it out, dragging the other shoe with it and emptied them into the lake.

"I don't think they'll come to any harm. We can dry them out. It's a good job he tied them together."

But Laura was not thinking about shoes. She was desperate to join Elizabeth in the rescue, but that would mean leaving Poppy alone in the boat. She dared not do that.

Stuart's voice came out of the bush again, sounding quite cheerful.

"I'm alright Laura. At least, I think I am. My arm hurts a bit. I slipped. Somebody will have to pull me out. I can't get a hold."

She saw an arm come up and try to push a branch aside.

"Ouch! It's no good. I've really twisted my arm. I landed on it. And I've lost my shoes."

If you have to fall into a bush, a gorse bush is positively the worst kind to chose. By the time she had pulled him out, Elizabeth was almost as scratched as Stuart. He limped barefooted down the bank and winced as he stepped into the water.

"I saw a frog," he said. He was going to explain more about the frog; then he saw the look in Laura's face.

They helped him gently into the boat and Poppy leaned over him.

"You've probably broken your arm. You should stretch out on your back. That's what they do in hospital. I've seen pictures of that. You'll have to have it put in plaster of Paris."

"Oh, do shut up Poppy!" Laura shouted. "You don't know it's that bad at all."

Everyone stopped talking. They had heard Elizabeth say 'that's torn it.' For the first time that morning, they wondered what Mummy was going to say.

*

They decided the path from the beach up to the cottage would be impossible with the injured man, so Elizabeth brought the boat as far as the bay and waited while they all disembarked.

She watched for a moment as they slowly made their way along the road then let the sail out and set a course for the cliffs below the cottage, calling out, "I'll wait at the foot of the cliff until you get back along the road."

Laura waved as if to say yes - Mother would be worried if she saw only one of them coming back.

Ian and Poppy took it in turns to hold Stuart's good arm, but neither of them was really tall enough to be much help and in any case he was keen to manage on his own.

He was thinking perhaps Mother needn't know he had slipped, although now his heart had stopped thumping the arm had started to hurt quite a lot. He would have to explain about the arm.

The sight of him limping in from the road brought Mother running out to meet them. Stuart was a sorry sight - his legs and arms covered in scratches and his shirt and trousers torn. And he was nursing his arm.

Any idea of keeping the worst from Mother vanished with Poppy's cry of, "Stuart's broken his arm! At least I think he has."

After that, no one paid much attention to either Ian or Poppy. Mother gave a little cry of alarm, ran to the gate and helped Stuart into the house. Ian tried to help, but somehow always seemed to be in the wrong place. He jumped out of the way to let her hold Stuart as he limped painfully up the steps onto the porch. Then he was shooed out of the living room to make room as Mother sat the patient down and took his shirt off.

Elizabeth, who had walked up the cliff path thinking dark thoughts, stood watching at the open door. Poppy, offered to carry the bowl of hot water and the towel, but Laura was already carrying them in from the kitchen and pushed her to one side as she rushed past.

In the end, Ian went outside and stood on the porch steps. After a while Poppy came out and joined him.

"I suppose we should just let everybody get on without us," he said.

She settled down on the top step with her legs drawn up and started reading her book, but it was hard to concentrate. She looked up at him and gave a little nod towards the living room window. "It's no use trying to help. They don't want us."

She pulled him down to sit beside her. "What do you think they'll say?"

"I don't know. No one will say anything. Mother's in a dreadful stew. It's worse with Daddy being away checking moorings and things. Elizabeth offered to sail across and fetch him and Mother shouted 'No, you're to stay right where you are, my girl' in a really loud voice. It sounded quite fierce. Then she said sorry and asked Elizabeth if she would please go and stand by the gate to watch for the doctor. It was funny in a way: Elizabeth went as good as gold. She didn't even give one of her looks."

Poppy was trying to sound solemn, "It's what I said. He'll need one of those white plaster things."

"No one's going to do anything about eating," said Ian, "that's obvious. And it's getting really late. I only had an egg for breakfast."

*

When they heard the doctor's car they both ran down the path to meet him. Elizabeth pulled the gate open and was about to say something, but he just nodded and bustled by without even stopping to say hello. She ran along behind him, trying to keep up.

"It's not the usual doctor," Ian whispered, "remember, the other one always had humbugs in a paper packet."

"And he'd say 'Take your pick, children' although there was nothing to pick. They were all the same."

"Very nice though."

There had been a chatter of voices from inside the house when the doctor had first arrived. Now the noise suddenly stopped. All they could hear was the muffled sound of the doctor asking questions and Stuart answering, mostly saying yes or no, although they heard him say 'Ouch' once. After that there was silence.

Elizabeth had followed the doctor up the steps and gone indoors. She came out and sank down heavily on the step next to Ian.

"I don't think it's broken. He made Stuart lift it this way and that and he managed it all pretty well. He couldn't have done that if it was really broken."

She suddenly lowered her voice and the others instinctively leaned towards her.

"It's not good news, though. Your mother says he shouldn't have been climbing like that up a cliff."

"It's not a cliff," protested Ian, "it's a path. Just a path. We've been up it lots of times. It's nobody's fault the rain made it slippy … I mean to say, a bit slippy."

Elizabeth put her finger to her lips and they drew closer.

"It gets worse," she whispered, "Laura agreed! At least, she sort of nodded. Do you know what? I think they're going to stop us going to the tower."

"Oh, no!" Poppy shouted. "They can't do that! What about the camp?" She jumped up. "I'll go and explain to Mummy. He just slipped. Anybody can slip. And he isn't hurt at all. Well, not much. I'll go and explain."

"Best not," said Elizabeth, hanging onto her arm and pulling her back. "Best wait until the doctor's finished."

The three of them sat on the top step gazing out over the lake in mutinous silence until they had to jump out of the way to let Mother by. She walked with the doctor round the cottage to the iron gate and stood there for a second talking to him in a low voice. As the car drew away, they heard her shout, "Thank you very much," in quite a cheerful way.

But when she came back she was not smiling. They could see she was in no mood to smile at all.

"Well, the news is very good," she said, "and that's a mercy. Things could have been much worse. The doctor says Stuart's arm is badly twisted, but it's not broken. He'll have to wear it in a sling for a while, that's all. He has one or two cuts and a big bruise. But he'll live to tell the tale." She did her best to laugh.

"I simply don't know what next is going to happen this year."

"What's a sling?" asked Ian. Then, without waiting for a reply, added, "and what about the camp?"

Elizabeth shot him a warning look, but it was too late, the words were out. Mother seemed not to hear. He tried again.

"We can still go camping, can't we? You said we could."

But she had already turned to go inside, calling over her shoulder, "You'd better let me have a look at those scratches, Elizabeth."

Elizabeth waited until she had gone. "I told you things looked grim. It looks like camping's out … for a while, anyway. We'll have to settle for you staying here and me over at the Mill."

Poppy stared at her, horrified, and started to say something, but Elizabeth rushed on.

"That's not so bad. There's still plenty we can do. We've still got the boats. Even if we can't camp, we've still got the boats."

Then she heard Mother calling and ran up the steps, shouting, "Just coming." She turned for a second and looked back at Ian.

"Cheer up. It's not so bad. We've still got the boats, remember."

CHAPTER II

A KNOCK AT THE DOOR

"WE'VE still got the boats, remember," said Elizabeth, as she went inside for Mother to see to the scratches on her arms.

But even that turned out not to be true.

When Daddy got back from working on the boat in the bay Mother took him outside and the two of them walked up and down in the little garden talking together for a long time.

When they came back in, Daddy went straight upstairs to sit with Stuart. Mother went into the kitchen and closed the door. They heard her preparing the supper and looked at each other wide-eyed. Mother never closed the door.

"It's a sign," said Poppy darkly, but no one replied.

Later that evening, Poppy and Ian were sitting with Elizabeth in their favourite place on the porch steps. They were catching the last of the light.

They had eaten a rather silent meal, lost in their own thoughts: thoughts of the injured Stuart trying to sleep upstairs.

Daddy came outside and sat down on the steps beside them. They knew at once that something was wrong.

"We managed to sort out that second mooring line ..." He looked at Elizabeth.

"Your uncle's boat had a close shave you know. But ..."

He paused, suddenly looking very uncomfortable.

"But that's not what I wanted to say. I'm afraid the men from the Boatyard brought some bad news."

"His boat's not going to sink is it?" asked Poppy. "I'm sure Laura didn't hit anything. You can ask her."

"No, no, it's nothing like that. It's just that they have been surveying the lake. There's a lot of debris in the water. Logs of wood ... that sort of thing ..."

He stopped, shuffling awkwardly and fumbling in his pocket for his pipe. He took a long time to light it.

"Oh, we saw lots of that," said Ian, breaking the silence, "you mean brushwood and stuff floating about?"

"Yes, that's it." He stood up, suddenly looking very serious.

"Look, it's no use beating about the bush. They've asked us to keep off the lake. That is … no sailing. I'm to ask you …" He stopped, pulling on his pipe, "… Well, tell you really, because that's the message from the policeman. I'm afraid there's to be no sailing. No sailing at all until the flood waters have gone down."

"But that will be weeks and weeks," Ian shouted.

"Oh, no!" Poppy grabbed his arm. "That would mean no holiday. We can't have a holiday with no sailing. Oh, no!"

She got up, ran down the steps and stood with her back to them, breathing hard.

Daddy tried to put his arm round her shoulders, but she pulled away. They heard him mumble, "I'm sorry. I really am very sorry."

Then he went inside.

*

After Mother had tucked the injured Stuart up in bed, he lay thinking about the frog for the hundredth time. If he had not seen that frog he would never have slipped. If only he'd waited for Elizabeth. If only they had all climbed up together and spent a perfectly normal day and come home hungry with nothing much exciting to talk about.

When the doctor had gone, Mother came upstairs to sit with him. She pushed the door closed and sat down at the foot of his bed. For a long time she just looked at him. The same look Laura had when she was trying her very best not to cry. He had not thought about it before, but grown-ups never seemed to cry.

He pulled himself up in the bed, wincing a little, and tried to smile. But Mother didn't smile back.

"Well, it's not broken at all. That's one good thing."

She stopped and sat looking out of the window for a long time.

"You know, Daddy can't stay very long. Captains can't take a holiday from their ship whenever they feel like it. He only came because of the floods and he didn't know how we would cope. He must get back to his ship. But I have to talk about all this with him before he goes."

She stopped again and leaned over to straighten the cover on his bed. He could see she was making up her mind to say something. Suddenly his heart turned over. He knew what was coming. He'd really known ever since the doctor arrived.

"Look Stuart, I think we should all go home ... now the flood is going down a bit, there's a train every day ..."

He gulped and tried to think of something to say, tears starting up in his own eyes.

She ran her hand through his hair, "... No, let me finish. You're the oldest, that's why I'm explaining things to you."

She got up and went over to the window and stood there for a moment while he found a handkerchief and blew his nose.

"We can always come back, of course. But think about it - you have to rest your arm. You can't go running around with your arm in a sling. Certainly no camping - that's what the doctor said. You must see I can't let the others go off on their own. Daddy's been and looked. He says the only way to the tower is up that path. It's dangerous..."

Stuart started to protest, but she shook her head.

"No, hear me out. I know it was an accident. But if you can slip, so can Ian or Poppy. Even Laura. Just think about it - it's too dangerous."

"Elizabeth said she'd worked out a way of getting across the causeway. She did a drawing. We were going to show it to Daddy."

Stuart could see Mummy was not even listening properly. She sat down on his bed and took his hand.

"I was going to tell you. The Constable was over at Mr Bradley's boat this afternoon, talking to Daddy. While you were all away. He says there's to be no more sailing on the lake until the flood waters have gone right down ..." She saw the look in his face.

"No, it's nothing to do with you falling. Nothing at all. It's just that with all these floods, and then the storm, the lake is full of logs and things. If one of your little boats hits something like that you could sink."

She sat looking at him, waiting for him to say something. He shifted on his pillow and for a moment was so lost in misery the little stab of pain from his arm seemed far away.

Mother watched as sad thoughts chased themselves across his face.

"I really am very sorry Stuart, but it might be for the best. Daddy has to get back to his ship, you know that. And I've been thinking how we could perhaps all go together with him. Make a proper expedition of it. That would be nice, wouldn't it?"

Stuart was looking down, trying to straighten the sheet across his legs. He didn't lift his head.

She stood up and said, as brightly as she could, "Now, what would you like for your supper? You'd better stay here the rest of the day. I'll bring you a tray. What about something hot? Is there anything you would like?"

She went over to the window. The rain had started again, pattering against the glass. She tried to laugh.

"Honestly, you're not going to miss much this year. Here's the rain again."

But Stuart said nothing. He could think of nothing to say.

*

Later on, when he had finished his tea, the others came crowding into his bedroom. Ian sat down on the bed, bouncing up and down, until Poppy pulled him off.

"Mother said you could have visitors," she said, "a bit like in hospital. But you're not to have a plaster." She was trying her very best not to sound disappointed.

"You'll be as right as rain in no time," said Elizabeth.

Laura stood silent and miserable at the back of the group looking at Stuart propped up in bed. Today had been a catastrophe. Even before the doctor arrived she had known their holiday was over.

Elizabeth grinned at her.

"Why the long face? Something will turn up, you'll see. It always does."

"Not this time. Mother says we have to go home."

She let the dreadful words hang there. Stuart looked up, but said nothing.

"But here's home," shouted Ian, "and I don't want to go anywhere else. Why have I got to go home? It's Stuart's arm that got hurt. There's nothing wrong with my arm. It's not fair."

"She's made her mind up," said Laura, "I know when she's like that."

"It's all these things happening at the same time. They just got on top of her," said Poppy. She was looking at Elizabeth. She felt she should excuse Mother. "Sometimes grown-ups are like that, they can't help it."

Suddenly no one could think of anything to say. Elizabeth broke the silence.

"I wasn't going to tell you this, because I'm not sure what it means, but Uncle was talking to the men from the Boatyard about the storm. They didn't want me to know, but I wormed it out of them. That's about all I can say. They kept winking at each other and grinning. They didn't want to tell me anything."

"Anything about what?" said Stuart.

"Uncle's planning something. I just know he is. They said he kept looking at that box where Laura found the anchor. Then he said something, but they wouldn't tell me what. They just laughed and said 'You wait and see, you'll find out.' That's all I know."

"He was probably wondering how the anchor got stuck," said Laura, looking hard at Elizabeth. "But you weren't there, and anyway I didn't do anything except push the anchor over the side. Nothing special."

Elizabeth shook her head.

"Don't you go saying it was nothing. Uncle's jolly grateful to you. And so he should be. You saved his boat for him."

"And all his pictures," said Poppy. "Don't forget his pictures. I suppose he would have been sorry to lose them after painting them."

"But planning what?" said Stuart, who was starting to get a headache, "I'm sure Mother's not going to change her mind, if that's what you're thinking."

He tried to shuffle down into his bed and winced as his arm caught the pillow.

"If only I hadn't spotted that frog."

"You don't suppose he's going to get the motor in the boat going?" asked Ian. "If he did, we could go on a voyage round the lake. I'd like that."

But Elizabeth shook her head.

"The *Arethusa* doesn't even have an engine anymore. It was taken out years ago. She can't go anywhere unless you tow her. So it can't be that. But just you wait and see. I know him. When he sets his mind to something, he's pretty good."

Mother came bustling into the room.

"There's too much of a crowd in here. Come on, let the patient get a bit of rest." She turned to Elizabeth.

"That's Mr Grice back again. He says he can tow your boat across the lake to the Mill if you're quick about it. The light's going fast."

Elizabeth went very red. The thought of *Fairway* being towed behind the policeman's little motor boat was too humiliating to contemplate. She stood there, filled with black defiant thoughts, not knowing what to say. Mother smiled.

"Although you're more than welcome to stay here for the night if you like. There's a spare bed in Laura's room if you don't mind sharing. I can ask Mr Grice to take a message to your mother. What do you say? The bed's made up ready."

Poppy grabbed her arm. "Yes, do stay."

Elizabeth suddenly remembered it wasn't very polite standing there thinking harsh things about Mr Grice's boat.

"That would be lovely," she said, "thank you very much."

*

Much later that evening Stuart lay in bed looking wearily through the window. The sun was about to set and the room was filled with a soft red light. He usually liked the sunset, but it seemed strangely gloomy tonight.

His arm had stopped hurting so long as he kept it in one position. He would have to sleep on his back tonight, but that was alright – he was very tired.

That evening there was none of the usual cheerful chatter from downstairs. Just the clink of plates as Mummy cleared the table and the occasional echo of footsteps across the hallway. It was not nice at all lying in bed like this, knowing everybody downstairs was keeping quiet on his account.

He might have been asleep for a second, but he remembered waking to the sound of a knock at the door downstairs. The door at the front of the cottage that nobody ever used. And not a quiet knock at that – a very solid rat-a-tat.

There was the scrape of Daddy's chair on the floorboards and footsteps across the hall. Then the muffled sound of voices and people moving about.

There suddenly seemed to be voices everywhere. The cottage was alive with whispers. People moving about on tiptoe and doors opening the way they are opened so as not to wake you up.

Once, he heard Daddy laugh out loud and Mummy say 'shush,' then laugh herself. And there was another voice, almost familiar, but he felt too drowsy to bother whose it was. Anyway, why were people laughing when everything was so miserable?

He slipped back into an uncomfortable sleep, sitting up and listening to the endless voices whispering away.

*

It was the lamplight that woke Stuart. Somebody was opening his bedroom door very quietly. A beam of yellow light fell across his face. Mother's voice, whispering.

"He's awake I think." She came over and sat on the side of his bed.

"I thought you might have dropped off. Would you like some more visitors?"

For some reason she looked very cheerful. She was smiling.

"Who is it? I could hear Elizabeth and Laura talking for ages, but they've stopped now. Is it Daddy?"

She pulled the door open wide. Daddy and new Uncle Albert shuffled in. The two of them together seemed to fill the little room. They stood there looking a little awkward but very pleased with themselves.

Stuart tried to push himself up in bed then fell back. Mummy gave him a little pull and plumped the pillows behind his back.

Daddy perched himself on the end of the bed.

"Mr Bradley has suggested something very exciting ..."

For a second Stuart wondered who Mr Bradley was, then Uncle Albert winked at him and gave a little nod as if to say, that's me.

"Why don't I explain?" he said. "Then if you want to blow the whole idea out of the water it can be my fault."

He crouched down next to Stuart's bed and went on in a low voice.

"Best not wake the house. It's like this. I almost never spend summer up here on the lake. This is the first time in twenty years or more I should think. I'm always away in France. I'm only here this year because of that awful problem with my boat." He grinned at Stuart.

"But I don't need to tell you about that. You know more than I do, I imagine, because there's still a story to be told about that night ... now, where was I? Yes ... well I have to get back in a few days. On Saturday, to be precise. What I've suggested is that I take a bunch of explorers back with me. My house is big enough. And I think you'll find it interesting ... " He chuckled.

"And one thing I can promise you - it won't rain. Because we never get more than a couple of spots at this time of the year."

He looked at Stuart, waiting for a response.

"So that's the proposition. A holiday in France. What do you think?"

Stuart sat up in bed, his heart pounding, but he could not think what to say.

Uncle Albert glanced round anxiously at the others.

"After all, I owe your four my boat ... if Laura hadn't been there and got that anchor overboard, I'd have lost the lot for sure."

He looked down at Stuart.

"It's the least I can offer ... if you like the idea, that is ..."

"We think it's wonderful! It's a wonderful idea!" It was Elizabeth's voice. Two figures in pyjamas were standing in the doorway.

"Don't we Laura?"

Mother started to shoo them out.

"What on earth are you two doing out of bed? And neither of you with anything on your feet."

But Daddy got up and closed the door behind them.

"They're welcome to stay. But cold feet is what you get for listening at keyholes."

"The door was open," protested Laura, "and there isn't a keyhole." But when she saw Daddy was smiling the two of them shuffled onto the carpet as the next best thing to slippers.

Uncle Albert was still looking at Stuart.

"Well, what do you think? Do you feel up to it? It's a long way, I must say. But you've a few days yet to recover ..." He turned to Elizabeth.

"And you've made the trip before. We'll have to ask your mother of course, but since she'll be wanted on the voyage I dare say she'll say yes. Your father's still in Paris, helping sell my paintings. I'll write and tell him what's going on. He needn't come back here. It's time he had a holiday – I'll jolly well make him turn South and visit us."

Elizabeth's face lit up. She turned to Stuart.

"I told you he'd come up with something. But this is the best ever. France. And all of us. It's wonderful!"

"Not quite all of us," said Daddy, "I have a ship to get back to, remember. I'm not on holiday." He sat on the end of the bed.

"You're awfully quiet, Stuart. You haven't said what you think of the idea. I'm really very sorry about the trip to your tower ... but there's always another year for that."

Stuart felt a little dizzy. He had been almost asleep. Then all these people had appeared crowding into his bedroom, looming over him.

He looked at Elizabeth, grinning from ear to ear, tugging at Uncle Albert's arm, asking him about trains. He suddenly felt very tired and very happy all at the same time. He smiled, almost to himself, and nodded his head.

"Yes, please. I think it's a splendid idea."

*

It was barely dawn when Stuart woke up. He had decided to wriggle down in bed, forgetting about his arm. A familiar jab of pain had interrupted a very muddled dream about people running about in his room in the middle of the night. Why on earth had he been dreaming about Uncle Albert?

He pushed himself up onto his pillow, pulling the rumpled sling into shape. Then he remembered Laura and Elizabeth had been in the dream. And Mummy and Daddy as well. In fact, a room-full of faces all talking in the dead of the night.

He looked across at the window. A little cold sunlight was filtering round the curtains, spilling onto the floor. It must be dreadfully early. The house downstairs was quite still.

Mother had left a glass of water by his bedside. He drank it down in one go, realising he was very thirsty. But the headache of yesterday had gone and his arm only hurt if he stretched it. The bruise on his back didn't hurt anymore. All in all, he felt so very much better it was hard not to smile.

As soon as he heard Mother moving about downstairs he would get up and have his breakfast with the others. He thought how she had tried not to cry when she explained how they all had to go home. It was really very odd - they had to go home, but somehow it didn't seem to matter anymore.

There were footsteps creeping past his room. It was Elizabeth. She had been making good progress tiptoeing past his door when she had tripped and fallen against it with a thump. There was a ripple of barely stifled giggles. Stuart grinned to himself. Laura must be there as well.

The stairs creaked as the two of them crept down and made their way into the kitchen. He heard the clink of teacups and the rattle of cutlery; and above it all an excited chatter of whispers. They seemed very cheerful. He slipped down a little into the warmth of the bed, feeling snug and comfortable.

Why was Elizabeth here? Why had she not gone home? He'd forgotten. And why did he feel so content, just happily lying here, in a comfortable warm glow? He let thoughts slowly stitch themselves together in his head. He remembered the tilt of the yellow light from the lamp in Mother's hand and the shadows dancing on the bedroom wall. That wasn't a dream. And if that had really happened, Mother must have been there. Perhaps it hadn't been a dream at all.

He lay quite still, barely daring to move. Something was there; something wonderful, lurking at the far edge of his thoughts, just waiting for him. He sat up in bed, ignoring the twinge of pain, his heart thumping like a steam engine as he remembered.

They were going to France! Uncle Albert was going to take them to France.

*

But there was no sign of Uncle Albert when Stuart went down to breakfast. Mother was setting things out on a tray as he limped into the kitchen.

"I was going to let you have breakfast in bed, but it's just as well you're up. We're all at sixes and sevens this morning. You can help and carry your cup through - you've one good hand at least. Go and sit down. I'll bring the other things."

Ian was sitting at the end of the table earnestly trying to cut the top off his boiled egg. He collected runny egg from the side of the shell with his finger and licked it off, grinning up at Stuart.

"Mummy said I had to do it myself. And she said Poppy was making too much noise so she's been sent into the garden to do her celebration dance."

He glanced towards the kitchen and lowered his voice to an urgent whisper.

"It is true, isn't it? What Daddy said about France, I mean. It's not all pretend? We're really going to France?" Ian wasn't at all sure how far that was, but the way Poppy talked about it, France seemed like somewhere an awfully long way away.

Stuart nodded. "Trust Elizabeth to come up with something. Where is she?"

"With Laura and Daddy in the shed. They're looking for suitcases. We can't take boxes on the train."

Mother came hurrying in, carrying a plate of toast and a teapot.

"Finish up as quickly as you can Ian, we need a bit of space in here. You can take your breakfast outside if you like."

Ian buttered a last bit of toast, piled it onto his plate, perched the egg cup next to it and carried the whole lot across to the door. He pulled it open with his foot and looked back at Stuart.

"Coming?"

"Stuart's alright here for a minute," said Mother, "you go on."

They watched Ian walk out onto the porch and lower himself onto the step, balancing his breakfast precariously on his knees. Mother sat down at the table close to Stuart.

"There's something I ought to explain." She got up and closed the door onto the porch. Stuart suddenly felt very anxious.

"Everything was arranged so quickly last night I hardly had time to think. I like Elizabeth's uncle very much, but he does rather rush you off your feet."

She was watching Elizabeth through the window, brushing a pile of cases and laughing as she knocked cobwebs out of her hair.

"In fact they're two of a kind, really."

Stuart could see Mother was working herself up to say something. He felt his spirits sink. But she smiled at him and patted the back of his hand.

"I know what you're thinking. No, it's not that. I said yes and yes it will be ... and Daddy said yes as well. But I must say, there is a problem." Stuart looked up, preparing for the worst.

"No, don't get upset ... it's just that I won't be able to travel with you ... that's all ... not if you're to go on Saturday - and Mr Bradley says that can't be changed. Daddy and I have to close up the cottage here and I have to wait to see him off. And then I have to go back South and see to things at home. What it all means is I can't possibly come at the same time as you."

She saw the look in his face and hurried on.

"But there's nothing at all to worry about. I'll be coming out to join you just as soon as I get things straight. A few days; a week at the most. And I think Elizabeth's father will be coming as well, so it will end up as quite a house-full. I must say, the thought of a bit of sunshine is very appealing."

"But you mean we're to go on our own?"

"Not exactly on your own. Mr Bradley – I mean your new Uncle Albert – is taking Ian and Poppy on the night train with him on Saturday. You and Laura will be going a couple of days later with Elizabeth and her mother." Mother chuckled quietly to herself.

"Apparently she said she was very happy to go and she was more than used to Uncle Albert's surprises. But she needed more than a day to arrange an expedition abroad - I'm not surprised!"

The relief was so evident in his face that she laughed out loud.

"So there you are, you see - you'll get on perfectly well without me."

She was suddenly serious. "But you must promise me one thing. You must promise to be good. You'll be in somebody else's house, remember. And you and Laura must look after the other two."

"I promise."

The door burst open and Elizabeth backed in, carrying one end of a huge suitcase. Laura, at the other end, caught the look in Stuart's face.

"Promise what?"

"Never mind now," said Mother, "Stuart will explain. Now … how about a hand clearing these things away? Then we'd better start thinking about what clothes to take." She looked at Elizabeth. "Your uncle says it's going to be very hot."

"It wasn't hot at Christmas. In fact it was jolly cold. But Mum will just pack light things this time." She grinned.

"And I bet anything Uncle's told her not to pack sou'westers. No problems with night rescues on this holiday."

"Where is he?" asked Stuart.

"Over at the Mill. He begged a lift with one of the boatmen last night. But I know where he'll be now. Saying goodbye to Caesar … you know, the farm dog that always comes looking for him. He'll have gone to throw sticks in the lake for him … and to say goodbye."

"Speaking of goodbyes," said Mother, giving Laura a little push, "go and fetch Daddy. Somebody said something about sending the lot of you to France."

"HE'S AWAKE I THINK."

CHAPTER III

FRENCH INSECTS AND GREEN PAINT

AT first Ian thought it was just a leaf that had somehow fixed itself to the wall. It hung there, magically waving in the breeze. But as he got close, he saw it was an insect. The biggest insect he had ever seen. Bright green with long wings folded across its body and a diamond-shaped head. Large eyes. Eyes that seemed to be looking at him right now.

He stood stock still, not knowing what to do. If it had wings it could fly. And if it could fly it might bite. Even if it couldn't fly, it might very well jump. It was silly to have got so close but it was too late now.

He lifted his left leg, dragging his sandal back in the dust. The insect seemed to hear and turned its head towards him. It crawled a little higher up the wall, lifting its front legs and scraping them against the stone.

Ian thought it suddenly seemed altogether too big. He wondered how many legs it had - it seemed to be a lot. The creature rotated its strange head and looked at him.

"Poppy, can you hear me?"

Across the platform, Poppy was standing in the shade behind Uncle Albert, watching him paint. He had fixed a big white sunshade next to his easel and Ian could only see his arms as he stabbed at the canvas with a long brush.

Poppy looked up and saw Ian standing on one leg wobbling a little and waving a hand urgently behind his back.

"Of course I can hear you. What's the matter?"

"I can't move. Come and look. Only don't come too close. It's a French insect. A monster insect." He was trying his best to sound unconcerned.

"I'd better just stand here until it goes away." He paused, wobbling desperately. "I wish it would go away ... but it isn't ... it's just standing watching me ... I'm alright ... but I think I'd better wait until somebody comes ... you know ... in case it jumps."

Uncle Albert peered across from under his shade. He wiped his brush on a cloth then took off his hat and wiped his forehead, leaving a smudge of green paint over one eye.

"There aren't monster insects, Ian. Really, there aren't. Not even in France. Although I must say there are some big ones. Surprisingly big, some of them."

He put the brush down, pushed the little chair back and stood up, stretching his back.

"I needed a little rest anyway. I'm getting stiff sitting in the sun. Let's see what you've found. Just stay where you are."

"I think I'll have to put my foot down or I'll fall over."

Ian gently lowered his leg but could not stop himself starting back as the green monster seemed to copy him, rearing up and lifting its own legs high in the air.

Uncle Albert walked as quickly as he could, trying to stay in the shade of the station wall (he was quite fat, after all, and even walking was not very comfortable in the heat).

"It's a mantis. A big one. You don't get them that often. You're lucky to see one on your first day out."

Ian would have been quite happy to be less lucky. He put out a hand to steady himself and found he was holding Uncle Albert's hand.

"They call them praying mantis. I suppose it's that way they have of lifting their front legs. There – she's doing it now."

Ian was about to ask why it was a she, but he caught his breath as the insect reared up, lifting its huge green head to get a better view. It was holding its hands against its chest as if it was praying.

"Can they fly?"

He had managed to shuffle back to stand next to Poppy.

"Yes, they fly. But she won't hurt you. It's the little insects that bite, you know. The big ones usually know better. She's just sunning herself. It's hot, after all."

He patted Ian on the shoulder.

"I must get back to that picture – paint dries in no time in this weather."

"You've got green on your face," said Poppy.

"Better than red," laughed Uncle Albert, "or people would think the monster had bitten me."

He rubbed at his face and looked at his hand to see whether there were signs of green, then shrugged and pulled his straw hat down over his eyes. He walked as fast as he dared back into the bright sunlight at the end of the platform.

"I didn't really think it would bite," Ian whispered. "But you never know, do you? It's not as if we'd been here before. France is very nice … so far … although I didn't think it was going to be so awfully hot all the time."

Poppy tugged at his arm. "Why don't you come and watch Uncle Albert paint? It's very interesting."

"Not right now. I was watching a lizard just before I saw the mantis. There's one behind that door. I'm sure he's still there. If you don't move and wait long enough, he sticks his head out and looks at you."

Poppy was staring wistfully across to where Uncle Albert was squeezing paint out of a fat tube onto his palette and scraping at it with a flat knife. It looked a lot more exciting than waiting for a lizard. Ian looked at her.

"You go back. I'm alright. I wasn't really frightened. It was almost too big to be frightening. I just wondered whether it could bite, that's all."

She glanced up at the stone wall.

"Well, you've lost your mantis anyway. She's gone. Must have flown off somewhere."

They looked up, scanning the yellow stone blocks where the letters SNCF had been carved over the doorway. There was no sign of the green insect.

"Nothing to worry about, anyway," she added, patting him on the back as if she had arranged it all. Then she ran back to Uncle Albert.

*

Ian was left in the dappled shade of the station platform wondering whether it was altogether best that the mantis had flown away. That was the trouble with insects. When you couldn't see them it made you wonder where they were hiding.

Fierce sunlight flickered down through the leaves hanging over the station wall. Immense trees rose high into an empty blue sky, their knobbly branches sticking out like crooked arms peeling with blotches of white bark. They were like no trees he had ever seen before.

He stepped through the stone doorway into the entrance of the deserted railway station. There was shade in here, but out of the fresh air the heat was worse and the little hallway was stifling. There was no one about. The wooden hatch where you bought tickets was shuttered and closed. Somebody had left an ancient bicycle leaning against the wall.

Everywhere was very quiet. The doorway on the other side, where you came into the station, framed the view of a dusty lane and a silent house with a red tiled roof and painted shutters.

Far away, the bell of a clock rang lazily in the afternoon haze as if it was almost too much trouble to call out the hours. Slowly, slowly, it measured out five strokes and left the final chime hanging in the air.

Ian stepped back onto the platform and sat down on a low wall to wait for his lizard to peep out from behind the door. Streamers of hot air were swirling above the metal tracks of the railway line. A drowsy kind of smell, a mixture of hot tar and dust, rose up from the wooden sleepers.

It was very nice being in France. He tried to remember what the map of France looked like. There was one in the atlas at home but he had never looked at it very carefully. It must be a tremendously long way off. A picture of Mummy sitting in her chair looking across the lake flashed into his mind and his heart lurched at the thought of it. It was true - they really were miles and miles away in a strange and foreign land.

*

And France *was* rather a strange place. Not just the insects. For one thing, everywhere smelled different. Not nasty at all; but very strange. The faint scent of some kind of sweet flower seemed to be everywhere. It was the first thing they had noticed when they had jumped down from the train the day before yesterday.

They were feeling a little stunned by the heat and the very first thing Poppy said was, 'What's that lovely smell? Just like flowers everywhere.' Then she had added, 'But it's awfully hot, isn't it?'

And they had stood together gazing around and breathing in the sweet smell of scented flowers everywhere, the glare of the morning sun bathing them in sticky heat.

Ian's lizard peeped from under the door, blinking in the sunlight, its tongue flickering out. It held its head up like some prehistoric beast – a sort of tiny dinosaur. You could see its heart pulsing fast in its chest.

It was best to watch out of the corner of your eye. If you looked properly the lizard somehow seemed to know. He would stare at you and scuttle back into the shade. The two of them sat there, warily weighing each other up: Ian perched on his wall; the dinosaur with half his body poking from under the door.

A tiny breeze got up, enough to rustle the leaves above his head. It was completely quiet apart from a low murmur of voices from the other end of the platform, mostly Poppy, but Uncle Albert as well. Poppy was always asking questions. Now and then they would both laugh. Once, he heard the scrape of the chair as Uncle Albert got up to light one of his little cigars.

The church bell rang again. Only one chime this time. That would be half past five. He shifted his legs to get a bit more comfortable. The lizard disappeared in a flash behind the door. He'd forgotten the lizard. Never mind, he would come out again eventually. There was just room on the wall to stretch your legs out. Ian leaned back and closed his eyes.

*

He must have dozed off for a second. His back felt stiff where it had been leaning against the station wall. The church bell had been ringing again. He could still hear the last few chimes echoing like the end of a dream. Ian shook his head.

He jumped down from the wall. The sun was lower in the sky and it was a tiny bit cooler. He wandered back into the station hall, rubbing the sleep from his eyes.

Through the entrance on the other side of the hall the quiet road dipped down. It was hardly a road at all really – just packed dry clay baking in the last of the sun, with clumps of tall plants at its edge covered in little yellow flowers. There was no pavement, just a dusty track winding between the flowers. Clouds of red butterflies circled round, restlessly landing and taking off.

"Where's Ian?" That was Uncle Albert calling.

"Where on earth has he managed to get to? He was there a second ago. I was thinking if we hurry there's time for a cold drink."

Poppy came running into the hall, her feet echoing on the bare boards of the wooden floor.

"Here you are. We were looking for you. Uncle A has finished for the day. He's been packing up his paints and things. Come on."

"Where to? There's nowhere to come on to. And it's still very hot. Why's the train so late?"

Uncle Albert came into the hall dragging his easel and putting it down next to a big canvas. He perched a leather bag on top of his tiny wooden stool and pushed the whole pile against the wall next to the bicycle. He fastened up the buckles and patted the leather bag, saying, "Safe enough, I should think." He grinned at Ian.

"The train is due at half past five. That means half past six or a bit later. No use asking why; that's what it means. It's not even late, because everyone knows that's when it comes." He laughed, "In fact if it was ever on time, everyone would miss it." He dusted off the back of Ian's shirt.

"How on earth did you manage to get covered in all this dust? No, don't try to explain. I was a boy myself once. And we don't have time."

*

They followed him across the station hall and out into the little square. On their left, nestling against the wall, was a café with two tables set out in front. There were no customers. A man in a white apron stood in the doorway wiping a glass on a cloth. He looked as if he had been there a long time. Poppy was tugging at Ian's arm.

"Come on, lemonade mixed with that pink stuff. Like yesterday. Hurry up - I'm thirsty."

The three of them sat at the table nearest to the station entrance. Uncle Albert talked to the man in the apron for quite a long time. It was funny listening to them speaking French, even if you didn't know what they were saying. It all sounded very friendly.

"The pink stuff is grenadine," said Uncle Albert, "it's made from pomegranates. You know. You get them at Christmas."

"With hundreds of little red seeds like tiny jellies?" said Poppy.

Uncle Albert nodded as the man in the white apron came out with three glasses of lemonade and put them on the table. He showed Uncle Albert a fat little bottle filled with dark red syrup, then added a little to each of the glasses, stirring it round with a long spoon. He seemed to be asking a question, but when Uncle Albert replied they both burst out laughing.

"He was asking why I bother to paint the railway station when there's such a pretty view down by the lake. It's an interesting question but I'm a bit too tired to explain." He took a long drink of lemonade. "Anyway …"

But the sentence was never finished. A bell started ringing inside the station. It was loud enough to hear all over the square. A door opened and footsteps echoed across the entrance hall. They could hear the sound of the train now. A long way off but clear enough, struggling up the hill, puffing and snorting.

"Drink up, Ian. As fast as you can. They'll be here in a few minutes. If we want to see the train coming in, we'll have to get a move on."

"I can't go any faster. I get bubbles in my nose. And it's a big glass."

But only Poppy understood what Ian said because he was talking and drinking at the same time. She stood up waiting impatiently while he tipped his glass back and licked out the last few sticky pink drops. Then he hopped down from the chair.

"I'm coming. I'm coming."

Uncle Albert put some coins on the table, shook hands with the man in the white apron, then stretching out two arms sailed across to the entrance of the station like a galleon with two small boats as escort.

*

There was a little huddle of people waiting on the platform. Everybody seemed to be wearing black: black hats, black coats, black dresses, dusty black trousers, black shoes. She felt everybody was looking at her summer dress because it was not black. Ian's shirt was as white as a day's lizard hunting would allow, and seemed awfully bright.

She took his hand and edged him away from the knot of people towards the end of the platform where Uncle Albert had been painting.

"We can stand here. We're bound to see them – it isn't as if it's a huge station. There's only one platform."

They stood and watched as the train ground its way past, towering above them, filling the platform with the smell of woodsmoke and steam.

For a second there was a glimpse of the driver, way above, his face streaked with black, hanging onto a brass rail and shading his eyes to look at the other end of the platform. Then a tremendous noise of grating wheels and the line of brown wooden doors that was moving past jolted to a halt. Some were already half open. Faces stared down at them.

"I can see her!" Ian shouted. "It's Elizabeth! There she is!"

He set off trotting alongside the train trying to keep the familiar face in view. She was grinning cheerfully down at him from the window. Laura's face appeared at the carriage door, trying to get it open.

"Here we are! Over here!"

Elizabeth was shouting to Uncle Albert who was standing further up the platform. He must have decided it would be less effort in the heat to wait for the train to reach him rather than run to meet it. As the carriage stopped he reached out and swung Laura's door open.

"Nicely judged, I must say." He held out his hand to catch her.

Laura hesitated a second then jumped. He staggered back as she bounced against him, steadying herself and looking relieved to be on firm ground. She glanced anxiously towards the back of the train where a crowd of people were picking over jumbled piles of suitcases and bags.

"Stuart's helping Mrs Bradley. They've gone to look after the luggage."

A man with a crate filled with chickens rushed past. Laura could not see Mrs Bradley, but now and then caught the white of Stuart's sling through the crowd.

A porter was wheeling a bicycle across the platform. He stood at the edge of the crowd patiently waiting for a chance to load it onto the train.

Another man in a peaked cap tottered his way towards them pushing a strange wooden contraption with tiny metal wheels piled with bags and suitcases. Following behind, her hands resting on the topmost suitcase, was the diminutive form of Mrs Bradley. Her other arm was round Stuart's shoulder.

She was very hot and very flustered, looking carefully from face to face as people pushed past. She spotted Uncle Albert at last and gave him a funny sort of smile, half relief and half something else.

"Well, here we all are," she sighed. "Though why my favourite brother–in–law chooses to live all this way away, I'll never know. And I'd quite forgotten how hot it is. It seems hotter standing here than in the carriage – and that was hot enough. You can ask to have a window down until the cows come home, but no one will oblige."

She caught Ian's eye and couldn't help breaking into a smile.

"Hello Ian. And yes, I know quite well what you're going to ask. It's about the cows coming home isn't it? Now's not the time. Later."

Ian grinned back.

Uncle Albert was standing puffing one of his little cigars and smiling at no one in particular. He strolled over to join them.

"I got used to the journey years ago. You do forget how long it seems when you don't do it very often. But you're here now. Have you got all the bags? It looks like an awful lot."

He said a few words to the Porter who shook his head and muttered something in reply. Uncle Albert shrugged.

"That's a pity. We'll just have to manage." He clapped his hands.

"Come on Lucy, time we set off home. We'll have to walk it. It's a tidy step and we'll have to share the bags round. This chap says we can't borrow his cart – he needs it for the next train."

"Who's Lucy?" whispered Poppy who was standing next to Elizabeth.

"Oh, nobody. That's just Uncle talk. When he's rounding people up, everybody's called Lucy."

She grabbed two cases off the cart, handing one to Laura. The Porter helped Stuart get another one down.

Mrs Bradley looked at him.

"Can you manage it with your arm like that?"

"It's stopped hurting. Anyway it isn't heavy at all. I can carry it easily with my good arm."

Uncle Albert took the next two cases and stuffed a package under his arm. Poppy picked up a cardboard box and gave it to Ian. She took the last little suitcase herself.

"I must say that's very nice of you," said Mrs Bradley, "I've nothing to carry at all."

"So far, Mother," said Elizabeth, laughing, "so far … but there's a way to go yet."

She set off at a mighty pace, her footsteps clattering through the station hall. At the doorway, she paused for a second, the golden light of the sun streaming past her.

"Come on, slowcoaches, follow me. I remember the way. The first bit is worst, it's uphill all the way."

Ian and Poppy were walking next to Laura.

"We got here yesterday," Ian said. "You can see the house when you get to the top of the hill. We call it the pink house; you'll see why. It's very big."

"But a bit odd," added Poppy, "lots and lots of rooms, but hardly any furniture."

"COME AND LOOK"

CHAPTER IV

THE PINK HOUSE

ELIZABETH had run up the hill and stood waiting at the side of the road. Laura, a little dizzy with the heat, stopped to catch her breath. She was trying to imagine what a house without furniture would be like. Surely there were tables and chairs and things … and beds … she would really like to stretch out in a bed.

Although she had tried hard not to, she had fallen asleep for the last part of the journey and still felt she had not quite woken up. The carriage had been so hot you could hardly help it.

She had been reading her book and the next thing she remembered was Mrs Bradley shaking her shoulder and saying 'Laura, Laura, you'll have to wake up. We're coming into the station. Jump to it, I have to go and look for the cases.'

Her book was lying closed on the seat next to her. Whoever had shut it had stuck a little bit of paper to mark where she'd got to.

She started up, wondering for a second where she was. There was noise everywhere with people shouting as they ran alongside, trying to keep up with the carriage. Now and then somebody even jumped up to look at her.

Elizabeth had run to the window and Laura remembered her calling out, 'There they are! Why can't they see us?' And the faces of two little figures anxiously looking up at the carriage had flickered past.

Mrs Bradley had given her an encouraging little smile then hurried out into the corridor, calling over her shoulder, 'I'm going to look for the cases.' And then she was gone.

The carriage jolted to a halt, throwing Laura forward, then changed its mind and jerked a few more feet before it stopped. Although she hadn't meant to, she had sat down with a bump hanging on to the seat. Then the carriage door was open, bringing a gust of smoke mixed with the sweet scent of flowers, and she was looking down at the smiling face of Uncle Albert.

*

Laura was well behind Elizabeth and the others. They had stopped at the top of the hill and were watching as she struggled up, red-faced and panting in the heat. Uncle Albert put his load down and stretched his back. Stuart waved with his good arm and called out.

"There's no hurry, Laura. Don't try and run; it's too hot. I'm going on ahead. I'll wait for you down there."

He pointed vaguely down the hill and set off, half-walking and half-trotting, his suitcase banging awkwardly against his legs.

Laura reached the top of the hill at last and stood there gazing open mouthed at what lay in wait.

Stretched out before her, as far as she could see, as far as the hazy mist of the horizon miles and miles away, was a vast swelling ocean of green. Huge birds circled lazily over wave upon wave of trees. Everything was bathed in a soft golden sunlight. The road dipped sharply down and threaded through a patterned quilt of tiny fields squeezed between the trees. They were pink with poppies.

She could see Stuart now, a good way off. He had reached a place where two tall stone pillars, not quite upright, flanked the road. A sandy track broke away between them snaking through deep woods towards a clearing.

You could not see all of it because trees were in the way, but there was the house. A very big house. Walls of peach-coloured stone were half-hidden in ivy; bright red geraniums hung from window-sills; faded blue shutters stood closed against the sun. A thin line of grey smoke climbed lazily up into the sky from one chimney.

Mrs Bradley stood looking down.

"It's lovely, I must say. I'd forgotten. It's years since I was here. But nothing's changed. Nothing at all."

Uncle Albert was picking up his load of cases.

"Well, you'll find a few changes I dare say. But things change slowly here."

"And everywhere's so quiet," she added. Then, turning to Elizabeth, "I don't know; perhaps it's too quiet. Do you think you'll find enough to occupy your time? I was wondering about that on the train. Perhaps it was a mistake after all, dragging you all this way."

Uncle Albert's laugh boomed out and a flock of little birds circling a tree at the side of the road wheeled round and chased each other down the valley.

"You're a bit late to decide that now! Anyway, if they don't find something to do here I'll eat my hat." He turned to Ian.

"What do you think, Ian? Is my hat safe? It's quite a useful hat, I don't want to eat it."

But Ian was peering through the shimmer of heat rising up from the road. Straining his eyes way beyond the house, to the distant horizon where the trees seemed to melt into a faint line of blue-green mist. He pointed and called to Uncle Albert who had already started to walk down the hill.

"What's over there?"

But all Uncle Albert said was, "You'll find out. Come on you lot, this pack horse needs its food."

*

Stuart had walked on ahead, leaving the others chattering and looking at the view. He wanted a few minutes on his own, to get the stuffiness of the train out of his lungs, but also, to tell the truth, to try his arm without the sling. On the train, every time he had started to ease his arm out, either Mrs Bradley or Laura had looked at him.

That was the trouble with being a patient, people wouldn't leave you alone. It had only been an accident; the sort of thing that could happen to anybody. And now it was as if everybody expected him to fall over all the time. Even Mother. In the cottage, he had only to set off upstairs for her to say 'Take care' as if he was a baby. It really was very frustrating.

He walked as fast as he could down the hill between two lines of massive trees. At first, they threw patches of shade in front of him, but as the road dipped down further, the sun disappeared below the hill. A tiny breeze got up and his shirt,

"EVERYWHERE'S SO QUIET"

sticky with sweat, suddenly flapped cold and shivery against his back.

He reached two stone pillars where a sandy track split off from the road to his left. This would be as good a place as any. He turned the suitcase on its side and sat down on it. The others had started walking down towards him, but they were taking their time and were a good long way away.

He was quite alone.

He eased his arm carefully out of its sling and tried gently lowering his hand. His shoulder felt stiff but nothing seemed to hurt anymore. So far, so good. He wiggled his shoulder. Stiff and creaky, but not painful at all. He tried lifting his elbow and at once felt a flicker of pain.

He dropped his arm and sat there for a second, his hand resting on his knee, breathing hard. He pulled the sling across and straightened it out more or less the way Mrs Bradley had tied it. It could be worse. His shoulder was throbbing a bit, but it was certainly getting better. He would give it seven out of ten.

He dragged the case across to one of the pillars and sat down again, leaning against the crumbling stonework, waiting for the others. Tall iron gates stood flung back across the path. They looked as if they had not been closed for years. Little tendrils of weed had wound themselves round the lower rails.

Through the gate, the path disappeared into dense trees. The woods all about him seemed cool and dark and inviting. The shade under the trees had brought another scent into the air. There was still the smell of flowers, but now something else: something fresh and damp and earthy.

It was very quiet; even the birds had stopped singing. All you could hear were leaves far above your head whispering together. He felt slightly giddy. For a moment he could not quite believe where he was. He smiled to himself. If it had not been for that frog they would not be here at all. You can never tell how things are going to turn out. He must not forget that frog.

*

As the others got closer, Stuart heard Poppy asking questions and Mrs Bradley answering, the two of them talking happily together. Now and then Ian would say something and Elizabeth would laugh. They all seemed very cheerful.

Uncle Albert had fallen behind a bit. You had to admit he was rather fat. He was taking his time and had stopped to catch his breath, looking very red. It looked like hot work with two suitcases, even downhill. He was watching three huge birds slowly circling high above an empty field.

"Look up here! They're buzzards. There's always some at this time in the evening." He caught them up and stood there breathing heavily.

"I suppose they're hunting, but I must say, they've an awfully lazy way of going about it. I think they eat lizards mostly ... come to think of it, I really could eat something myself. I was not cut out to be a bearer of burdens."

"I know one lizard they won't eat," said Ian. "He lives at the railway station. It would take a pretty quick bird to catch him."

He ran across to where Stuart was sitting and pulled him to his feet, brushing the dust off his back.

"You must have got awfully hot running like that. What were you doing here on your own?"

"I wasn't running. And I've been thinking."

"Thinking about what?"

"How we got here mostly. I can't quite believe we're really here. I keep thinking it was only yesterday when we were ..." He stopped and Mrs Bradley burst out laughing.

"Yes? ... go on Stuart ... where were you?" But since he really couldn't remember, he just stood there looking puzzled.

She came across and looked first at his sling, then at him.

"Someone's put this thing on inside out. Now I wonder how it got like that?"

He went red and started to explain, although he could see she was smiling. She untied the sling and straightened it out.

"Remember what the doctor said ... it really is best left alone. We'll see how it is tomorrow after a night's sleep." She was still smiling.

"Anyway, now you've disobeyed orders, you'd better tell us all ... does it feel any better?"

Stuart gave a guilty sort of grin.

"Quite a lot better, thank you." He saw Laura looking at Mrs Bradley's face.

"But I won't take it off again, I promise. Anyway, not till tomorrow."

"I remember once when I had my arm in a cast," said Uncle Albert, "it was itching so much inside I got caught trying to scratch myself with a knitting needle ..." He jumped up as one of his suitcases was snatched from under him. "Well that's very obliging I must say ..."

Mrs Bradley had grabbed the case and set off down the path at a cracking pace, calling over her shoulder, "Come on – I want my supper, even if I have to sing for it."

Elizabeth picked up Stuart's case.

"Here, give me that. I can carry two just for the last bit. It's not far now. The sooner we get going, the sooner we'll be able to have a nice cold drink. I'm parched."

"We had pink lemonade at the station while we were waiting for you," said Ian, then thought that didn't sound very polite, so added, "although we had to pour it down too fast to taste properly because the train came."

They were wending their way between trees in deep shade, the path flanked with banks of yellow flowers. Uncle Albert pulled his hand through them, leaving a line of tiny black seeds on his fingers. He held his hand out for Poppy to smell. She sniffed,

"Oh! It's aniseed ... how peculiar."

"Let me!" shouted Ian. He grabbed some of the flowers for himself and sniffed. "It's just like aniseed drops. Can you eat them?"

"Better not," said Uncle Albert, "although I think you can – if you've washed them, that is. But now's not the time. Come on, it can't be far now."

Suddenly the trees ended and they were walking across the springy turf of a lawn. They stopped at a little paved square in front of the house. A flight of stone steps led to the biggest door Ian had ever seen. A double door, opening in the middle, made out of some ancient wood. Perhaps it had been painted years and years ago – he thought he could still make out faded patches of paint, but it was quite impossible to know what colour had been.

One half of the door was held ajar by a big clay pot full of geraniums. Red flowers had climbed up and wrapped themselves round the brass door handle. It looked as if that bit of the door was open all the time.

Long ago, there must have been a fountain in front of the house. All that remained now was a statue of a lady with a sad expression on her face pouring nothing at all out of a vase into a circular stone basin. Stuart peered over the side. It was quite dry.

Uncle Albert dropped his case on the ground and looked up at the house.

"Where is everyone?"

He saw Poppy jumping up to look into the fountain.

"No – it's no use looking in there. At least, no use looking for fish. No use looking for water, in fact. Water's precious here - there's none left over for fountains."

He looked round again, muttering to himself.

"I can't think where she's got to. I know we're a bit late … I was hoping someone would be here to greet the thirsty camel train."

But even as he was speaking, a little woman, rather plump and dressed in a long blue apron, came rushing out to greet them. She stood on the top step, wagging her head and tapping her wrist where there might have been a watch if she had ever worn one.

Uncle Albert whispered to Poppy, "I'm afraid we are a bit late … and we'll be for it if that means supper's spoiled." She watched him do his best to run up the steps and tried not to smile.

He was dabbing at his face with a paint-stained handkerchief and saying something in French at the same time. He may have been explaining why they were a bit late, but the little old lady was hardly listening. She was looking past him at the new arrivals; first at Mrs Bradley then at the others. When she saw Elizabeth, her face lit up with a wide smile. Uncle Albert called down to them.

"It's alright. Supper's on the way, but there's still time. Come and say hello to Madame Berri."

He turned to Laura, "That's Berri with an i, not the other sort of berry. Not that I imagine you'll have to spell it. But you'll remember to call her Madame Berri. We grown-ups call her Pia, but you'd better not. You explain, Laura, I'm relying on you."

Laura wondered why everybody always said they were relying on her. But she nodded and shook the outstretched hand, mumbling, "Hello Madame Berri," and looking awkwardly at Mrs Bradley. The name didn't come out at all the way Uncle Albert had said it, but the lady gave her a very friendly smile.

Mrs Bradley was looking anxiously at Uncle Albert.

"You know, it's a bit of a mouthful for the little ones, I don't think she'd mind at all if they called her Cook. They're used to that."

"That's what I called her at Christmas," said Elizabeth, "she likes that name."

"I'll ask her."

"I didn't think berries had eyes ..." said Ian to himself, but he caught the look in Laura's face and quickly skipped out of the way. "Anyway, she lifts me up and lets me do the shutters. You'll see."

Uncle Albert finished speaking and turned to Mrs Bradley.

"That's settled then, 'Cook' it is. You know, I couldn't manage to work here without Pia. She does everything ..." He grinned as she started tapping her wrist at him again.

"If there's going to be any supper for us tonight we'd better jump to it and get things sorted out. Poppy and Ian are already settled in. Elizabeth, you're in the room you had at Christmas - you know where that is. Laura and Stuart, you're next to the other two. You can toss for which room you get. They're more or less the same. That's one thing we're not short of - rooms."

He turned back to Mrs Bradley, "I thought you'd like the big one on the other side, over the studio? You've been in there before. You'll be comfortable and quiet there, away from the pirate hordes. Will that suit?"

Mrs Bradley picked up her case and was about to set off when Cook stumped slowly down the steps and planted two big kisses on Elizabeth's face, one on each side.

Stuart stood watching, feeling very awkward. He wondered whether she was going to kiss him as well. He wasn't sure he could manage that.

He glanced nervously at Laura, but there were no more kisses. He just found a very friendly arm round his shoulders steering him up the steps towards the door. Laura, finding the other arm round her own shoulders looked round searching for a familiar face.

Elizabeth skipped up the steps and whispered, "We're old friends, Cookie and me ... she's very nice ... I'll show you where the kitchen is later. There's pretty well always something going ... if you feel a bit peckish that is ... leftovers, bits of tart or cake, you know, that sort of thing. You don't need to ask – just stand there and look hungry."

"I couldn't ask anyway," Laura whispered back, "I don't know how."

"No point trying," said Elizabeth with a little shrug, "I tried a few French words last time, but she laughed so much I thought I'd better stop. We started French at school last year. But we've not reached speaking it yet." She watched Cook smiling at Ian.

"She's really taken to Ian, you can tell ... look, you'd better get on. We were late getting here, what with the train and then having to walk. You go ahead; I'll be up in a minute. I know where my room is. I just want to ask Uncle something."

CHAPTER V

SETTLING IN

LAURA stood on the top step, glancing back awkwardly and feeling more than a little lost. It was alright for Elizabeth, Uncle Albert was her uncle after all, and she had been here before. Cook had even kissed her. But it was not the same for her, or for Stuart. She could see Stuart biting his lip. He only ever did that when things got on top of him. If only they could understand what people were saying, perhaps it would all seem less strange.

What she could see of the hallway through the huge front door seemed to be very dark. It was as if the house was shut up.

Cook said something to herself then gathered her two charges, one under each arm and led them inside. Ian and Poppy had run on ahead and you could hear them shouting and calling to each other. Poppy was laughing. Their voices seemed to echo round the walls.

True, it was very dark inside the house, but you soon got used to that. And it was not empty of furniture: there were chairs and tables and cupboards everywhere. It was just that everywhere was so very big.

As her eyes got used to the dark, shafts of afternoon sunlight broke through cracks in the shutters and winked up at her from red tiles stretching away as far as she could see.

Between jutting bits of ancient stonework the walls were painted a mottled yellow colour. They were covered with pictures, no more than framed splashes of vague colour in the darkness.

Doors opened off the hall on both sides of a flight of stairs that disappeared up into the gloom. There was a big table in the centre of the hall with a bowl of flowers on it just finding room among piles of books. Laura was reminded of Uncle Albert's cabin on the *Arethusa* and how there had seemed to be books everywhere.

Cook took her arms from round their shoulders and left them standing as she climbed the staircase clapping her hands. Ian came running to meet her, hanging onto her hand. Poppy followed him and stood looking down at the two of them hesitating at the foot of the stairs.

"Come and watch," she called. "What are you waiting for?"

Stuart turned to Laura, "Watch what?"

But Laura had already set off saying, "Come on, hurry up, or we'll lose them."

The hallway at the top of the stairs was so dark you could barely make out the other end; just the dim outline of a line of doors on one side and a line of shuttered windows on the other, both dissolving into the distance.

Cook stopped in front of the first window and picked Ian up. He pulled the window open then reached out pushing back tall wooden shutters. They clattered open, flooding the hall with dazzling sunlight. A sudden rush of hot scented air surrounded them.

"This is my job now," Ian shouted, "I'm going to do the shutters every afternoon."

Laura blinked. It was as if somebody had switched on an electric light.

"Why not leave them open? It's lovely now you can see things properly. Really lovely. But a bit gloomy at first, with everything shut up like that."

"It must be to keep the heat out," said Stuart. "If you think about it, that's why it's cool inside."

The shutter-opener was working his way down the hall, counting windows as he went.

"That's five," he said, grinning back at them. "I like doing this."

They were standing in a wide corridor with a polished wooden floor. At the far end was another staircase running upstairs into shadow.

"I bet you thought it was a bit spooky in the dark like that," said Poppy. "We did at first, but you get used to it." She suddenly grabbed Ian as he started to push past her.

"No, that's not fair. We agreed I was going to do the doors."

"Go on then."

Poppy threw open the first door.

"This is Ian's. Nobody has to share ... and the rooms here are all ours. Elizabeth's at the end there. And the bathroom's down there round the corner. We're up here on our own. Mrs Bradley is somewhere else. We haven't discovered where Uncle Albert's room is yet."

Stuart and Laura were still gazing round trying to get their bearings.

"Everything's very big here" Ian added, thinking this might be his last chance to explain where things were. He pushed his door open further and stood to one side to let them look inside.

"This is my room." He slid across the polished wooden floor and skidded to a halt, spinning round. "It's positively enormous. Although, like Poppy said, there's not much inside."

They went in and stood looking round. The floor boards were black with age and not quite level, but they had been polished until they gleamed.

Apart from a bed covered with a patterned quilt there was very little furniture; just a wooden table with a basin on it, a chest of drawers painted with flowers, and a high-backed cane chair standing in an alcove next to the window.

Laura went over to the little chest and started to look inside drawers.

"Where have you put your things? Not in here? There's not room."

Ian ran across to a door set in the wall, pulled it open, and went inside. "I keep them in here," he called, "it's all mine."

He was standing proudly inside a tiny room lined with shelves up to the ceiling. He had emptied his case and laid things out neatly on the bottom shelf.

"Plenty of room, you see ... Poppy's next door. Her room's pretty much the same as mine. She doesn't have a little room like this, but she's got a bigger chest of drawers and a wardrobe, so that makes us even."

He went back into his cupboard.

"I like it in here. Uncle Albert said you had to toss with Stuart for one of the other rooms. But there's not much point – they're both the same. We've looked."

Laura went out into the corridor, picked her case up from where she had left it, and walked down until she stopped at the door next to Poppy's. She opened it and glanced inside then turned to Stuart.

"I'll go in here, if that's alright. I think I'll lie down for a minute. I'm a bit tired. She went in and closed the door. They heard her dump her case on the floor.

*

Stuart had unpacked his case and put his things into a tall wardrobe with a mirror on the front. The shutters were already thrown back. Somebody had fastened the window open a few inches with a little metal catch. He lifted it, pushed the window wide, and gazed out at the view: a lawn, edged with bright red flowers, and beyond that, an endless expanse of trees, tossing and waving in the breeze.

The sun had almost set but the air was still thick and sticky. Distant fields past the forest melted into a milky blue haze.

Ian and Poppy appeared at his door.

"Laura told me to go away," said Ian. "I knocked and she said she's tired. Cook always rings a little bell when supper's ready. At least, she did last night. It will be any time now. You can hear it up here, but you might not. We could go downstairs to be ready if you like."

"Go and wash your hands and face. You too, Poppy ... I'll be along in a minute."

Stuart closed the door behind them and sat on his bed. He let himself lie back. His arm had started to ache a bit. He felt tired and a little lost. He listened to the clatter of feet on the bare wooden boards outside as Ian and Poppy ran happily down the corridor. He closed his eyes for a second.

So this was France. He was not disappointed - not at all - although, to tell the truth, he had expected something not quite so different.

Sunlight glinted from the wooden floor. The boards looked as if somebody had polished them for years until they shone. Even the air in the room smelled faintly of old wood - a strange, foreign, smell. And now the warm breeze drifting through the open window brought another smell: the unmistakable smell of somebody cooking something. But even that was not quite familiar.

He went over to the big china jug, peered into it, then poured some water into the basin. The soap had the scent of violets. He washed his face, splashing cool water up from the bowl, and stood at the window, letting the soft evening light dry him.

From far down below there was the sound of a tinkling bell. The sound moved through the house floating up to them. At the same time he heard Elizabeth taking the stairs two at a time and pounding along the corridor outside.

She was banging on Poppy's door shouting, "Grub's up. What are you all doing? Come on! Cook gets cross if you're late. Come on!" Finally, with a little rap at the door she appeared breathless standing in his doorway, peering in.

"What are you lot doing? Is Laura next door? All she did was grunt. It's jolly quiet up here. Are you alright? It's time for supper."

There were more footsteps. Poppy and Ian appeared at the door, then Laura, looking a little tousled.

"I'm awfully sorry. I fell asleep, would you believe it? You lead the way; we don't know where we're going."

*

They followed Elizabeth downstairs and across the hall, filled now with the last of the evening sun. There was a strong smell of cooking. She pushed through a swing door and almost ran down a narrow corridor lined with pictures.

All at once they were outside in the fresh air, standing on a terrace, listening to birdsong and the soft swish of wind in the trees above them. A table with a white cloth flapping ran down the length of the terrace.

Cook was already ladling out tomato soup into bowls. Uncle Albert and Mrs Bradley were sitting close to each other, talking in a very excited way. They heard Uncle Albert say, "That's settled then," and burst out laughing until he noticed them and nudged Mrs Bradley. They looked very pleased with themselves and were doing their best for it not to show.

Mrs Bradley looked up.

"Oh good! So you're here at last. We'd almost given up and decided you'd been kidnapped. Just sit down anywhere. I always think it's best with the sun behind you. But the sun's almost gone, so it hardly matters."

She had already taken Laura's hand and pulled her into a chair next to her own.

Uncle Albert got up and went round the table lighting the oil lamps. As they flared up, the evening seemed to close in. The trees across the lawn suddenly seemed darker. They were sitting in a little yellow island of lamplight.

"I hope you like soup," said Uncle Albert, grinning at Ian.

He looked at Mrs Bradley as if to say, 'Can we start?' She smiled and nodded. He took a spoonful and jumped back as if he had been stung.

Uncle Albert burst out laughing then checked himself.

"I'm sorry. I shouldn't laugh, but you did look very comic. Was it such a surprise?

"But it's cold," said Ian, "I mean really cold. Cold like it's not been cooked yet."

"It's cooked alright. It's just not hot."

Stuart had taken his first tiny spoonful and was looking thoughtful. He darted an uncertain glance at Mrs Bradley.

"It's no use looking at me," she said "I didn't make it. Although I must say there's really no reason why a soup has to be hot. It tastes just the same cold." She took a spoonful.

"And this tastes delicious."

Ian tried a little more. It was true. It was a little odd at first, and you couldn't really say it tasted just the same, but it was alright. Just one more native custom to get used to.

Cook had started to work her way round the table, ladling out second helpings. Ian looked into his bowl. There was a long way to go before she reached him and he was not altogether sure he liked cold soup enough for seconds.

He looked up to find Uncle Albert eyeing him with a very encouraging grin so he spooned it down just in time to let her fill his bowl again. She tapped him gently on the head with the handle of the ladle as if to say don't bolt your food.

Stuart managed his second helping, but Laura was so lost in thought that when her turn arrived she had hardly started on her first.

There was a long loaf of bread lying on the table. Uncle Albert picked it up, snapped a piece off with his hands and passed it to Elizabeth. She tore a chunk off in a very piratical way and passed it on. Laura found herself holding the loaf. She looked round the table.

"No bread knives," said Uncle Albert, "that's what you're thinking, isn't it Laura? But it's the custom here. We had hands before we had knives you know. Go on. You'll get used to it, honestly."

Laura carefully broke a little piece off, trying to keep the crumbs at bay. But it was impossible. She scraped them into a little pile at the side of her plate when nobody was looking. It did seem rather untidy, but somehow friendly as well.

"Lots less washing up," said Ian, tearing off a big chunk. He had finished his second helping of soup and was just thinking he could manage another when he noticed Cook had gone. She had collected up all the plates and vanished.

They sat there in the last of the daylight, listening to the sound of the wind in the trees.

"I saw a bird," shouted Ian. "It flew right down over the table." He was waving his piece of bread in the air. "Over there." He leaned over and whispered to Laura, "Do we just have soup?"

Laura was wondering the same, when a shaft of yellow light from the kitchen door fell across the terrace and Cook reappeared. She stood for a second under the stone arch holding the largest platter they had ever seen and the table was suddenly enveloped in a wonderful smell of hot cooking. Uncle Albert shouted "Bravo!" and they clapped.

She put the dish, filled with little chops still sizzling, in the middle of the table and trotted back to the kitchen to come back almost at once with a bowl brimful with sliced beans running with hot butter.

Cook held out a big spoon to Uncle Albert but he shook his head and pointed to Mrs Bradley.

"While we were waiting I managed to organise some lemonade," said Mrs Bradley. "Not quite like you get at home, but nice enough, I dare say. It's in that jug. Help yourselves."

She was scooping up the little chops and putting two on everyone's plate, spooning a little juice over them as she went.

"Shall we just dig into the beans ourselves?" asked Elizabeth.

Uncle Albert was pulling the cork out of a bottle of wine. He poured a tiny drop into his glass and sipped it.

"If you don't want to starve," he said. He nodded to Mrs Bradley, "The wine's lovely." He filled her glass and topped up his own, then saw Poppy looking at him. He beamed back at her.

"Yes, we're altogether at last. Eat up. Eat as much as you like. I'm not allowed to tell you what's for pudding, but remember to leave a bit of room for it."

*

For Poppy that first supper in the old house together was like something out of a storybook - the kind you read especially slowly to make it last. The meal seemed to go on for ever. She even forgot to talk very much. Instead, she sat there wide-eyed and watching.

People pulled chairs closer in as the evening settled itself into night, until it was dark enough for Uncle Albert to fetch two more oil lamps and set them down on the table.

A half moon had risen over the trees. Soft amber lamplight flickered over faces as everyone tried to talk at once. Stuart described the train journey again, and they all laughed when he reached the bit about no one opening the window for Mrs Bradley.

Elizabeth pointed every now and then into the dark where the lawn dissolved into the trees, trying to get Stuart to see something.

Uncle Albert came and perched on the edge of Poppy's chair next to Ian and showed him how to pick up his chops by the end.

"That's what this bit of paper is wrapped round the bone for. It's so that you can pick it up."

Ian had made very little progress with his knife and fork. He glanced at Laura then quickly grabbed a chop and looked at it. He took a bite.

"Lots easier," he said, before she had time to speak, "what's more, you can get at the bits you can never manage with a knife."

Laura wondered what Mother would say. But the knife she had really wasn't very sharp, so she gave up and copied Ian.

Mrs Bradley spooned two more chops onto her plate saying, "There's plenty of beans left."

Ian watched moths beating against the side of the lamp. Some so big you could hear a little chink as they hit the glass. They fell back exhausted onto the tablecloth, spinning round until they started up again driving in against the yellow globe.

Orange insects as big as bees shot in over his head diving towards the light, only to veer away into the darkness as they caught the heat of the lamps.

When the chops were finished and the juices had been mopped up in a very friendly way, everyone dipping bits of bread into the big platter, the pudding arrived. A huge dish of strawberries.

"I don't know why they grow so big here," said Uncle Albert, "the heat I suppose. You'd think it would spoil the taste." He picked one up and popped it into his mouth.

"But it doesn't. Cook must have a secret supply, they're always like this. She must have been saving these for us - the season's almost over."

"I'm always sad when the strawberry season ends," said Mrs Bradley, "but then I remember that means the start of something else. What's next? Melons, is it?"

She started spooning the strawberries out, pouring a little splash of thick cream on top of each dish. "If you want seconds, just help yourself."

She gave a nervous little cough and looked briefly at Uncle Albert. He nodded and tapped the side of his glass with a knife. The table fell silent.

Mrs Bradley coughed again then said, "There's something I want to say before you're all off to bed. It's about tomorrow."

"They'll be so tired tomorrow, they'll spend the day in bed, I'll be bound," said Uncle Albert.

"Oh no we won't," said Elizabeth. "You'll be seeing us bright and early. There's things to be done."

"Well you won't see much of me," said Mrs Bradley, "I shall be away most of the day tomorrow." She stopped, leaning forward and looking rather awkward. Her eyes flickered towards Uncle Albert again then she rushed on.

"Actually, it's an old friend. That's it - there's an old friend I want to visit ... or rather, I have to visit. I thought I'd better get it done right away. Anyway I don't want you running about wild on your first day."

Elizabeth started to protest, and she added, "Alright, I'm sorry, running about exploring if you like."

"I wasn't going to say that at all," said Elizabeth, "I was going to say ..."

But her mother broke in before she could finish. "I just thought you'd all like a quiet day, that's all. Anyway, I know your uncle has a surprise for you." She leaned across and ruffled Laura's hair. "At least for four of you."

Elizabeth tried to say something again, but Uncle Albert held out the dish of strawberries towards her. He pushed his chair back.

"That's right, a surprise. Tomorrow morning. After breakfast. But take your time, there's no hurry at all."

"What surprise?" Ian said, then catching Laura's look, turned to Poppy.

"How big a surprise is it?" said Poppy. "Is it something you can carry? How big is it? Just give us a hint."

Uncle Albert winked solemnly at her and pulled his mouth down.

"Sorry, I'm saying no more about it. My lips are sealed."

Poppy tried looking into his eyes.

"It's no use," he said. "You'd never guess that way. And I'm not splitting. Just put it under your pillow before you go to sleep."

"But that's not fair," said Ian, "you haven't given us anything to put."

"Well you can put guesses under your pillow. That should be enough."

He started to collect the plates together, handing them to Mrs Bradley.

"Now … do you think you can find your way?" He looked at Ian, "You know, I've quite forgotten what your bedtime usually is. Your mother did tell me, but it's slipped my mind." He held his hand up as Ian was about to speak.

"No, don't tell me. Best not. Just get along and sleep well. You too, Elizabeth. I want to sit here a bit and talk to your mother."

He struck a match, the flame flaring yellow into his face, and started puffing a little cigar. Off you go. Good night to the lot of you. Sleep well. Breakfast's when you want it. We don't keep strict hours here. But do knock on the kitchen door before you go rushing in."

*

Much later, Ian stood at the open window in his bedroom looking out into a misty landscape. The moon shining through the trees threw mysterious crooked shadows across the lawn.

He was thinking how nice it was to eat outside in the dark. Like camping, but better because you were sitting on chairs. He had forgotten to ask Stuart what time it was, but he didn't feel tired at all.

Small birds were swooping and diving across the face of the window. They flew straight towards him in twos and threes, then wheeled away. He looked again. They seemed almost too small for birds; perhaps they weren't birds at all. He watched one swoop across then dive down, changing direction almost too fast for him to keep up. If they were birds, they were not like any he'd seen before.

A light from Poppy's room next door shone out into the black for a moment then was switched off almost at once. Just for a second he saw one of the birds swoop through the beam. It looked very odd. He leaned out and saw Poppy's arms resting on the rail across her window.

He called, "Poppy," as quietly as he could.

"I'm here. Isn't it lovely in the cool?"

"What are these birds flying about? They seem to be everywhere."

One suddenly flew past his face, close enough to feel a little puff of air. He wasn't at all sure he liked these night birds. They had a funny way of flying.

"They're not birds, silly; they're bats." Poppy's voice came back to him out of the darkness. "They won't hurt you. They're chasing insects to eat. Go to bed. It's awfully late."

"But one might fly in through my window." He was quite sure he wouldn't like these things flying round while he was in bed.

"They have more sense - they're looking for juicy moths for their supper. They won't eat you; you're safe. Anyway, they know their way around. Just don't go switching your light on and inviting them in. I'm going to bed. You'd better do the same."

There was another voice, Laura's, small and faint, but sounding rather cross.

"Are you out of bed Poppy? And is that Ian talking?"

Ian scurried back into bed and curled down. Now that his eyes were used to it, the room was quite light.

A fox barked in the forest, a long way off. He knew that cry. He had heard it many times when they were camping by the old tower. It was a lonely sort of sound usually, but hearing it here was somehow comforting. It was nice to know they had foxes in France as well.

He saw a shadow fly across the window, then twist away upwards. There was nothing to be frightened of. After all, Stuart and Laura were here, and Poppy was just next door. He pulled the sheets up tight round his shoulders and then up a little more so that only his nose poked out.

He was wondering how often a bat might lose its way when he fell soundly asleep.

CHAPTER VI

THE SURPRISE

POPPY woke to the sound of horses coming towards the house. She lay on her back, listening to a steady clopping sound. No, it was just one horse, she thought. Rather a rather small horse at that; light on its feet. Then, as the hooves scrunched off the gravel onto the paved terrace she heard wheels clattering across stone.

She jumped out of bed and ran to the window. Sunlight was just starting to slant into the room but it seemed very early. She leaned out, feeling the cold stone of the window sill wet with dew under her hands.

Mrs Bradley was bustling down the steps, struggling to climb into the front of a tiny cart. A man was already sitting there holding the reins. He squeezed up against the side to make room for her then leaned down and helped her in.

It wasn't a horse at all: it was a donkey, standing quietly, nodding its head up and down and flicking its ears.

Mrs Bradley looked up at the house and saw Poppy. She gave a cheerful wave and tried to stand up, but promptly fell back into her seat as the man tapped the donkey with his whip and they jerked forward. They made a tight circle, the wheels cutting into the edge of the lawn, and set off down the long track towards the road.

Poppy stood there long after they had disappeared into the trees, listening to the retreating clop of hooves slowly fade into silence.

The sun was barely up. It was looking at her, a huge ball of red hanging low in the sky. The woods all around looked dark and mysterious, wrapped in streamers of mist. The bats of last night had disappeared. No birds were singing.

Now the donkey had gone, it was very quiet. It seemed too early for breakfast but she did not feel like going back to bed. She picked up the soap and towel from next to the basin, gathered up her clothes, and tiptoed to the door.

*

Somebody must have closed the shutters in the corridor after they had gone to bed, but a little light filtered through gaps in the wood, more than enough to see your way. She passed the other doors, trying not to let the floorboards creak, turned the corner, and stole past Elizabeth's room.

The bathroom door was wide open, spilling sunlight out onto the polished boards. There was a trail of wet footprints on the floor, enough to say she had not been the first to wake. She looked at them, thinking of Man Friday, wondering whose they were.

There was a huge stone bath at one end of the bathroom, standing on four legs carved like lion's paws. Somebody had hung a card from one of the brass taps with a little picture painted on it. She sat on the side of the bath and looked at it.

It was Elizabeth's boat, *Fairway*. There was even a tiny Elizabeth hanging onto the mainsheet for dear life. But the waves breaking against her hull were waves of sand, and the boat was in a desert, perched on the top of a hill under some palm trees, with a camel looking at it with puzzled expression. Under the picture Uncle Albert had written,

Here's how we'll be if you use too much water – the shower is behind you!

There was nothing at all behind her, but after all it depended on where you were looking in the first place. Poppy looked round. Then she saw it. At the far end of the room there was a big copper spray, like the spout of a giant watering can sticking out of the wall. It was still dripping. She hopped out of her pyjamas and stood underneath it.

There was only one tap: a massive brass ring jutting out of the tiles. She gripped it with both hands and turned. Water gurgled out of the holes above and plopped down onto her head. Just a few drops, then more and more, until she felt she was swimming. It was cool, almost cold, and very pleasant at first, splashing onto her head and bouncing off her feet to disappear down a little grille in the floor. But she soon started to get shivery and jumped out of the way to one side, only to have to get wet all over again leaning across to turn the tap off.

The shutters were propped half-open on three sides of the room. As she dried herself, she could hear somebody singing. The faint smell of coffee floated in through the windows.

There were other sounds as well now: the rattle of china; people talking quietly.

A door opened and she heard footsteps clatter across the hall. She remembered the wet footprints. Perhaps everybody had been up for ages.

She finished drying herself, dressed as fast as she could, then grabbing the soap and towel, scampered back to her room. As she ran downstairs she remembered she had forgotten to comb her hair.

*

But she was not late. The table on the terrace was laid with a fresh white cloth and Uncle Albert was there, sitting in his favourite seat talking quietly to Cook. She had pulled up a chair next to his and the two of them were holding big china bowls spilling tiny wisps of steam into the crisp morning air.

"Good Morning Poppy. First as ever. We're having coffee and settling the order of the day. There's a fresh jug of hot chocolate there - dig in."

Poppy looked round the table. Breakfast at home was things like porridge and boiled eggs, or sometimes fried bacon and eggs, or fried bread and sausages. There was nothing like that here. Not even tea cups – just brightly coloured bowls, big enough to swim in, with pictures on them.

There was a basket in the middle of the table filled with strange flaky rolls wrapped in a white cloth to keep them warm, and a loaf of bread almost as long as she was. And bowls of fruit: strawberries, peaches and some little purple things she didn't recognize.

What looked like raspberry jam had been set out in a china dish shaped like a tortoise lying on its back. It had a little china spoon resting on its head. She chose one of the bowls and held it up to look at the painting before pouring hot chocolate into it out of the jug.

"Do you like it?" asked Uncle Albert. "That one's my favourite; I don't know why."

"I think they're all lovely. I've never seen anything like them."

"Well, that's true enough. I made them myself. When the weather gets a bit cooler I make pottery things like that. But you can't make pots in the heat – too much like hard labour. I'm not really very good at it, but it keeps me busy."

Poppy pointed to the little purple things. "What are these, please?"

"They're figs. Not ours, though. It's too early for them. I think they come from Italy. But they're almost as good. Try one."

Poppy picked one out of the bowl and sat looking at it, puzzled.

"Just break it in half and bite the stuff out."

She dug her nails into the fig and broke it open, a glistening mass of pink and white jelly. She nibbled some.

"Very nice."

"There's not much in one. Have another. It must seem an odd sort of breakfast – hot chocolate and figs. But you could do worse. Try some of the jam."

All the time they were talking, Cook sat looking from one to another, shaking her head at the strange language. Then, hearing the sound of cheerful voices echoing from inside the house, she sprang up and made for the kitchen door.

Stuart and Laura came running out onto the terrace, followed by Elizabeth with very wet hair and a rather indignant Ian.

"You've started already," he shouted. "I thought you would. I hope you've left something for us. I heard you get up. You never wait for me."

"Good morning," said Uncle Albert. "Who was last with the shower? I should have told you. The water's pumped up into the roof in the day to let the sun warm it up. It's hot enough, but it does get a bit colder the more you use."

"It was me, I think," said Elizabeth, pretending to shiver. "I'd forgotten the water was cold in the summer. But it wasn't too bad."

"I know you slept well," said Uncle Albert, "so I won't ask. It's impossible not to here. I have to go to my studio in a second. Help yourself to whatever you like for breakfast. Poppy will show you what's what. More hot chocolate is on the way. And when you've finished, come and find me; I've something to show you."

"Is it the surprise?" asked Ian.

But Uncle Albert seemed not to hear. He finished the last of his coffee and stood up saying, "now, where did I put my hat?"

Poppy picked it up from where it had rolled under his chair and handed it to him, waiting for his reply. But he simply perched the straw hat on his head and patted it, making a hollow sound. He gave Ian a huge wink and said, "that's for me to know and you to find out, young man. All in good time."

He marched off across the lawn, humming to himself, and disappeared round the corner of the house.

"But we don't know where to go," said Laura.

"The studio's round there," said Elizabeth, waving a piece of bread. "He's awfully fussy about who goes in, so this is something special. He said it was for you four anyway, so I suppose it's to do with rescuing his boat. I wonder what he's up to? He's always up to something."

"There's no need to do anything about that," said Laura, "I'd really rather he forgot all about it."

Elizabeth was sorting among the bowls on the table. She picked one painted with a red cockerel and poured hot chocolate into it. She glanced across at the kitchen door and whispered, "I wish there was more for breakfast. I don't think they eat breakfast in France."

"The cocoa's nice," said Ian.

"I mean things to eat. There's just fruit and jam and these." She unfolded the cloth and picked something out of the basket.

"There's a name for them. I knew it at Christmas, but I've forgotten. They're alright – a cross between bread and cake. Uncle dips them in his coffee. He does it on the sly when he thinks no one's looking."

Ian grabbed one. "Oh, it's hot … well, warm anyway." He looked at Stuart.

"Can I dip it in my cocoa? … just to see."

"You'll have to ask Cook," said Laura, and Stuart grinned.

"But I don't know how to ask her anything. She only speaks French and we haven't even started that at school. And I can tell already I'm not going to be able to."

Stuart had been sitting quietly sipping his chocolate and looking across the lawn. It was lovely eating outside in the cool of the morning. Of course, you did that when you were camping, but then you didn't have tablecloths and painted china bowls.

"Plan for the day," said Elizabeth, spooning jam onto her bread.

"Visiting Uncle Albert," said Poppy, "he said we have to."

"I mean after that. I think we should explore first. When I was here at Christmas it was so cold you couldn't really go very far. But I did work out where I wanted to go."

She scraped a collection of knives and spoons together into a pile and laid them out in a rough square on the tablecloth.

"Right … let's say this is the house."

She looked round and grabbed a piece of bread.

"This can be the woods on one side of the house." She placed it on the table.

"It's woods there as far as you can go; and that's a really long way. I've been down there."

She picked up another piece of bread and propped it up on the table to stop the jam falling off.

"It's the same this side - more woods. Just woods and woods for ever and ever. That's done two sides of the house."

She looked around and picked up a spoon.

"Let's say this is the front. That's down there," she waved the spoon in the direction of the lawn, then put it on the table. "That's the way we got here. You can go down the path, of course, but that wouldn't be exploring. If you go off the path, you come to a little stream – dried up now I should think – and a fence. After that it's just fields, but they're nothing to do with Uncle."

She picked up another piece of bread. "It's here I don't know about."

"That's the back of the house," said Stuart.

"Yes. I asked Uncle what's there and he just said, 'Why don't you go and look?' So it's a mystery."

"Can that bit of bread stop being woods?" Ian asked. "I want to eat it. It was my breakfast."

Elizabeth nodded. He picked up the bread and continued his breakfast.

"Alright, let's start that way," said Stuart. "It will be more fun to go where no one's ever been."

"Somebody must have been there before," said Ian. "People live here. There might be houses there."

Elizabeth spread some jam on another of the woods and started to eat it.

"That's just it, we don't know. There could be anything there."

"Shouldn't we go and find the studio?" asked Poppy who was starting to feel anxious. "He's been gone a long time. Perhaps he's waiting for us."

Elizabeth took a last swig of chocolate and looked wistfully at the breakfast table.

"Dinner's much better. Usually something hot. At least it was at Christmas." She jumped up.

"Come on, I'll show you the way. It's not far."

They followed her along the terrace and under a stone arch covered in trailing purple flowers. They came to a door. She was about to tap on it when she stopped.

There were voices inside: two men speaking French. Uncle Albert seemed to be doing most of the talking; the other voice just managed to say a few words now and then. Suddenly there was complete silence, then they both burst out laughing. They heard Uncle Albert chuckle and say, "You're right, you know. I bet that's what they do. We'll have to see." At least this last bit was in English, but that didn't help because they had no idea at all what it meant.

Elizabeth stood there, uncertain what to do. She was about to knock, when the door opened and a startled little man with a large moustache stood there looking at her. He was pulling on some white leather gloves. In fact he was dressed very neatly all over and carried an ebony walking stick in his arms, as if it was too precious to touch the ground.

Finding five assorted explorers crowding round the door, he stepped back into the studio, looking confused, then managed to smile in a very friendly way. He turned to Uncle Albert.

"And here they are. Just when we're talking about them. Speak of the devil, as you say, it's always the way."

Ian stared open mouthed. He was speaking English, but it had a very odd sound. Like something he'd never heard before.

He caught Laura's eye and hurriedly looked down. Best not to stare. But very odd, all the same. The strange man was clearly in a hurry. He continued in rapid French, speaking almost to himself until Uncle Albert came across to the doorway and beamed out at them.

"This gentleman is the Mayor. He's a very important man. He's also the village doctor and lots of other things as well. I won't say all your names, he's in a hurry. I'm painting his portrait, although not this morning. We were talking about something else."

While he was speaking, the Mayor was looking at each of them in turn, echoing, "Something else … yes, something else," and grinning to himself.

He gave a quick bow to Elizabeth and Laura and hurried past, stepping carefully across the damp grass to keep his shoes dry. He disappeared round the corner of the studio.

They heard an engine starting and the sound of a car bumping its way down the track towards the road.

*

Uncle Albert beckoned them all inside. It was a huge space, painted white, with big windows high up on one wall. It looked like several rooms knocked into one, with bits of old wall sticking out here and there. Ian had expected to see pictures everywhere; after all, the house was full of them and this was where they were painted. But the whitewashed walls were almost empty, apart from a few canvases and a calendar pinned above a desk in the corner.

He glanced round quickly. There was no sign of a parcel, just a big carpenter's saw propped up against the wall and that couldn't be the present. It must be hidden somewhere, but there were so few hiding places it must be something quite small.

There was a huge table cluttered with bottles and brushes, strange jars filled with coloured liquids and hundreds of tubes of paint, most of them squeezed out. It was all a bit untidy, but clear enough there was nothing there that looked like a present.

Paintings were stacked at the far end of the room, turned with their faces to the wall. Perhaps it was hidden there, but it didn't seem very likely. There was a big mirror on a stand with wheels. You could see right underneath it: there was nothing there.

You couldn't help feeling a bit disappointed.

In the centre of the room, next to a little stool, was a huge easel. Two canvases stood leaning against it on the floor. Uncle Albert sat down on the stool and they crowded round him.

"I have to thank you four for the rescue of my boat." He tipped his hat back and looked hard at Elizabeth.

"It would have been five of you I suppose, if someone hadn't been left behind to wait for an Uncle who never arrived."

Laura was starting to feel very uncomfortable. If only people wouldn't go on so much about the boat in the bay and the rescue. It was best all forgotten. If he was going to make a speech about that it would be awful.

He was looking at her with quite a serious expression, almost as if he knew how she felt. He leaned towards her.

"I can't see that presents would make much sense, so I've been trying to think of something a bit different. Something for me to remember you by."

He looked a little awkward, then shuffled round and added, "I settled on this. I've done half the job. Here … what do you think?"

He hoisted one of the canvases up onto the easel and turned the whole thing round so that it was left facing them.

It was a picture of a hillside with a few bent trees braving the fierce sun. Tufts of yellow grass poked out between outcrops of white rock. Near the top of the hill, against a familiar sky, there were the ruins of a building. All that was left of an old chapel, a wall or two rising out of piles of stones where other walls had fallen down. There was a stunned silence.

Laura was the first to speak.

"It's awfully nice of you ..."

But she could go no further. She looked at Stuart. He was biting his lip. What could they say? Then she saw Uncle Albert was trying his best not to laugh out loud.

"Poor old Laura, polite to the last. No, you needn't worry, I'm not saddling the crew with anything you'll have to cart home." He laughed.

"Well, not exactly. I'm not giving you the picture. In fact, quite the reverse."

"But the reverse doesn't work. You can't say a picture is giving something. It doesn't make sense ..."

Stuart caught Laura's look and went very red. "I'm sorry. I mean we really are jolly grateful ... and ... well, thank you very much." He felt dreadfully uncomfortable.

Elizabeth had been feeling a little bit out of things and had wandered across to the window. She glanced back at the painting then looked at Stuart with a wide smile.

"Oh, I don't know. Perhaps the reverse works after all."

Ian was feeling lost. "I don't understand. What's everybody talking about? The painting's the surprise, isn't it?" He looked at Laura and mumbled, "... Isn't it?"

It wasn't at all his idea of a surprise. It wasn't wrapped up for one thing. But he did his best, saying as valiantly as he could, "J olly nice really. A picture."

Elizabeth was enjoying herself now. She stood next to Uncle Albert and the two of them grinned at Ian.

"It's alright for you," she said, "but it must be hot in that sun for those two. Good job they've got some shade ..."

She started giggling to herself.

All this time Poppy had been looking at Uncle Albert. She could see he was very pleased with himself but also a bit shy, the way people look when they give you something and know for certain you will like it a lot. Why was he looking like that? It was all very puzzling.

She got up and looked at the picture again. Then she saw. It had been there all the time. There, standing next to a pile of stones, was a tiny Stuart. He had his hands in his pockets and was looking far away into the distance. The way he always looked when he was checking the weather. He had his back to you but that was exactly how he looked; he always looked like that. And next to him, Laura, sitting on a low wall, her head bowed, reading her book.

For a second Poppy didn't know what to say. She swung round and looked at Uncle Albert, her eyes swimming.

"But it's wonderful. Stuart and Laura in the picture."

Ian jumped up and pushed his way past her.

"Where? Where? I can't see them."

Then Stuart saw. How could he have missed it? His heart gave a little lurch as he recognised himself. Or rather the back of himself. But he was quite sure who they were - the two tiny figures looked as if they had always been there. They would be there always now - as long as the painting.

Laura was looking at the picture. She stepped back a little with a soft smile on her face and looked at Uncle Albert.

"Well? What do you think?"

She started to take his hand in hers then feeling shy, turned it into an odd little handshake. "Thank you very much. What a lovely thing to do."

Elizabeth was starting to get impatient. "That's all very well. I'm good at spotting these things. But where's Poppy and Ian? They were in the rescue as well, you know." She was looking at the other picture on the floor next to the easel.

"Are they there? Let's look."

"No use," said Uncle Albert. "Couldn't be done. Not from memory anyway. Tricky pair, those two. Always hopping about like monkeys. So you'll have to wait a bit. It's my next trick."

He hauled the painting up onto the easel and Poppy ran across to look at it. It was like the other one. A dusty path winding up a hill, the grass brown with the sun. On one side a stone arch, part of a ruined church, framed the view beyond of endless pale blue hills. A few blobs of creamy white, that for some strange reason looked exactly like sheep, were grazing peacefully on the hillside.

Uncle Albert was standing at a table at the other end of the studio squeezing tubes of paint and sorting through a big bottle full of brushes. He somehow managed to fit three little brushes through the fingers of one hand and pick up the wooden palette with the other. He nudged Ian in the back with his elbow.

"Just go and stand over there a second. By the window would be best."

Poppy ran up close to see what he was going to do. She almost missed it. It was all over in a few seconds. Uncle Albert dipped a brush into something dark and touched the canvas. Then another brush and another colour. Another dip into a little bottle. He put the palette down, shook his head and scratched at the paint with his nail, wiping his hand afterwards on a cloth. Another brush. A final dip into the little bottle, a tiny blob of paint, and he stepped back.

"All done. That's it, you can come back."

Poppy came up close and looked at the tiny patch of wet paint. It was only a few lines, the colours all mixed up, grey, brown and pink, smudgy and running into each other. A thread of black ran down through it all. He was looking down at her, his face creased into a smile and his eyes twinkling.

"You're a bit close," he said quietly, "get too close and you can see the stitches. Best step back a bit."

Poppy fixed her eyes on the picture and took a few steps back. The little patch of paint was so small if you took your eyes off it you would lose it altogether. It would just disappear into the dusty hillside. Then her heart turned over in a most alarming way. There was Ian. He was standing as he always did in that funny way of his, half-perched on one leg. And he was looking straight at her. She could even see he was grinning.

"How did that happen?" she said. "Is it a trick? It's like magic." She walked up close again, then stepped back, stumbling into a chair.

"It's Ian. How did you do that?"

All this was far too much for the subject himself. He came running over, almost bouncing into the easel, standing up on his toes and staring into the picture. He shook his head. Poppy pulled at the back of his shirt. "Now you'll see it."

And he did. A broad smile suddenly lit his face. "Jolly clever. I wish I could do that."

"Poppy's turn," said Elizabeth.

Uncle Albert threw a few cushions on the floor. "Just sit on these. Any way you like. Look over there but whatever you do don't imagine someone's painting you. Just think about your dinner."

A few minutes later they were all clustered round the second picture. A boy and a girl, tiny against a huge sky, looked out at them as if they had been there for ever. A smiling Ian next to a solemn seated Poppy.

"JUST THINK ABOUT YOUR DINNER"

CHAPTER VII

THE HOUSE IN THE SKY

UNCLE Albert shooed them into the morning sun, smiling and waving as they called out goodbye. They were halfway across the lawn when Elizabeth suddenly stopped and turned.

"I've forgotten something. I won't be long. You go on ahead."

She ran back, found the door to the studio still open, and pushed it wide to peer round. Uncle Albert was humming to himself, putting a pan of water on a little stove. He turned and pulled a face at her.

"Back already, niece? What can I do for you? I must get on – I've things to do."

She came in and sat down at the little table next to the sink.

"Hello you. What sort of an uncle do you think you are?"

"Well, do they come in sorts? I never knew that. Would you like some hot chocolate? I was making coffee for myself but I can make you some – the water's hot."

"I'm not to be got round that way. You're up to something. What is it? It's not fair leaving me in the dark. I can keep a secret you know."

He gave her an innocent wide-eyed look then burst out laughing.

"Not much gets past you, that's for sure. But as for keeping secrets, I don't know about that. I'll have to ask your mother."

"I saw you wink at her last night. The others didn't, but I did. What's all this about her visiting friends? Mother doesn't know any people here. She hasn't got any friends here. She's not visiting anybody, is she? That was just a story. Poppy saw her this morning, you know; she told me. First thing, when you thought we'd all be fast asleep. Sneaking out like that. Where's she gone to? Come on, out with it."

It was a long speech and Elizabeth stood there red-faced and a little out of breath.

"I really couldn't say. Somewhere special, do you think? We'll know soon enough. She'll be back before supper."

"Back from where? You must know. Look, what's going on? Why the mystery?" Elizabeth tried her most engaging smile.

"Come on, I won't tell, cross my heart."

But Uncle Albert had said all he was going to. He perched on the edge of the table, pushed his hat to the back of his head, and took a long slow drink of coffee smiling sweetly at her over the top of the bowl.

"Lovely morning out there I expect ..."

Elizabeth tapped her foot in frustration and walked across to look at the picture on the easel.

"Is it something to do with these pictures? I bet it is."

"Is what to do with them?" He put his bowl down and pretended to look at an imaginary watch.

"Well, I really do have to get on. Won't the others be waiting for you? What are you all up to this morning?"

"You'll just have to guess. Two can play at that game. You'll just have to guess - I'm not telling you."

She stood for a second in the doorway giving him her sternest expression and trying to think of one final crushing thing to say. But words failed her and she turned away in frustration, calling over her shoulder, "I know you're planning something. I just know it." She left the door open.

*

The others were waiting for her on the lawn. Elizabeth looked flustered and very red.

"What did you forget?" asked Ian. He could see she had nothing in her hands. "What's the matter?"

"Never you mind. It's probably a secret. Everything's a secret here. Altogether too many secrets." She went on trying to look fierce for a while but could not help breaking into a laugh.

"Oh well, never mind. It doesn't matter. Grown-ups can be infuriating sometimes. And uncles are the worst of the lot."

"We've been talking," said Stuart. "If we explore behind the house, we'll have the best of the shade. It's starting to get awfully hot. We have to get back for dinner, so we can't go all that far."

*

There was a wall of dark trees at the back of the house with just a single break in it, no more than a narrow gap between two huge oaks. Barely a proper path, more like a track made by some big animal in the night.

He led the way, with Elizabeth bringing up the rear. Once among the trees, it was much cooler. The little path, no more than rutted dried mud, curved gently up ahead of them. A few months before there must have been a stream rushing down here, gouging out a deep scar in the earth. Now, the ground was baked hard and covered with a thick mat of dry leaves. Tiny threads of some thorny weed had sprung up everywhere, catching your ankles.

The explorers came to the top of a little rise and stood looking down. The path ahead widened out, with clearings on either side stacked with neat piles of logs. Apart from the insistent chirp of some small bird, it was completely quiet. The leaves above almost blocked out the sky.

Far off to their right, where trees had blown over in some winter storm, shafts of sunlight made little basins of green.

Stuart led them down into a bigger clearing. Years ago, somebody had felled trees here, leaving stumps cut close to the ground. They were covered with a thick layer of greenish-white lichen.

At the edge of the clearing there was an odd sort of hut covered all over with bracken and open at both ends. The roof was criss-crossed with dry branches and more bracken. Ian ran across and peered inside.

"There's nothing in here," he said. "It's empty. Just like a big tunnel."

"Best not go in there until we've looked all round," said Stuart. They followed him, scrambling through dense weeds looking at the outside.

"There's a fireplace," shouted Ian, pointing to a ring of stones filled with a heap of dead ashes. He poked into it with a stick.

"Ages old by the look of it. Why is it outside the hut? Do you think people lived here?"

"They'd get awfully wet," said Poppy. "The roof wouldn't keep the rain out. It would leak. And there's no door. Anyway, there's nothing inside. What on earth's it for?"

"It must have been built before Uncle lived here," said Elizabeth, "and that's ages ago."

"I think it's a hide," said Stuart, "you know, a place where you watch birds."

"They don't watch birds here," added Elizabeth. "They shoot them."

"That's awful," said Poppy.

"Well, they eat them afterwards, so I suppose it's alright. We eat chickens and somebody must kill them."

She went inside and peeped through the gaps in the wall of bracken, thinking of lines of men silently waiting for the birds to arrive.

"It just doesn't seem fair to lie in wait like that."

*

While the others were looking at the hide, Ian had wandered off to the edge of the clearing. Two tree stumps had been cut higher than the rest, almost as high as him. He went over to look at them and found himself staring at a length of thick steel wire lying at the bottom of a weedy ditch.

He slithered down and looked at it, then at the base of one of the tree stumps. The wire was wrapped tightly round it, with bits of wood stuck down to stop it cutting into the stump.

He waded along the ditch, strands of prickly weed catching at his feet. What was the wire for? It all seemed very mysterious. The second stump was exactly the same as the first, with a steel wire looped tightly round and a trailing end lying loose in the ditch.

The two wires ran up from where they were tied and disappeared high into the dark of the trees above. They were as taut as bowstrings. He leaned back, shading his eyes. The wires simply vanished, dissolving into the leaves miles above his head.

He struggled up out of the ditch, ignoring the nettles stinging his knees, and pushed between two bushes, tearing his shirt. It didn't matter; he had discovered something. Possibly something really important. Something the others had not noticed at all. He looked up again.

Far above, a dark shape seemed to loom out of the branches. He shouted across to the others, "Come and look! I've found something! Over here!"

They heard the excitement in his voice and came running out of the hide. Ian was standing, half-buried in undergrowth, pointing up into the sky.

"Great big wires, two of them. Just disappearing up there. And there's something in the tree."

He tilted back, looking straight up, then let himself topple over onto his back, lying there looking triumphant, with a wide grin on his face. "I can still see it. What is it?"

Laura came running over.

"Do get up Ian, you've got dirt all over your trousers. And you've torn your shirt again."

He managed to scramble up, wincing as he grabbed at a bunch of tall nettles. He stood there looking extremely pleased with himself.

"Your knees are all green," said Poppy, "you'll have to have another shower."

This was not at all the greeting the explorer had expected. Particularly the explorer who had discovered the wires. He was about to protest when Elizabeth said, "He's right, you know! Good for you, Ian! How could we have missed that? Look up there!"

From the top of the bank it was easier to see. Three trees had been pulled together with wires to support a platform of planks. And perched on top of them, a little wooden house appeared to be floating against the sky.

"It's a tree house," said Poppy. "But how on earth do you get up to it?"

Stuart crossed the ditch and walked a little further into the wood. "There's another wire here," he shouted, "and a ladder. Pretty old and all covered in green." He put his foot on the bottom step and pressed.

"But it's not rotten; it seems solid enough."

"I don't think it's a playhouse at all," said Laura. "It's got that same bracken stuff all over it. It must be just another place to shoot at the birds. I don't like it."

"We're not shooting birds," said Elizabeth. "You're not going to let this go to waste, are you? It's much too good for that."

She chopped her way through the weeds with a stick and came to stand next to Stuart. They looked at each other. Her eyes were dancing.

"Shall we?" she said. "What do you think?"

Stuart looked at Laura and saw an odd mixture of disapproval and curiosity in her eyes. She frowned at him.

"I don't think you should. It's awfully high and we don't know it's safe." She saw the disappointment in his face and added, "Anyway, there's your arm. You can't go climbing ladders with your arm in a sling."

Ian had already clambered up the first few rungs.

"I can climb it. My arm's alright. And it was me that found it."

"No," said Laura. "Come down. No one's going up." She looked at Elizabeth and hesitated.

"Well, you're not anyway. If anybody's going up I suppose Elizabeth might." She stopped, then mumbled almost to herself, "But really it's best nobody does."

Stuart was looking carefully at the ladder. It was made from two slender tree trunks, the crosspieces underpinned with thick wire. It didn't run straight up at the start but was fixed at a shallow angle, almost like a bridge. He slipped his sling off and handed it to Laura.

"Honestly, it hasn't hurt much since yesterday. I can take it easy. It looks safe enough."

Elizabeth had already jumped on and started to climb, carefully testing each rung of the ladder as she reached it.

"It's very solid," she shouted, her voice starting to echo back from the trees as she went higher. She paused, staring down in front of her.

"That's odd - somebody must have been here. This rung has new wire along it. It looks shiny." She looked down at Stuart.

"What about it? I'm going up. If it starts to get all shaky, I'll just come back."

Laura bit her lip. If Elizabeth was going to climb up she could hardly stop her. She just hoped Stuart stayed behind. She held the sling out to him. He took it, but just draped it over his arm and sat down on the bottom rung of the ladder, looking up to see where Elizabeth was.

"I could give it a try," he said; then added quietly, "one of us ought to, you know. We can't just let her go up on her own."

"Not me," said Poppy. "I wouldn't climb up there if there was a tiger after me."

"You don't get tigers in France," said Ian. He looked at Laura, suddenly doubtful, "Do you?"

"Wait a minute, Stuart," Elizabeth shouted. She sounded very cheerful, "If you get on the ladder as well, things start swaying about."

He stepped off as carefully as he could and looked up at her. She was leaning out with one arm round the side of the ladder. It was much higher than he thought. Just her head was visible through the leaves, looking down at them, hanging on with one hand and grinning happily.

"It goes straight up from here. Easier really, it was a bit giddy-making looking down through the rungs. It's not hard at all, honestly. But wait till I reach the top before you go jumping on."

Laura looked at Stuart. Only one of the explorers was going to climb up to the tree house. It always seemed to be that way. Even when they were racing on the lake – it was always Elizabeth who won. This time they were all going to be left behind.

Ian had already wandered back to the hide calling out that he wasn't really interested in tree houses anymore. But his voice gave him away. It didn't seem fair.

Laura watched him trail across the clearing dragging his sandals in the dust, kicking at clumps of weeds. He was doing his very best not to look up.

A cheery voice, oddly thin and distant, floated down from above them.

"Phew, I've made it." The noise of shoes on wooden planks echoed through the woods. "Gosh, you can see for miles and miles."

Stuart handed the sling back to Laura.

"Look, I'm going up. I've got to try. If my arm hurts too much, well … I'll just have to come back." He clambered onto the ladder and started up, climbing on all fours.

"But it won't. It hasn't hurt at all today."

"Alright. But do take care. And don't hurry whatever you do. We'll wait here."

*

It was surprisingly easy going at first. The slope of the ladder was so shallow it was more like crawling than climbing. Elizabeth was right, though: it was not very nice looking straight down through the rungs at the ground below. He saw Laura's face staring up at him. She waved, moving her hand just a little, as if to say, 'No need to wave back'.

Poppy had fetched Ian and he stood there with a big smile on his face. The angle of the ladder suddenly changed. You couldn't crawl on your knees anymore. There was nothing for it but to stand and climb vertically. He pulled himself up, pressing his chest against the wooden rungs in front.

He reached up with his good arm and took the first step. He raised his other arm gingerly towards the next rung, letting go and clumsily dropping down onto the step below, standing there while the pain slowly subsided.

As he lowered himself back down, crouching on the flatter part of the ladder, Poppy called out, "Are you alright?"

He put his arm across his chest where the sling was meant to go.

"I can't make it. My arm still hurts if I lift it up. It would be silly to try. It's the bit where you have to climb straight up. It's too steep."

He scrabbled his way back down, crawling awkwardly on two knees and one arm. At the bottom, Laura took his hand and helped him off. She handed him his sling, seeing the look in his face.

"It can't be helped; you tried, and that's what counts."

He sat down on a log, hot and miserable.

"Why don't I have a go?" said Ian. "It looks pretty easy. Elizabeth got up in no time at all."

"You know you can't," said Stuart, still panting from the climb. "It's miles higher than you think and you're just not big enough."

Ian started to walk away. Stuart jumped up and followed him, catching him by the shoulder.

"Don't go on about it, Iggie," he whispered. "You know you can't go up there on your own. You're being silly. I promised Mummy we'd take care of you. What if you fell down?"

"You're the one that goes falling down things."

Stuart grinned sheepishly, "Well, alright. So neither of us can climb it. And Poppy can't climb at all." He lowered his voice.

"Laura could, but she just doesn't want to. I think it's because of the great storm and all that. Don't go making things worse."

"If she doesn't want to, why's she up there?" said Ian, pointing back.

Stuart had not noticed. While they had been talking, Laura had jumped onto the ladder. Faster even than Elizabeth, she had crawled across and was already disappearing through the leaves far above their heads.

*

Perhaps it was that way Poppy had of not saying anything. Laura found herself scampering like mad across the ladder, a fleeting glimpse of the ground below turning her stomach over in the most peculiar way.

She stopped a moment to rest, out of breath and panting hard. It had only been a few minutes, but she was already far too high to go back.

She cricked her neck, straining up to see how much further. Above was a blur of shifting green, a mass of leaves curving in an arc over her head.

The angle of the ladder started to change. Beams of wood criss-crossed under her. A thick wire, close enough to touch, ran alongside the ladder, threaded through a huge metal staple hammered deep into the tree. She fixed her eyes grimly on the rungs of the ladder in front and pulled herself onto the next step.

It wasn't at all like the ladder up to the *Arethusa* in that dreadful storm. For one thing there was no rain stinging her eyes. And there was no wind - it was very quiet and calm hanging in mid-air, feeling just a tiny breeze across the back of your legs.

Somewhere high over her head she heard the sound of Elizabeth's shoes. She tightened her grip, feet swaying slightly with the ladder. She was climbing vertically now, looking through the rungs at the bark of the tree covered with little beetles scuttling about.

She risked a quick look down catching a fleeting glimpse of figures a tremendous distance below: tiny white faces, upturned.

The wood at the side of the ladder was polished smooth by all those other hands that had gripped it. Hunter's hands, used to the climb.

She felt, rather than saw, the dark shadow of something close above her head: the underneath of a rough wooden floor. The ladder continued on through a square hatch into the little house above.

And staring down at her was Elizabeth's smiling face.
"Where's Stuart?"

But Laura could not answer. She looked up, her legs aching, wondering how she could pull herself into the little house.

Elizabeth kneeled down, stretching out a hand.
"Just keep climbing. Hold on to me if you like."

Laura shook her head and started to climb. Leaves brushed against her back. A shower of ants and beetles cascaded down. She felt something quite big stick in her hair and shook her head.

You could see inside now - a floor made of rough logs nailed together; walls of bracken. She was still hanging onto the ladder, breathing heavily.

It should have been easy enough to step across and stand on the floor. That was what the hunters must have done. They would have pushed their way through and jumped across onto the platform without a second thought. But she was not a hunter and somehow it was difficult to persuade her legs to reach out across that bit of empty space.

She backed down the ladder a little, reached across, and crawled onto the floor of the hut on all fours. It was not very dignified, but at least she had arrived.

Elizabeth crouched down and took her hand. They heard the sound of voices from below.

"Hurrah! She's there!" That was Ian shouting; he sounded miles away.

Then Poppy's voice, "Laura, can you see us? What's it like?"

The two of them sat side by side on the ribbed wooden floor and looked at each other. Elizabeth leaned forward and knocked a beetle out of Laura's hair. Her face was alive with excitement. Laura managed a little smile.

"Stuart couldn't climb up. Not with his arm."

"But you climbed it. That's just as good. We've climbed it. That's what counts. Right to the top!"

In fact, sitting on the floor, surrounded by walls of bracken you could imagine you were not high up at all. Certainly not on top of a tree! Laura managed to get onto her knees, leaning forward uncertainly and hanging onto Elizabeth's arm.

Square slots, like windows, had been cut out of the bracken on each side. There must have been a roof once, but all that was left now were a few clumps of bracken in one corner. The rest had blown away leaving the little house open to the sky. Above them was a thin canopy of leaves, endlessly rustling in the breeze, and beyond that, a bright blue sky.

"It's like flying," said Elizabeth, hauling herself up. "It's wonderful."

As she moved, the whole platform gently swayed beneath them and Laura grabbed at the ladder.

"It's a bit like being in a house in the sky. Or a boat, I suppose. I wouldn't like to be up here in a gale."

Two massive branches poked through the floor of the platform. About halfway up, the wood on each side had been worn to a smooth white with the grip of countless hands. Laura crawled away from the ladder to the nearest branch.

For a few seconds of panic she had nothing at all to hold on to. Then, very slowly, she hauled herself upright. She had a strange tingling feeling down her back and into her legs.

Elizabeth was already standing beside her, leaning through one of the little bracken windows. She stretched a hand out. Laura took it and inched her way to the window.

They were on top of the world, looking over wave upon wave of trees. An endless restless ocean of dark rippling green for as far as they could see. There was a gentle hissing noise streaming round them. Laura grasped Elizabeth's arm.

"Can you hear? It's like the sea." She was whispering.

"Let's look through all of them. Perhaps you can see the house, it must be over there."

They held on to each other and shuffled round to the next window in the bracken. But there was no view of the house; only a bank of green rising even higher than the tree house.

As Elizabeth leaned out, a bird swooped towards her, about to land. It saw her startled face and veered off, disappearing overhead.

The view from the next bracken window was the same: treetops stretched out to a far horizon, broken only by lines of thin clay tracks.

Elizabeth was feeling bolder now. She let go of the branch and stood looking at the ladder stretching down to the floor of the forest.

"I think we've seen all there is to see," she said. "I wonder how best to get back onto that ladder? We should go one at a time."

"There's still one window. I'm going to look." Laura edged round to the last of the square slots cut in the bracken walls and peered out across the trees. Elizabeth whirled round, hearing her cry out.

"Come and look! You won't believe it!"

The two of them stood, wide-eyed and silent. There was a narrow band of trees below. But beyond that, reaching out to the curve of the far horizon was a wide expanse of sparkling blue, flecked with white. She reached out and grabbed Elizabeth's arm.

"Look! The sea! It's the sea!"

"BUT YOU CLIMBED IT. THAT'S JUST AS GOOD"

CHAPTER VIII

THE SIESTA

"SO that's what he meant," said Elizabeth. "You know, when he said 'You'll find out' to Ian. I did wonder. Well, we've found out."

"I thought it was the leaves making that noise," said Laura. "Of course it sounded just like the sea. It *was* the sea!"

They perched against the bracken walls clinging onto each other; a salty freshness filled with the smell of the sea streamed through the window.

Down below, so close it seemed just a few yards away, the woods petered out into straggly lines of trees. Sand had piled itself up into vast dunes dotted with coarse grass. Tiny waves flopped over onto the sand, leaving a white line on the beach.

And beyond that, the swell of a great ocean heaving out to the horizon.

Elizabeth tried to poke her head between the bracken.

"There's something over there ... I can't quite see it ... it's a building I think ... something dark anyway. The trees are in the way ... no, I can't make out what it is."

She tried to lean out further, hanging onto the branch behind her head, until Laura pulled her back."

"Careful! You're going to fall."

"No ... it's no use, you can't see what it is. We'll simply have to come back and look. We'll come right back after dinner."

She straightened up, her face flushed with excitement.

"Just think, the sea right here on our doorstep and we never knew about it. Come on ... let's get down. The quicker we get dinner over, the quicker we can come back and explore. We're going to be a bit late anyway."

Laura glanced down at her watch then remembered she had left it in the house. "You're right. The others will be wondering what's happening." She looked at the ladder sticking up through the floor of the platform and then at Elizabeth.

Elizabeth smiled back. "Do you want to go first?"

"I'd rather, if you don't mind. How do I get onto it?"

"Just don't think about it."

Laura crawled over the floor and grabbed the top of the ladder with both hands. There was a moment's panic as she dangled her legs down, kicking into thin air, then she knocked against something hard with her foot.

She reached down and wriggled both feet onto the ladder. Her legs were trembling with the strain, but Elizabeth could not see that. She looked up and managed a weak sort of smile.

"Well, here goes," she gulped, and dropped out of sight.

*

The others had soon grown tired of peering up into a tree, even a tree with a house on top. They heard the faint sound of voices and once heard Laura call out, but you could not make out what was said. Poppy had called up twice but no one had answered.

In fact, nothing at all seemed to be happening apart from the occasional echo of feet on the platform and the shiver of the tree trunk as the explorers above moved about.

Ian and Poppy wandered back into the hide and stood inside waiting for passing birds. Stuart tied the sling back round his arm and sank down onto his log wondering what had made Laura climb the ladder. There were things about Laura he never got right.

There was a rattling noise and the wire running down into the ditch started to flex. He jumped up. There was a rustle from up above, then the tree trunk itself swayed and Laura's legs appeared, painfully feeling their way from rung to rung.

She reached the place where the ladder flattened out and lowered herself onto hands and knees. It was slow work inching backwards, but eventually she drew level with him.

He held out a hand, but she swung her legs over the side, and jumped down, brushing some ants off her front. She gave him a brisk smile and called up to Elizabeth,

"Can you hear me? It's alright. I'm down!"

There was a muffled sound in the tree above and all three of the tree trunks swayed violently. Ian and Poppy came running across.

Elizabeth appeared, hanging out from the ladder with one hand and waving cheerfully with the other. She scampered down and jumped the last few feet, landing next to Laura.

Poppy was looking at them as if they had returned from the moon.

"What's it like? What did you see?"

"Well ... we saw something ... but Ian saw it first," said Elizabeth.

"Remember, when he asked Uncle what's over here? I heard him ask."

Ian was trying to remember. "But there wasn't anything. It just looked all misty."

"You'd never guess where that mist comes from," Elizabeth said. "I'll tell you. It's the sea!" She looked round to get her bearings, then pointed to the woods behind her.

"Through there. You could walk it easily."

Poppy looked at Laura. "Really the sea? Not a pretend thing?"

Laura nodded her head. She suddenly felt a little sick. Her legs had started to tremble. She set off down the path, walking fast.

"Wait for us," shouted Ian. "Aren't we going to look at the sea? If you can walk there, why don't we? I want to see the sea."

"Not right now," Stuart called, running ahead to catch Laura.

"We have to get back for dinner. We'll come again when we've got time to explore properly. You do want your dinner, don't you?"

*

Even so, they were late. Laura made them stop while she tried to get the worst of the mud and grass off Ian's legs. Then there was a row about the correct path. When they were coming there had seemed to be only one way to the tree house, but now they were facing the other way, there were innumerable tracks forking and splitting off in all directions between the trees.

Ian had been so sure of the way they had followed his choice until it petered out in a wall of brambles and they had to struggle back over unfamiliar ground, grumbling at him, until they reached the main path.

"We'll just take whichever way goes uphill," said Stuart, "that must be right."

When they eventually came out over the rise, the house was in view, but much further off than they expected, and it was a very footsore and bedraggled bunch of explorers that eventually struggled out onto the lawn.

The table on the terrace had already been laid with glasses and china. It looked cool and peaceful. Uncle Albert was sitting quietly in a deckchair under the shade of a huge walnut tree, reading a newspaper. He heard them coming and put it on the ground at his side, then jumped up to stamp on it as the breeze started to blow the pages apart.

"Sorry we're a bit late," said Elizabeth cheerfully, "we got held up." She went over to the table.

"Is this water? Is it alright to help ourselves?" He waved a hand to say yes. "We're parched, you see." She started filling glasses and handing them round.

Uncle Albert tapped a letter lying open on the table.

"The post's slow here … but it's good news … from your father … still busy in Paris … but you'll be seeing him soon enough … he says he's on his way at the end of next week."

He watched as she filled another glass.

"What have you all been up to? Exploring?"

Ian finished his drink. "Were we just!" he blurted out, "you'll never guess … ouch!"

The hurried kick from Elizabeth had been a little harder than she intended and Ian hopped out of range.

"Ah," said Uncle Albert, "I can see I'm not to know. Never mind. I'm used to conspiracies."

Ian was going to ask, but couldn't quite manage the word.

"It's not that," said Poppy, "but we have made the most tremendous discovery. Really."

She glanced at Stuart. But Elizabeth looked as stern as she could and firmly shook her head.

"Well you keep quiet about it," said Uncle Albert. "When I was a boy I used to get sore ankles from secrets that way." He pulled a face at Elizabeth, "Mind you, I've been accused of plotting things myself. And that was only this morning."

The kitchen door opened and Cook appeared carrying a big white dish and a tiny china bowl with a lid. She looked at Ian's green legs and shook her head.

"Come on Ian," said Poppy, "we'd better clean up a bit. I'll go with you."

"I'll race you," said Ian, but Uncle Albert waved his newspaper at them.

"There's no hurry so don't you go racing anywhere. It's far too hot. The food can wait."

*

When they got back, Elizabeth and the other two were already sitting down. Uncle Albert was standing at the head of the table holding a loaf of bread close to his chest and cutting round it with a sharp little knife.

He piled slices up onto a plate and sat down, only to spring up again and whip the top off the china bowl.

"Thought so - the butter's here, (looking hard at Elizabeth) by special request. I had to explain our strange ways to Cook. You don't put butter on bread in France."

One end of the big dish was covered with something that looked a bit like bacon; the other end was piled high with slivers of pink melon.

Poppy put some of the meat on Ian's plate then served herself. Uncle Albert leaned over and spooned a few slices of melon onto their plates.

She was not at all sure about the meat. It had a powerful taste almost like something raw. Ian was prodding his with a fork.

"Try, Iggie," she whispered, "it's a sort of French sausage I think. It won't kill us."

She popped some in her mouth and swallowed as fast as she could. She had done her best, but it would be difficult to eat another piece.

"But it's not cooked," said Ian, "I only like bacon cooked."

He folded a slice into his bread making a sort of sandwich and sat looking at it. Elizabeth was eyeing him with a mischievous look on her face. She had picked up a piece of melon and was chewing along it biting as close as she could to the bright green rind. He made up his mind. He bit into his sandwich, swallowed a mouthful whole, barely tasting it, and washed everything down with a big swig of lemonade. He took a piece of melon and grinned back at her.

"It's not too bad."

But Laura was in difficulty. The meat really was very strange. Ian was right - it tasted uncooked somehow. She glanced up. Elizabeth and Stuart, oblivious of the others, seemed to be eating happily.

She rolled a piece round her fork and sat looking at it, her head bowed. She glanced timidly up at Uncle Albert. He smiled back.

"Don't worry. If you try everything once, that's the best you can do."

"I quite like it now I'm used to it," Ian said. He had buttered his bread and was making an elaborate sandwich of ham and melon. He started to take a bite then changed his mind and added another piece of melon.

Under cover of the tablecloth Elizabeth reached out and took Laura's hand. She gave it a little tug and started to speak.

" Uncle … we were walking in the woods behind the house."

She pulled at Laura's hand again, looking hard at Uncle Albert. He didn't seem very interested.

"We went right down as far as the hut made of bracken."

"Oh yes. Find anything down there? It's ages since I looked."

He was staring wide-eyed at her, daring her, the ghost of a smile crinkling his eyes. He leaned back in his chair, tipping it up on two legs until Poppy reached out in alarm.

"That hut down there … isn't it an old hide?"

"He knows all about it!" said Elizabeth shaking her head in exasperation. "He knew all the time."

"Do you know what it's for?" asked Stuart.

"It's not all that nice. Years ago, before I bought this place, men used to lie in wait there for migrating birds."

Poppy was about to say something, but he waved his fork towards her.

"No, before you say anything; you can't blame them that much. It was something to eat, after all."

"But the tree house," shouted Poppy, "that's not fair. Birds don't expect people up there," then seeing Elizabeth's face she remembered it was a secret. She stared hard into his eyes.

"You knew all about it, didn't you?"

He nodded. "It's the same sort of hide. They climbed up there in the evening and waited for pigeons to fly across."

Poppy was about to protest, but he took her hand and patted it.

"It's alright, it's stopped now."

"Pigeons," said Ian, "you can't eat pigeons! So why did they do it?"

Laura smiled at him. She was making very slow progress with her meat. She remembered the book Mother had given her for her birthday, *Recipes for the Hunter*.

"I think you can eat them. There's different ways of cooking them in my book."

"Well you won't catch me eating them," he said.

"Of course, it wouldn't surprise me at all if people climbed up there just for the view." Uncle Albert was looking hard at Elizabeth again.

"Venturesome people, that is. But they'd ask first if it was safe, wouldn't they?"

Elizabeth had gone rather red and was suddenly very occupied picking a piece of melon off her plate. It was taking her a long time.

"We were most awfully careful," said Stuart. "And the ladder was very strong … it was quite safe."

He stopped, feeling very awkward. Uncle Albert burst out laughing.

"We knew it. We knew it. I was talking to the doctor about it only this morning. He said he was just the same when he was a lad. But don't worry, he got some men from the village to look at it yesterday. A ladder's irresistible for some folk. They only have to see one and up they go."

Elizabeth had been looking very uncomfortable.

"It's not Stuart's fault. He didn't even climb it. Blame me. Anyway, it was safe, and it would have taken all day coming back here to ask permission. We were careful. We always are."

"So that's why there was that new bit of wire," Stuart mumbled, almost to himself, "I've been wondering about that."

"I was just like that when I was a boy. Do it first and ask afterwards, that was my rule. Best that way round in case the answer's no. Mind you, it got me into a fair number of scrapes."

He nodded at Stuart's sling.

"I knew you wouldn't get up with that thing on your arm. And I know my niece. She's safe enough - she can climb like a monkey."

"But they saw the sea," shouted Ian.

"And who's 'they'? I thought I only had to account for one miscreant." He looked anxiously at Stuart.

"Now don't tell me you got up there after all. That wasn't very sensible, you know."

Laura spoke up. "Stuart tried, but his arm hurt too much ... so I went up. Only to see ... and it did seem quite safe ... anyway Elizabeth had done it," she finished lamely.

He sat staring at her, his fork frozen halfway to his mouth.

"Well, good for you," he murmured, then checked himself, looking across at Stuart. "That's right is it? All the way up?"

Stuart nodded and Uncle Albert turned to Laura.

"So you know all about it. The secret of the wooden watchtower."

"The sea," said Ian, "that's the secret! It's the sea. When can we go?"

"It's no distance at all," said Elizabeth.

"Further than it looks. I would guess a couple of miles."

Ian had jumped down and was tugging at Uncle Albert's arm.

"But we can go, can't we? Why not right away?"

"You've not eaten anything, that's one reason. I can't have your mother arriving to find you've shrunk. There's lots more to eat." He saw the look in Ian's face and laughed.

"No ... leave that if you don't like it ... no more raw bacon ... I promise you'll like what's coming."

And even as he spoke, Cook appeared carrying plates and a dish of roast chicken, still crackling hot. She set it down and poured something over the meat from a jug. Uncle Albert handed Elizabeth the serving spoons.

"I suppose you'd better dish it out, with your mother away."

Cook came trotting back with a bowl of lettuce. She ruffled Poppy's hair as if to say 'Tuck in' and tapped Ian on the head as she went by.

It's not easy cutting joints of chicken on a little plate. Things have an alarming way of skidding about. Elizabeth was making heavy weather of it.

Uncle Albert leaned past her and plucked a leg out of the dish with his fingers. He winked at Laura.

"I told you; local custom. It's the only way. Mind you, don't go doing this at home. Your mother might not approve. But I think it's alright if you're outside."

Ian grabbed a chicken leg before Laura could speak. She went on trying to tackle her own piece with a knife and fork, but gave in as she just managed to stop it spinning off her plate altogether.

Silence fell on a happy table of cannibals, eating delicious chicken with their fingers, only stopping now and then to nibble a piece of lettuce and dip their meat into the juices in the common dish.

*

Uncle Albert pointed to the last piece of chicken, but even Ian shook his head.

"I don't think I have room …" He paused, looking wistfully at the dish, then added, "But I could try … if nobody else wants it?"

Laura shook her head and pushed her chair back.

"I'd like to go and have a little rest for a while. Is that alright? You too, Ian. You ought to rest after all that food. And it's getting dreadfully hot."

"Rest?" said Elizabeth. "Why on earth? There's lots of time to rest tonight. What about exploring? We've got all the afternoon? You can't just let it go to waste."

But Laura was already halfway across the terrace. She turned and managed a thin smile and a little apologetic nod to Uncle Albert, then walked resolutely away under the stone arch and into the house.

There was a pause. No one knew quite what to say. Elizabeth looked at Stuart and rolled her eyes.

"It was that climb," he said. "She doesn't like heights."

"She's quite right, you know" said Uncle Albert. "It's unusually hot, even for here. It's the dog days. Far too hot to go tramping through woods. You should take a rest till it cools down a bit. It cools off once the sun starts to go down."

"Why dog days?" asked Ian, "there aren't any dogs here, are there?"

"No; no dog - more's the pity - I miss old Caesar. But I used to know why it was called that; something to do with a star. The dog star. Ask your brother – he's the one with the star book. There's an old story it makes people do things they're sorry for afterwards." He looked hard at Elizabeth.

"Like climbing into tree houses."

"But they're not sorry afterwards about that," shouted Ian. "They found the sea."

"Sea or not, that's what people do here in a hot afternoon - sleep." He got up and stretched.

"Not me, though. I've got a painting to finish."

"Can I come and watch?" asked Poppy.

"Honestly, you'd be better lying down a bit in your own room; they call it a siesta. But you can come if you really want to. I warn you, though, there's not much to watch."

He grabbed an apple out of the bowl on the table, picked up his hat, and set off across the lawn at a great pace. Poppy ran after him catching him up at the corner of the house. He turned and called back to them.

"A siesta – that's what you need. Off you go. You can explore later. Get a bit of rest."

CHAPTER IX

THE PAINTING LESSON

IT was a little cooler inside the studio, although the breeze through the open windows was fiercely hot, filling the place with the smell of resin from the trees outside. Papers fluttered restlessly on the table.

Uncle Albert squeezed a long line of white paint out of a fat tube onto a battered wooden palette.

"It's like toothpaste," said Poppy.

"I suppose it is a bit." He pushed the straw hat out of his eyes and looked round the room.

"There's not much for you to do here, you know. If you get bored you just trot away; I won't mind."

"No, I like watching. It's very interesting." She screwed the tops back onto the tubes where he had tossed them in a pile on the table and sat there reading their labels.

"Would you like to have a go?"

Poppy's eyes lit up. She had hardly dared ask, but that was exactly what she most wanted in the world.

"Could I? Really? Just a little bit. I'd like to try."

Uncle Albert rummaged among the things on the table and found an old china plate. He wiped it with a piece of rag then, taking one tube of paint at a time, squeezed a ring of six tiny blobs round the edge. He pulled a brush out of the jar on the floor, gave it to Poppy, then grabbed it back.

"No, that won't do; it's too big. I forgot, you've got little hands. I'll see whether I can find you something better."

It took some time, but eventually he found a small brush. He poured some clear liquid into a little bottle and stood it next to her.

She sniffed at it and started back, vapour stinging her eyes. For a moment she was back in the cabin on the *Arethusa*. The whole boat had smelled like that - the sharp, clean smell of turpentine.

"Dip your bush in to clean it. Just wipe it with this bit of cloth. It's a messy business, painting, you can't help getting it on your hands." He looked round the studio.

"There's an old apron over there on the back of the cupboard door. Put that on. It will keep the worst off. I don't want to get into hot water sending you back to the tribe looking like a Red Indian."

The apron was much too big but Poppy managed, wrapping it round herself twice and tying it up as best she could. She hobbled back to the table trying not to trip over. Uncle Albert grinned at her.

"Very professional. All you need is a black beret, but I don't have one." He handed her a piece of card.

"You can work on this. It's not very clean, but it'll do. You decide what you want to paint - it's up to you."

Poppy took her treasures to the other end of the table, spread them out and sat down in front of the piece of card. She looked about the room, trying to decide what to paint. Uncle Albert watched her for a second then picked up the apple he had left lying next to his coffee.

"It's no use trying to paint the room. You want to get close to something. Here, have a go at painting this." He put the apple down in front of her. She looked at it doubtfully.

"No, see what you can make of that. Come to think of it, I was going to eat it, but you can have it for a while. Now, I really must get on."

He bent over his palette, furiously mixing paint with a brush that seemed enormous next to Poppy's. She watched while he dragged a huge canvas across from where it had been left propped against the wall.

He heaved it up onto the easel, and fixed it with two wooden clips. He winked at her.

"You can eat it if you like. But paint it first."

*

For a long time Poppy sat watching him work. The apron was so stiff she could barely move her arms. She slipped it off and laid it out on the floor. She would just have to be careful.

It was very peaceful in the studio. The chatter of voices outside had long since stopped. The only sound was the repeated chirp of hundreds of cicadas and the echo of Uncle Albert's shoes on the old wooden floor. His picture had its back to her and he was darting about like a dancer, jabbing at the canvas. The brush made an odd little scratchy drumming noise.

Now and then he would grunt to himself, and scrape something off with a flat little knife, wiping it on his overalls. He caught her watching and grinned sheepishly.

"Don't you go doing that, mind. That's what I gave you that bit of rag for."

Poppy went back to looking at her apple. There were blobs of green and red on the plate and apples were mostly that colour. Although the green on the plate didn't look much like the apple at all. In fact, now she looked at it, there wasn't much red and green to this apple. Quite a large bit looked more yellow than green - a sort of brownish yellow.

"I'm not sure you should eat this," she said, almost to herself, "it looks soft." But Uncle Albert seemed not to hear.

She put her elbows on the table and rested her head on her hands. Now she looked at it, the half of the apple away from the light, almost the whole of one side, was a faint purplish colour. And even where it was green it wasn't one green at all - there was a minty bit, right at the top, and that dissolved into a grassy sort of colour before it stopped being any sort of green she could describe at all.

The more you looked, the odder it seemed. She shook her head.

She dipped the brush into a blob of green and swirled it round on her plate. It was much too bright. She wiped the brush and mixed in a little black, making a tiny pool of muddy green. Yes, that was lucky; it was exactly like the bit at the top where the stalk came out.

She dabbed her brush onto the card and tried to leave a mark as much like that bit of the apple as she could. Of course it was nothing like an apple, but it did look a bit like one part. If she got the parts right, the apple could look after itself.

She giggled to herself and Uncle Albert peered round his canvas to see what was going on.

"What's the joke? Shall I come and look?"

"No, not yet – I've only just started. I just thought it looked funny, that's all."

"I could never see the funny side of apples, myself. You're sure you don't want to play outside?"

But Poppy hardly heard him. She was cleaning her brush, frowning down at the plate. There was a yellow blob there, a bit like mustard, but not much like any colour she needed.

She smeared some over another part of the plate and added in a little white, forgetting to clean her brush. But it turned out alright. The mixture on the end of the brush was almost the colour of the next bit of the apple.

She wiped her brush and stopped to look, squinting her eyes together. Now she had dabbed the patch onto the card it seemed just right.

Far away, she could hear the cicadas and Uncle Albert humming to himself. But that was a world away; another world altogether.

*

How long had she been biting her lip like that? She rubbed where it hurt and remembered too late that she had yellow paint on her hands.

She peeped up at Uncle Albert on the other side of the studio. He had pulled two chairs next to each other and was sitting with his back to her, his feet perched on the other chair. He seemed to have been like that for a while, gazing through the window, smoking one of his little cigars.

How long had she been matching tiny patches of colour? It was hard to say. She had been lost in a maze of shapes, each one dissolving into a myriad others. Never in her whole life had she looked at an apple for so long. And that seemed so odd you could hardly help giggling.

Uncle Albert's chair scraped on the floor. "You've been very quiet over there. What's that you're laughing at again? You're not drawing something funny are you?"

The voice startled her, dragging her back from wherever she had been. For a second, everything seemed to be spinning. She looked up, feeling a little dizzy.

"I think I've finished it. I thought I'd do it in bits, but I can't get all the colours to come out. And there's a bit I just can't do at all. I keep looking at it and it seems impossible ... anyway, I can't do it."

Uncle Albert had been looking at his painting. He seemed to notice something and jumped up to scratch at the canvas, muttering to himself. He looked across.

"Sorry ... what was that? I spotted something ... just in time as well. You can't leave this paint a second, it's the devil for running away with you."

He slumped back down in his chair resting his palette on his knee and looking satisfied.

"What's that about you can't do something? What is it you can't do?"

"It's where the apple's on the table. If you look, there's a sort of shadow. I don't know what colour it is. Anyway, do shadows have colours? I've looked and looked. It just seems purple. A dark deep down sort of purple, but that can't be right. I can't do it."

He put his palette down and stared at Poppy sitting hunched at the table, solemnly examining her card and swinging her legs.

"Well, you're right. Shadows are a bit like that. But how...?"

He plopped his brush into the jar, wiping his hands on a bit of cloth.

"Here, let's see what you've done. How've you got on?"

He came and stood behind her chair, leaning forward to look at the card. He was silent for a long time. Poppy knew he was there because she could hear him breathing; but he said nothing at all. She suddenly felt awkward and half turned to look at him over her shoulder. He had a strange expression on his face.

"How long have you been doing this?" It was a question, but he seemed almost to be talking to himself.

"I don't know. What time is it? I lost track of the time a bit. I was concentrating. How long have we been here?"

She pushed the bit of card back on the table and squinted at it.

"It's funny, how things look like lots of little bits. I mean when you look hard. I'd never done that before."

But Uncle Albert went on looking puzzled.

"No, I didn't mean how long this afternoon, I meant when did you start painting."

Poppy looked at him. There was something in his voice that sounded odd.

"I didn't. I mean I haven't. Started, that is – apart from today. This is the first time. I do drawings of course. But they're just for me ... well, I show them to Ian sometimes."

Uncle Albert was hardly listening.

"But it's good ... very good."

He leaned forward and gently touched the painting with a stubby finger, blurring a place where two colours were running into each other.

"Oh, sorry, I wasn't thinking. It's your painting ... I just thought ..."

"No, it's better like that," she said, timidly dabbing her own finger onto the same spot. She lifted her hand. It was smeared with yellow paint.

She wanted to get up, but Uncle Albert stayed staring thoughtfully over her shoulder at the bit of card. She looked at it trying to see it the way he did.

"I can see that makes it better," she said pushing her chair back.

"Come and stand over here."

He picked the card off the table and stood with it in front of his easel. She jumped down and followed him. He propped the painting on the shelf at the foot of the easel and steered her across to the other side of the room.

She turned and looked. There, glowing back at her on the tiny scrap of card was the apple she had been thinking about all afternoon. It looked round and soft and almost, were it not for a few brown spots, good enough to eat.

"But I couldn't do the shadow," she mumbled, fumbling for her handkerchief.

"Nobody can, that's why you can't. But I can show you what I do ... if you like?"

She snatched the card down and rushed back to the table.

"Yes, please."

He picked up his big palette and Poppy watched as he mixed colours, mumbling to himself.

"You couldn't have managed anyway with the colours I gave you. That was half the trouble."

He splayed the brush out on the flat of his hand looking at a splash of colour in his palm.

"Here … this might do it … " He dipped the brush into the little pot.

"You've got to keep it fluid ... thin … like this."

And it was done. A faint smear of purple ran round and under Poppy's apple.

"That's it!" she cried. "I was wondering how you made it thin like that." She looked up at him, her eyes shining.

"I've got a lot to learn."

"Less than you think," he murmured.

He started tidying up, covering his canvas with a blue cloth.

Suddenly he burst out laughing and spun his hat across the room. It missed the hook on the back of the door by miles and fell to the floor. Poppy ran across and picked it up.

"Bless my soul! Who'd have ever thought it? Bless my soul!"

The faint sound of a bell drifted in through the open window. While she had been painting the sun had shifted right round. The light outside was cooler and lower now, slanting down onto the bare boards of the studio.

"Come on," said Uncle Albert, "that's the bell for supper already and your face is covered with paint." She looked up startled as he burst out laughing again.

"Not exactly a Red Indian, though. More a yellow and green Indian. Come on, or we'll be late. Oh, and don't forget to bring that apple. I was going to eat it, but I might change my mind."

"THERE'S A BIT I JUST CAN'T DO AT ALL"

CHAPTER X

THE DOG DAY WALK

AFTER Laura rushed off, Stuart, Elizabeth and Ian had been left sitting alone at the table. Cook pottered round collecting up plates and dishes. Elizabeth rescued a bowl of grapes just as they were being whisked away.

"I was talking to Uncle this morning. Trying to worm out of him where Mum's gone."

"She's gone to visit some friends," Stuart said. "Didn't she say that?"

Elizabeth laughed.

"That's what you think. She doesn't know anybody here. Uncle put her up to that tale. They're planning something, mark my words."

Stuart thought about it. For Elizabeth there was an adventure round every corner, but this time she must surely be wrong. Grown-ups weren't like that. Mrs Bradley had just gone off on a visit somewhere. And as for Uncle Albert - did uncles really plot things?

"How do you know he's up to anything at all? How can you tell?"

"I can tell. Anyway, where's Mum? That's the question. As for visits, visits fiddlesticks."

Although Cook had gathered up the plates, she had left Ian's in its place. He was about to hand it to her when he saw a piece of chicken had magically appeared on it.

She continued on round the table quietly piling things up onto a tray.

He stared at her and she returned his look with a very serious face. Then, just for a second, he almost believed she had winked, although Cooks never winked.

He looked at his plate and then at Stuart. The two of them were busy talking. And, after all, Laura wasn't here. She had mysteriously gone to bed in the middle of the day.

It was a pity to let a nice piece of chicken go to waste.

"It's all so completely odd …" Elizabeth went on. She had jumped up again and was walking round the table, snapping grapes off the bunch in her hand.

"First, she doesn't know anybody at all here. Of course she doesn't! It's simply ages since she came here. Second, she sets off before anybody was up. I heard the shower going in the bathroom. It's right next to my room. It must have been Mum. She used our shower so as not to wake people up. She thought we'd all be safely asleep. But not me. I heard the shower gurgling away."

"Poppy saw her getting into a little carriage," said Ian, happily nibbling his chicken bone. "Poppy always gets up early. She says there was a donkey. I wish I'd seen the donkey. Do you think it'll come back?"

"And another thing," said Elizabeth, ignoring him.

"A third thing," said Ian, "you were counting and you've already had a second thing."

Elizabeth scowled at him.

"Alright, third. Uncle knew all the time about the tree house, didn't he? He knew we were going to find it. He'd even arranged to have the ladder mended."

She stopped, struggling to remember something worse, "Oh … and the sea … don't forget the sea. He never let on about that. They planned it all behind our backs ..." She stopped again, red-faced and lost for words, then sat down, adding limply, "Anyway, don't forget how he had that ladder mended."

Stuart didn't know what to say. He had never had to deal with an uncle before. Perhaps uncles were like that. After all, perhaps it was a bit silly to go climbing ladders without asking. So just as well it had been mended. He tried to imagine Mother rushing off at sunrise in a donkey carriage and grinned to himself.

Elizabeth watched him and jumped up, walking faster and faster round the table, pulling grapes off one by one as she went. Suddenly she froze, her hand halfway to her mouth.

"That's it! It's no distance at all, why don't we just go and look? They didn't plan that. And there's nobody here to stop us."

"You mean the sea?" shouted Ian. "I said that ages ago. Let's go and look. You're the only one who's seen it ... well, Laura as well, I suppose, but she's gone to bed. Why don't we go now?"

He looked across the lawn to where Poppy and Uncle Albert had disappeared.

"I'll run and get Poppy. It must be boring just watching painting going on like that. Anyway, I don't need to rest. That's like going to bed. I'm allowed to stay up in holidays ... no one makes me go to bed ... well, not this early."

"Best leave Poppy where she is," said Stuart, "she'll come back if she wants to. But I suppose we should ask Laura."

Elizabeth finished the last of the grapes.

"Good idea. She can come. Let's go and grab her before she gets settled in. She can't really want to sleep. I can't see the point of lying in bed in the afternoon. Let's go and have a Council of War." She saw the look in his face.

"Well, he jolly well deserves a war; but alright, we'll just decide where we explore."

"So long as it's the sea," said Ian.

*

Once Laura had got inside the house she looked back to see whether Ian had decided to follow, but no footsteps came running down the passage. She could hear Cook in the kitchen singing to herself. It sounded almost like at home, although in French of course. A sad sort of song; the sort that never comes to a proper end.

The staircase was in its shuttered afternoon gloom. Cracks in the wood let a few thin beams of light slant red across the tiles. Just enough to see your way.

Somebody had pulled the shutters closed in her bedroom and it was quite dark. A thin bar of light fell across the bed. The room was hot and airless, filled with that same scent of flowers everywhere.

When they had first arrived in the train it had all smelled wonderful. A whole country drenched in sunshine and filled with the scent of fragrant flowers. But she had woken this morning wishing the sweet smell would go away for a while. That she could get away from it; just for a second.

She sat on the edge of the bed and let a curious wave of sadness sweep over her. Back at home at the holiday cottage, the light on the lake was always cold and bright, even in summer. True, there was a smell of pine everywhere, but you never wished that would go away. Not after the rain anyway, that was when it smelled best.

She smiled sadly to herself - they'd certainly had enough rain.

She pictured the old camp by the tower and the bitter smell of the smoke from the early morning fire. Nothing smelled as good as that; nothing at all.

She shook her shoes off and lay back on the bed looking at the pattern of shadows on the ceiling. A fly had got in and was buzzing lazily round. Far away there was a small murmur of voices. Everywhere was settling down into the heat of another afternoon. She ought to be happy, very happy. But she wasn't happy at all.

She rolled onto her side and looked about the room - at the door with its strange foreign catch; the black polished boards; the painted table.

A wave of misery engulfed her; to be here in this strange hot place with everything she loved a million miles away.

She sat up, leaning against the wooden head of the bed, running her hands across the stiff starch of the sheet. It was stupid going on like this. Everything here was lovely. And Uncle Albert was the nicest new uncle you could ask for. But she wanted to go home. More than she had ever wanted anything, she wanted to be at home.

A single tear rolled down her face and she felt it land warm and salty in the corner of her lips. As she rolled over to bury her head in the pillow, heavy footsteps sounded on the stairs and Elizabeth's voice echoed down the corridor.

"She can't be asleep. I can't see why you'd want to anyway, it's too hot to sleep. This is her room isn't it?" There was a huge banging on the door.

"Ahoy there! Permission to come aboard."

Laura sat up, wiping her eyes and struggling to wriggle her feet into her shoes. She wished there was mirror. She rubbed her face as hard as she could.

"Just a minute. I'm coming."

But too late. The door burst open and Elizabeth and Stuart piled in together laughing and talking. They fell silent, trying not to look at Laura sitting there, awkwardly pushing the hair out of her eyes.

"Phew, it's hot in here," said Stuart, "how can you stand it?"

He opened the window, reached out and swung the two shutters back. Fierce light filled the room, but also a tiny gust of fresh scented air.

Laura stayed sitting on the edge of the bed, her face very red and puffy.

"It's hot everywhere. I never expected it. It's too hot to do anything at all. I should never have gone up that ladder. It was too hot."

"But you saw the sea," said Elizabeth. "You're better doing something, I can't see the point of this lying down idea. You can get used to things. It's much hotter in Africa and places like that and real explorers manage alright."

She was staring at Laura. "What's the matter? You look like …"

She stopped, glancing across at Stuart who was leaning out of the window.

"We're here for a Council of War …"

Ian had been wandering along the darkened corridor outside looking at the shutters and wondering when it would be time to open them. He heard voices and came sliding through the door, spinning to a halt in the middle of the room.

"I've been looking. The corridor out there would be a perfect slide if only the boards went the other way. But they don't."

He jumped onto the bottom of Laura's bed and sat there swinging his legs.

"I wonder what Poppy's doing? She must have finished ages ago. Can we play outside, please?"

Elizabeth dragged the cane chair across from the window and sat down.

"Wait a minute. Shut the door, Ian ... you never know who's listening." She leaned forward.

"They're in the studio, the two of them. Conspiring I shouldn't wonder. I bet Poppy knows what's going on by now. He wouldn't tell me, but I bet he's told Poppy."

Stuart pulled his head in from the window and turned round.

"You can't blame Poppy. None of us know anything's going on, apart from you. And you're just guessing. You always see things going on, even when they aren't."

Laura sat silently picking at the sheet at her side. Stuart sounded cross and she knew it was because he'd seen she'd been crying. In some odd way he was standing up for her. She turned to Elizabeth.

"I was just feeling very sleepy (that was almost true, after all). Anyway I don't know what you're all talking about. Why is anybody conspiring? What about?"

"It's about Poppy," shouted Ian. "She's gone off all on her own ..."

He was going to say much more, but Elizabeth stopped him, shaking her head. She took up her usual stance, one leg on the chair.

"It's simple. I think Uncle's planning something for us ... and now Mum's started doing it as well. That's the two of them together. It won't do. It's no fun at all being explorers with somebody running about seeing you're alright all the time. It spoils everything. We're not children ..." She stopped, seeing Stuart's look.

"Well, I suppose we are ... some of us anyway (she glowered at Ian) ... but you know what I mean. It's awful not knowing what it is they're up to ... I almost got it out of him this morning. But now Poppy's in there with him ... either he'll tell her, and that's not fair ..."

"Or he won't tell her, "said Stuart with a broad grin, "and that's not fair either."

"Well I don't think that's much of a Council of whatever it was," said Ian. "I thought we were going to the sea-side."

Elizabeth had been trying to look fierce, but she could not help laughing. She looked at Laura.

"He's right. I'm sorry. But what do you think? We've got time. It's not too late to do a bit of exploring."

"You three go," said Laura. Her voice cracked a little, but she managed.

"I'm going to have a little sleep. Leave Poppy where she is. When she comes back, I'll tell her you've gone for a walk."

Elizabeth reached out and patted Laura's hand where it lay on the bed, then got up and led the others out of the room.

*

It took longer than they expected for the three of them to find their way back through the woods to the bracken hut at the foot of the tree house. The afternoon air seemed almost too heavy to breathe.

As they clambered up the hill they had to pause every few feet to rest. By the time they reached the top of the ridge even Ian had fallen silent. Stuart stopped and turned to see how far they had come.

"I forgot. We should have brought something to drink."

"We'll manage," panted Elizabeth, "we shan't be long. It didn't look that far. We can have a good drink when we get back."

"Just think. A glass of pink lemonade," Ian said, waving his arms. "A really enormous one."

They walked past the tree house along the path Elizabeth had pointed to that morning; the path that seemed to lead to the sea.

After fifty yards or so, it ended abruptly. They were faced with a wall of cut logs, covered in bramble. Another track ran off round the side, not quite in the same direction.

"Down here?" Stuart asked.

"It's the woodcutters' path I suppose," said Elizabeth.

"They must have come that way to stack the logs up. We'll follow it; if it veers off too much we can always come back."

They followed her, marching in single file along a tiny track between walls of brambles draped from the trees on either side. Now and then they had to push through places where weeds blocked the way.

The path dropped down steeply and reached a tiny clearing. Elizabeth was setting a cracking pace and Stuart felt hot and parched. They were out of the sun, but there didn't seem to be quite enough air to breathe. Walking jolted his arm; even with the sling it was starting to ache.

"It must be the right way," he muttered to himself, "we're going downhill and that must be right … it's downhill all the way to the sea."

"Which way now?" asked Ian, walking round the clearing. "There's lots of paths, and they all go down."

"That one's pretty well lined up," said Elizabeth, pointing to a path that plunged steeply down through the trees. She looked round uncertainly.

"It's that one I should think … anyway, it's going down fast enough."

Ian had already hurried ahead without waiting for them and they heard his feet skidding and sliding on the baked earth. The sounds stopped.

"You'd have to be an elephant to get through here," he called, "there's no way through. There's not even a path. It just stops."

He came slowly back up the hill and stood there red-faced and puffing.

"Which way next?"

"Stay with us," said Stuart. "You need to stay in sight. We don't want you getting lost."

Elizabeth grabbed a branch at the side of the path and snapped it, leaving a piece dangling down.

"That'll do to mark where you went … let's try along here."

It was not quite the direction they wanted, but looked a more promising path, wide enough for two and also dropping steeply.

They scrambled down, picking their way through snagging weeds. There was just a stony trench at the bottom; nothing but piles of pebbles washed clean by some winter stream long ago. The path turned sharply to the left and started to climb. They trudged on.

"It's not going down anymore," said Ian. "You said it was downhill all the way." He stopped to catch his breath. "This isn't down … it's up … wait for me … and I'm thirsty."

The two explorers up ahead exchanged looks, but they had not enough breath to speak. They waited for Ian to catch up then struggled on higher and higher.

The trees ahead slowly thinned out and there was more light. Patches of bright blue peeped between the branches. The tops of the taller trees had begun to catch the sun.

They had arrived in a large clearing dotted with the stumps of felled trees. Heat was rising up from the ground. Deep ruts, as hard as stone, were cut into the dry earth; ancient hoof marks showed where horses long ago had hauled logs away.

Stuart looked about him. The ground ahead was covered with tiny butterflies, grey shapes as they came to rest, turning bright red as they fluttered up. The only sound was an endless steady hiss of leaves over their heads. Trees reared up on every side out of a deep tangle of brushwood. He had no idea where they were.

"We can get our bearings now we're at the top," he panted. "We should be able to see from there."

The path had changed into a gravel road, broad enough for a cart. It ran to right and left along the crest of a dry ridge between banks of nettles, stretching out empty into the shimmering distance in two directions, as straight as a ruler for as far as they could see.

Ian stood looking along the track.

"Which way now?"

"I think we have to go back," said Stuart. "It's no good, I think we're lost."

Elizabeth stood close next to him, very red and out of breath. She had a grim expression on her face.

"Don't let Ian hear," she muttered, "but I don't think we can. Look."

She nodded down the way they had come. The path seemed to splinter into dozens of forks.

"It's the same as this morning. It looks like one path when you're coming up, but there's hundreds going the other way."

"We're not really lost, are we?" shouted Ian. "If you climb a tree you can see where to go. I know, because it's in *Robinson Crusoe*."

Stuart sat down on a felled tree trunk. A brown lizard scuttled away across his foot. His throat was dreadfully dry and his arm was throbbing.

"If only we had a compass," said Elizabeth. "Once you're lost, you end up walking round and round in circles."

She looked across the clearing and nudged Stuart. It was hard not to smile. Ian had managed to haul himself onto the bottom branch of an oak tree and was trying to stand on it, wobbling violently. He gave up and jumped down.

"But it's not a joke," she said in a low voice, "what are we going to do?"

Stuart did not answer. He was scraping dead leaves off the ground with his foot, clearing a little patch of dry earth.

"Let's make a map," he said, "start with a plan of the house. Like the one you did this morning. Can you do it again? Bits of stick would do. I can't with my arm tied up like this."

Elizabeth was going to ask what possible use a plan of the house was when she saw his face. She snapped off a few twigs and laid them out in a rough square.

"Now put a stick for where the woods are behind the house." He got up and gazed through the canopy of leaves.

"It was you saying we needed a compass that made me think. I've got my watch. If you can find the sun, it will do as a compass. We did that at school. I remember how it works."

"Well, the sun's easy enough," she said, pointing to the other side of the clearing, "it's up there."

Stuart jumped up, wincing as he tried to unfasten his watch.

"You do it," he said. Elizabeth pulled the little leather strap back and eased his watch off.

"Come on!" He almost ran across to the other side of the clearing. "It's a good job I wound it up. Right ... stand where you can see the sun and hold the watch so the hour hand points straight at it."

Elizabeth squinted up into the sunlight and pointed the watch at the sun.

"Now ... South is half way between where you're pointing and twelve o'clock on the watch."

He peered down then held out his good arm.

"South's there. We set off going that way, more or less ... so we just have to go North." He felt enormously relieved.

Elizabeth laid another stick on the ground pointing North-South and stepped back to look at the two paths.

"It doesn't point down either of them."

"But North's much closer to that one," said Stuart.

"I wouldn't have gone that way," she said, fastening his watch back on. She laughed. "So you're probably right. Come on, you can do the trick with the watch again if the road starts to turn." She grinned at him.

"Phew, it's a good job you thought of that. I was starting to think we were really lost." She lowered her voice. "I could do with a drink, though. I'm awfully dry."

It was easier walking now. The track was almost like a proper road. In places they found themselves looking across tiny fields cut out of the woods, hardly bigger than a garden, with the sun slanting fiercely at them over the trees. They scuttled past from one line of shade to the next.

After about a quarter of an hour, a farm track broke off to their side, plunging into the woods. Elizabeth stopped and peered down between the trees, checking the watch. She shook her head.

"Nothing. But it's a lot East that way. We can't risk it. It might be miles and miles before there's any building. Anyway, we're going pretty well due North already."

The path ahead swirled in waving plumes of heat rising from the baked earth. It was empty for as far as they could see.

Ian had started to limp. He sank down onto a big stone at the roadside. "I'm going to sit here. You can go on if you like. My legs hurt. How much farther is it?"

"We'll rest here a bit," said Stuart. "It can't be far now."

He looked at Elizabeth. She was standing in the middle of the road, shading her eyes and peering into the distance with a bleak expression on her face.

Wherever this path was taking them, it was not back home.

CHAPTER XI

LOST

ONCE they were sitting down, nobody felt like walking anymore. Stuart eased his arm out of the sling and rested it on his knees. His shoulder was throbbing and he felt very thirsty. His head had started to ache.

Elizabeth slumped down onto the ground and sat with her back against a tree. She started idly pulling at the stalks of a weed, tearing leaves off and letting them drop in front of her.

Ian perched uncomfortably on his stone for a while then dropped down and lay there, leaning his back against it. No one spoke.

Far overhead a slight breeze had got up, enough to bend the tops of the trees. With the wind, the steady hissing of the forest had changed to something different. As if somebody far away was saying 'shush'. A lonely sound that echoed endlessly round them.

"We're lost, aren't we?" Ian barely waited for a reply and did not turn round.

"You might as well say so. I know we're lost ... what are we going to do?"

Stuart didn't know what to say.

"I'm sure we're going the right way ... it's stupid ... we can't be that far away ..." He didn't sound very convincing. "Don't worry, we must come to somewhere we recognise soon."

Ian stayed leaning against his stone.

"You two can go and look without me. I'll stay here and you can come back when you find out where to go. I don't want to walk anymore ... my feet hurt ... and my legs. And what are we going to do to drink? I'm really thirsty."

"We have to stay together," Stuart said. "Anyway you said you were going to climb a tree." He was doing his best to sound cheerful. "We could try that. If one of us could only get high enough, maybe we could see the house." But he didn't move.

Elizabeth looked despairingly at the trees on the other side of the path: a tangle of knobbly branches densely twisted together.

It would be hard to think of less promising things to climb. She glanced at him and shook her head.

Ian had been listlessly kicking at the packed clay at his feet, raising little puffs of dust. He screwed his eyes up as a sudden gust of wind whipped sand into his face.

"Now I've gone and got something in my eye," he said, jumping up and rubbing it hard with his knuckles.

"Don't rub it," said Stuart, "you'll only make it worse. Let me look."

He started to wrap the sling back round his arm, but before he could struggle up, Ian stopped rubbing his eye and walked uncertainly into the middle of the path, the speck of grit forgotten for the moment.

"There!" he shouted, pointing down the road ahead. "A great big cloud of dust coming this way. What is it? Down there! Somebody's coming."

"Where?" said Elizabeth, springing up and wincing as her legs took the strain. "This had better not be one of your jokes."

She stood next to him, shading her eyes. "I can't see anything. It's just the wind blowing dust about."

But Stuart turned to her, his face filled with relief. "Listen! You can hear it. It must be a farmer with a horse."

There was not much to see, apart from a big ball of white dust, but they could hear it now; the steady clop of a horse and the squeak and scrape of wheels. Stuart set off as best he could on stiff legs, walking awkwardly towards the cloud of dust. Elizabeth called him back.

"It's coming this way. There's no point you going all the way down there. We're better to wait. We'll ask the farmer where we are. We'll go with him, wherever he's going."

"But he's going back where we've come from," said Ian.

"Anyway, you can't ask him. You don't speak French ... and I bet that's all he speaks."

"I'll find a way. One thing's sure - we can't stay sitting here. We are well and truly lost."

Stuart could hear the relief in her voice. At least the farmer would know where the Pink House was.

The cloud of white dust grew less as the horse moved onto a stretch of hard clay. They could see it more clearly now; a man holding a bridle, walking slowly alongside a little cart.

"I don't think it's a horse at all," said Stuart. "It's too small. I think it's a donkey."

He turned to Elizabeth, but she had already gone, hopping and limping stiff-legged down the path as fast she could, waving both arms and hallooing at the top of her voice. She stopped in the middle of the path and turned towards him, her face beaming.

"Who'd have thought of it?" she shouted, "it's Mum, and the donkey cart. It must be the one Poppy saw this morning."

Slowly the cart drew nearer until the man leading it tugged at the donkey and they stopped with a scrunch of wheels.

Mrs Bradley was sitting high up at the front, wiping dust from her face and gazing down at them wide-eyed.

"Well, this is a surprise. I must say, it's very nice of you to come and meet me. I never expected a reception party. How did you guess when we'd be coming? It's been slow going. Have you been waiting long?"

Stuart and Elizabeth exchanged glances. She went on looking at them with a puzzled expression on her face.

"I'm afraid you'll have to walk back the way you came."

Ian had been standing looking at the donkey. He was about to explain that they didn't know which way they had come, when he found himself being steered away with Elizabeth's arm firmly round his shoulders.

"Come on Ian," she said, trying to sound as normal as possible, "we can do our talking when we get home."

Mrs Bradley was still frowning at the three travel-stained explorers.

"The trouble is, there's not room for you in the cart. This donkey's very small. It's all she could do to get along with these things piled in the back." She waved her arm towards a heap of white linen sacks jammed into the back of the cart.

"And me, of course, but I'm too old for long walks in the sun. But you won't mind walking … I don't think it's very far, is it?"

Stuart was about to say he didn't know, when Elizabeth shot him a warning look.

"That's right. You lead the way, Mum. I suppose Ian could hop up, though, he weighs next to nothing."

At which, Ian ducked from under her arm and clambered into the seat next to Mrs Bradley. He sat there looking down at them, grinning happily.

The man shook the bridle but the donkey stood there twitching its ears. He flicked at her with the end of the leather and the cart rumbled on ahead.

"I didn't know what to say," said Stuart in a low voice. "I don't know where we're going. I think your mother suspects something."

It was hard to keep up. His arm was banging painfully at his side and sweat was running into his eyes. Elizabeth leaned towards him.

"Don't say anything ... maybe we can sneak away when we get there ... don't say anything to Mum yet, anyway... just walk along as if nothing had happened ... I mean to say, nothing has happened, really. Now we're found. Gosh, I'm thirsty."

But it's difficult to walk as if nothing has happened when your legs ache and the cart ahead is going too fast to keep up. Elizabeth hobbled wearily forward, wishing the donkey would go a little slower. Stuart followed, limping painfully behind the cart.

The donkey reached the point they had passed half an hour earlier where a farm track forked off to the right. She stopped and began to chew at the weeds alongside the path.

The man reached up and pushed at her head, persuading her to turn then pulled on her bridle. She looked at him, flicking her ears, chewing quietly.

Another tug on the bridle and the cart started forward with a jerk, leaned to one side, bumped over some deep ruts, and turned onto a sandy track, its wheels squeaking in protest.

Almost at once they were running downhill, leaving two footsore explorers far behind.

Ahead of them, Stuart heard the grating echo of cartwheels running onto stone paving and squeaking to a halt. Flashes of pink stone appeared between the thinning trees. Almost too tired to see where they were, they limped out of the shade and into the full glare of the sun.

Pigeons were cooing in the branches. The familiar scent of blossom was all around them; the Pink House stood there, peaceful and welcoming.

"We walked right past that track," Stuart murmured, "if only we'd turned off, we'd have been here ages ago. It was just a few minutes' walk. No distance at all!"

"Don't you go saying that to Uncle. He's always saying 'If only won't get you home'. All the same, to think we were this close. I could kick myself."

She leaned closer and whispered, "don't say anything to Mum just now ... there's no point getting everybody upset. Try and grab Ian before he starts telling the tale ... you know what he's like. He was going to start explaining everything back there but I caught him in time. It's not as if we were lost. Not really lost. We couldn't be lost when we were sitting just a few yards away."

*

But it was already too late. By the time Elizabeth and Stuart hobbled out onto the hot stones of the terrace, the man had led the donkey away into the shade and Mrs Bradley was standing listening earnestly as Ian described the afternoon's adventure, waving his arms and pointing in all directions.

Elizabeth looked hopelessly at Stuart. Mrs Bradley saw them and shook her head. Stuart saw she was very red. Perhaps it was from sitting in the sun all day, but perhaps that was not the only reason. He started to say something, but found his throat was too dry.

"What on earth am I going to do with you?" she said. "What's more, I'm pretty sure if the two of you had got hold of this little explorer in time I wasn't going to know anything at all about it."

This was so close to the truth that Elizabeth could only grin sheepishly and look at her feet.

"It really wasn't anybody's fault," said Stuart. "We knew the way ... at least, at the start. We'd been that way before. We just got lost."

Ian tugged Mrs Bradley's arm.

"Can I get something to drink, please? I'm thirsty."

She took him by the hand and the two of them set off towards the side of the house. Halfway across the terrace she stopped, giving Ian a little push to tell him to go on ahead. She watched him go and called over her shoulder.

"It's no use you two staying there sulking. Come on, you need something to drink as well."

The shamefaced couple shuffled towards her, hardly daring to look up. Stuart heard her laughing quietly to herself.

"I'm sorry; I know I shouldn't, it's not at all funny. And I'm not at all pleased. But I kept asking myself why you were both limping like that behind the cart. You looked quite comical, the pair of you."

She took Elizabeth's hands in her own and bent down to look into her eyes.

"If it wasn't so serious, my girl, I'd say it served you both right." She turned to Stuart. He was a sorry sight, a rumpled sling badly tied round his arm, his sunburned face smeared with dust and sweat.

He was staring at his sandals in misery, but glanced up to find her face quite close to his own, looking surprisingly cheerful. She was smiling at him in a very friendly way.

"Cheer up Stuart, I used to get into scrapes like that myself when I was a girl. I remember my grandmother used to say she didn't know what to do with me. I never knew what she meant."

She put a comforting arm round his shoulders. "I'm not going to ask who was to blame; you can go share and share alike with your fellow pirate ... or is it explorer? I suppose given what happened, it's explorer."

She straightened his sling.

"Come on the two of you ... we'll say no more about it for the moment ... I need to get something to drink before I expire – and so do you. What a day!"

*

Ian was sitting at the long table on the terrace waiting for them. He had already gulped down one glass of water and was pouring himself another. He wandered across the lawn, glass in hand.

Alongside the table, spread out on the grass, was a heap of white canvas bags.

"They're tents!" shouted Elizabeth, hobbling forward to pull at the neck of one of the bags. "Let's look."

"No, leave them please. Something to drink, first. That's the most important thing. And you two need to sit down. I've got something for blisters upstairs." Mrs Bradley grinned, "For those that had to walk the whole way."

Elizabeth poured out three glasses of water and fell back heavily in a chair, stretching her legs out. She poked at one of the canvas bags with her foot where the brass-tipped end of a pole was sticking out.

"They look a bit ancient. Where did they come from?"

"They belong to the scouts. It was all there was, and even then we had to ask the Mayor for help. And before you ask, this was not my idea; you have your Uncle to thank. Someone gave him the idea you wanted to go camping."

She looked at her watch.

"Come to think of it, where is everybody? It's getting on. It will soon be supper-time. Where's Poppy and Laura?"

"Laura's upstairs," said Stuart. "She didn't want to come ... I don't know where Poppy is."

"She's still in the studio," said Ian. I just went and banged on the door, and they both shouted 'Go away'. It's not fair. What's she been doing all this time?"

"Well you can ask her yourself now," said Elizabeth, waving her glass as two figures came towards them across the lawn.

Poppy had seen them and started running, pulling at Uncle Albert's arm. He lumbered up to the table, very out of breath, and reached out for the jug of water. He was clutching a piece of card.

"Water ... water ... I need something to drink. It's hot work, painting."

"You've been in there all afternoon, you know" said Elizabeth, "it's not fair you two planning things on your own. And what's that you're holding?"

"We weren't planning anything," said Poppy, "That's my first painting. I've been learning to paint. It's very interesting."

Uncle Albert propped the card against the jug on the table and they crowded round. Ian started laughing.

"It looks very blobby. I could do that. Can I have a go? Can I try?"

Mrs Bradley was standing silently at the back of the group looking at the little apple glowing in the afternoon light. When she had first looked at the card she had given an odd murmur of recognition, as if it had reminded her of something. Poppy looked up and saw her put her hand to her mouth, tears in her eyes.

Uncle Albert was nodding his head slowly.

"I know what you're thinking," he said, "I thought just the same. It's like my first efforts ..." he stopped himself, "although to be fair, I'd say a good bit better." He took a deep gulp of water and waved his glass towards the card.

"You can see what she's trying to do. She says she's been drawing. I'd like to see her drawings."

Poppy looked round unhappily and caught the expression in Stuart's face.

"How did you know...? How did you know how to do that?" he said in an odd sort of voice. It was almost as if he was cross with her for keeping a secret.

"But I didn't ... I've never done it before ... it's not that hard ... you only have to look carefully. But it takes ages and ages. You lose track of the time."

Ian had placed himself next to where Elizabeth was standing looking thoughtful. He squinted his eyes and stared at the card.

He was trying hard, but the apple still seemed very smudgy. It wasn't properly round, either. Apples weren't square.

"It's jolly useful if we have our own artist ..." he mumbled, "... if we need things painted, I mean ..." he sounded very doubtful.

"The hard bit is mixing the colours," Poppy went on. Now she had started, she wanted to explain as much as she could to anybody who would listen.

"They're never quite what you want. And then when you've got it right on the plate, it looks different when you paint it on.

Anyway, that's what we've been doing. Uncle Albert's been showing me how to make colours."

"A camp artist," said Elizabeth. "That's an idea. We'll have a camp artist."

"Why camp?" asked Poppy, noticing the piles of canvas bags for the first time. "Do you really mean camping? Are we going to camp? But where?"

"Yes, we're going camping. You've a few days before your mother gets here and it will pass the time. As for where," Uncle Albert pulled a face at Elizabeth, "well, it's a secret ... although come to think of it, I ought to tell you ... some people don't like secrets."

"No, don't tell," said Poppy, "I like secrets ... well, some secrets ... and this sounds like a good one. But there is one thing ..." She stopped, looking awkwardly at Uncle Albert. "I've remembered ... I have to take some colours with me ... if I can, that is? I want to practise."

"So long as it's not much," said Ian, "you've been practising all afternoon. That's plenty for now. If you're practising all the time, there'll be no time to play."

CHAPTER XII

SUMMER STORMS

MRS Bradley looked at her watch and then tapped it.

"Is that really the time? I can't believe it. I'm going to see what Laura's up to. This weather is so dreadfully hot and heavy, I think there's a storm in the air. I know it makes you sleepy, but she shouldn't still be asleep. I'll wake her up if she is." She stood up.

"And as for this tribe, you all need to get some of the dust off. I think a few nice cool showers are in order ... and if you find any blisters don't forget to tell me. Up you get! You'd better be quick about it, the bell will be going soon."

"But I'm not dusty," said Poppy. "And how did you all get so dusty? What have you been doing?"

"You've got yellow on your face," said Ian, "that's as bad as dust. Worse really, because I bet it won't come off."

Poppy gave in. She cast a last wistful look at her little picture and followed the others into the house, leaving Uncle Albert to pour himself another glass of water.

He sat there staring at the card and forgetting to drink. Every now and then he mumbled, "Who'd have thought it? Who'd have thought it?" and chuckled quietly to himself.

*

Laura was not asleep. The noise of the returning explorers had woken her and she was sitting in the cane chair by the window. She had pushed the shutters back as far as she could reach.

Little sounds drifted up on the hot afternoon air: the excited chatter of people all talking at the same time; the clink of glasses; Ian laughing. She could hear Poppy's voice, small and thin, above the rest, but not what she was saying. It all seemed to be a million miles away.

Her eyes were on the trim lawn edged with banks of red flowers and the dark trees beyond, but all she saw was a little whitewashed cottage perched over a sandy cliff far away. She felt unbearably lonely. Everything that mattered was in another place.

It was still as hot as ever, but the sun had shifted round. She would have to make herself go downstairs. Even as she caught her breath, a sigh managed to turn itself into a sob. And once there was one, there was another. The view through the window blurred as slow tears slid down her cheeks. She licked them away, tasting the salt on her tongue.

The terrace outside had fallen silent. She heard the sound of feet on the stairs and along the corridor outside, people chattering and the bang of doors. Ian's voice echoing plaintively down the hall complaining that the shutters had been opened without him.

Apart from a few footsteps the house fell quiet again.

There was a little tap on her door and Mrs Bradley's voice.

"Laura, are you awake? It's almost time to eat. Can I come in?"

Without waiting for a reply the bedroom door eased open and a cheerful red face peered round it at the empty bed. When she saw the figure slumped at the window her expression changed. Laura had snatched up a handkerchief and was pretending to blow her nose.

"What on earth's the matter? Don't you feel well?"

Laura only managed a little grunt in reply. Mrs Bradley picked up the painted wooden chair from by the bed and came to sit next to her.

Laura had let her hair fall over her face and sat there, peering miserably out, pulling her handkerchief through her fingers. Neither of them spoke for a long time.

"I'm going to guess," said Mrs Bradley, "I'll guess and you can just nod if I'm right. Can you do that?"

There was the smallest of nods, barely a twitch, from the bowed head.

"I think you're feeling homesick. Am I right?"

Another tiny nod and Laura let two more tears fall unchecked down her face.

Mrs Bradley said nothing more. She leaned over and pushed the window open as far as it would go. Late afternoon sun threw dark red patches across the room. The shouts and squeals from the corridor outside had fallen silent.

"I'm going to tell you a secret, but you'll have to promise you must never tell anyone. Will you?" Laura glanced up for a second then bowed her head.

"I've never told anybody this story. When I was a girl – about your age I'd say – I went away on my own to school. Sent away, you could say, because I didn't want to go. It was a long train journey. I might as well have been sent to the moon ... now ... I was a shy little girl ..."

Laura started up.

"Yes, you can look like that, but it's true all the same. In those days I couldn't say boo to a goose. And there were lots of geese at that school." In spite of herself, Laura smiled.

"Well, for a week at least – it seemed a lot more – I thought of nothing but home. My sisters; my mother; the places where I used to play; and my toys of course. The toys I wasn't allowed to take with me because I was too old for them. And it's true, I was too old for them. But I thought of the toys I'd left behind ..."

She stopped speaking for so long Laura thought she had finished and she peeped up. Mrs Bradley was gazing vacantly through the window, as if she was dreaming about something that happened a long time ago.

She suddenly took Laura's hand and squeezed it.

"Sorry ... I was miles away ... where was I? Yes, toys ... one toy in particular. It was just a silly model of a palace, but I was very fond of it. I cried myself to sleep thinking of that wooden palace. The funny thing was, I'd stopped playing with it ages before. It had been put away in a cupboard somewhere. But there you are; round and round it went in my head, until I could hardly think of anything else. That and home, of course. I didn't know what was the matter with me. This went on for days until I was a little bundle of misery. One day, one of the teachers found me where I'd hidden myself away in a classroom. I was crying all by myself. She said I was homesick, 'sick for home', that's what she said. I can hear her saying it now."

"Did it go away?" Laura asked.

"Well, that's the interesting question. And I asked the teacher the very same thing. Just like you."

"And what did she say? The teacher, what did she say?"

"She said something I never forgot. She didn't say 'poor thing' and she wasn't even very nice to me. She just said it would go away the very second I wanted it to."

Mrs Bradley leaned back in her chair and laughed quietly to herself.

"How I cried. I thought she was most dreadfully cruel."

She let go of Laura's hand and murmured, almost to herself, "But she was right, you see. Absolutely right."

Laura sat for a long time staring at her hands in her lap. She pushed the hair out of her face and managed to look up. Her eyes had filled with tears again; she started to say something then stopped and sat silent and unhappy.

The faint tinkle of a bell drifted in through the window and grew as it progressed round the house and into the hall. Mrs Bradley jumped up.

"Heavens above! That's supper and I have to wash my face. I'm covered in dust. You'll have to run down and tell them not to wait for me. Tell them I'm on my way."

Laura reached down and started to pull her shoes on.

"Here, I'll tidy you up a bit." She poured water from the big jug into Laura's bowl and soaked the corner of a towel in it.

Laura stood, eyes closed, to have her face sponged and dried. She let Mrs Bradley turn her round and straighten her clothes. The air on her face felt cool.

"There you are; you'll do."

"You won't...?" Laura hesitated.

"Not me. Your secret's safe with me. And remember you promised about mine. Now, off you trot. Go and eat something; you must be starving." She glanced through the window.

"You know, I think the weather's going to break. It looks like we're in for a storm. We could do with a nice fresh breeze."

At the door, she turned, her hand resting on the catch, looking back at the forlorn figure of Laura standing by the window.

"Look, do you want me to come down with you?"

Laura shook her head. "No thanks, I'll manage." She hesitated, "What that teacher said to you? When she said it would go away? I mean ... did it?"

Mrs Bradley rushed across and took Laura's face between her hands.

"Of course it did, you silly goose! I woke up one morning and found I'd forgotten to be miserable. And now you're going to ask me how long, and I can't say. I forget. It was all a very long time ago ..."

She gave Laura a little hug, laughing to herself, "... longer ago than you think." She bent down and planted a kiss on the top of her head.

"I was just thinking to myself ... perhaps I should say 'poor thing' ... do you want me to?" Laura managed a little smile and shook her head.

"Right ... off you go, or they'll think you've been kidnapped. I dare say they have a few stories to tell. About this afternoon. But you'll find out all about that."

*

Laura dreaded going through the garden door and out onto the terrace, but she need not have worried. No one even noticed her arrive; no one even glanced in her direction. Food was set out on the table but nobody was eating. An argument was raging across the table like a storm. Everybody seemed to be trying to get the last word and the last word grew louder and louder.

She sat down next to Elizabeth in time to see her jump up, scraping her chair back on the stones. She was giving Uncle Albert one of her very best looks.

"No, let me say something. It's just not fair! First you go plotting things without telling us ..."

Uncle Albert threw his arms up, appealing to the sky.

"Honestly, what's the use of plotting if it's not a secret?"

He was trying to get her to smile, but Elizabeth was having none of it. She pressed on.

"And then you get Mum to join in. And to cap it all ... and this is the worst ..." she looked round the table for support, "... we get sent off to bed." She paused for breath, "Well, perhaps not all of us. You go and lock poor Poppy up in that studio of yours ..."

"But I wasn't locked up," protested Poppy, "I wanted to be there. More than anything ... it was lovely."

There was an uncomfortable silence. Elizabeth stood looking round the table, her face very red. Uncle Albert shuffled in his chair.

"Alright, I'll grant it wasn't very sociable. I'll give you that ... but it was in a good cause. How was I to know that young Poppy here ..."

It was Ian's turn to break in, "So long as she doesn't do it again," he said plaintively. "I always get left out if Poppy's not here."

Poppy threw a despairing look at Uncle Albert, but he was staring awkwardly at the tablecloth, crumbling a bit of bread between his fingers. Both of them knew they had already arranged to spend time tomorrow in the studio. They had even stayed back to mix paints so she could get a head start.

Poppy looked at Ian, feeling guilty and hoping at the same time Uncle Albert would not confess.

"We'll have to see ... we'll see," he mumbled.

"No use at all saying that," shouted Elizabeth. "That's the very worst thing you can say. That's what grown-ups always say. What you say when you've decided to do something anyway."

She turned to Stuart. "Isn't it? It's what they always say ... isn't it, Stuart?" She looked down at him with hot eyes, waiting for him to speak.

He let his gaze fall, saying nothing and feeling awful. She shrugged and sank back into her chair looking very cross.

When the door swung open and Mrs Bradley came bustling through the stone arch she was greeted by a completely silent table, no one daring to say anything.

"My word, it's very quiet here. You really shouldn't have waited for me."

She shot a glance at Laura who shook her head as if to say it had been impossible to deliver her message.

"I simply had to get some of the day's dust off." She started passing plates round.

"Serve yourself Ian, just take what you like ..." She paused, looking hard at Uncle Albert.

"What's up? Why is nobody saying anything? I'm not that late!" She threw another anxious glance at Laura, raising her eyebrows this time in a sort of question, but Laura gave another tiny shake of the head.

"Come on Elizabeth, out with it, don't tell me the cat's got your tongue … it never got it before. What's amiss?"

It was Uncle Albert who broke the silence.

"It's all my fault, and I'm sorry for it. Thinking it would be a nice surprise – that's what went wrong; and now I think we're both in trouble. But my fault … it's what comes of having good intentions … I might say the of best intentions …" Elizabeth gave a little snort. "No … we meant well. But sometimes surprises are a bit selfish, I can see that … leaving you to your own devices that way was a bit unfair."

He turned to Mrs Bradley, hoping she would rescue him, but she shook her head.

"It's no use looking at me. You talked me into going off like that - you and the Mayor. All I can say is, he should have spent the day being bounced about in a dust cloud behind the slowest donkey in France." She pulled her chair forward.

"And I only have to go away, and what happens? Stuart looks as if he's been fried, Ian is hobbling about like a man who's forgotten his stick … and as for this explorer …" She put her arm round Elizabeth's shoulders, "She takes it into her head to lead an expedition into the jungle. To the back of nowhere. I must say, if they hadn't come across my donkey cart …"

"You've forgotten Poppy. What about Poppy? Who was it kidnapped Poppy?" asked Elizabeth, very anxious to move the subject away from the afternoon's exploration.

Mrs Bradley looked puzzled.

"What on earth has poor Poppy done to upset anybody?"

Poppy was feeling very uncomfortable indeed. She glanced timidly up at Uncle Albert.

But Uncle Albert had caught Elizabeth's imploring look at her mother and was determined to find out about the expedition.

"What's this about a jungle? What jungle? And where's the back of nowhere? I'm confused. I thought you were all safely in your beds. Wasn't that what you were complaining about? Here's me saying I was sorry to be the cruel Uncle that sent you off to bed and now it seems there was no siesta anyway." He frowned at Elizabeth.

"Explanations … please."

But she seemed not to hear. She was deeply occupied with her supper, earnestly digging into the china bowl and serving herself. She smiled sweetly at Stuart and passed him the spoons.

"Surely they've told you the story," said Mrs Bradley. "What on earth have you been talking about if it wasn't about that? It's simple … you're right, they weren't resting in bed at all … well, Laura was … but the rest of them were out in the forest. In this heat. Getting thoroughly lost. I thought you knew."

Uncle Albert's expression suddenly changed.

"No! Not in the woods over there? Not on your own? Nobody goes in there in the middle of the day!"

He swung round to Elizabeth, and she met his glare with a timid smile. He shook his head.

"No, that won't do. That's not good enough … really, it's not funny at all … what on earth were you thinking of?"

Stuart was shuffling in his chair, wishing the ground would swallow him up.

"Here, Stuart, you've a head on your shoulders. You'd better explain. I'll only get half the story out of this miscreant, if that. What's this all about? Come on, spit it out."

Uncle Albert grabbed Ian's hand and patted it, grinning ferociously. "Not now … not now … I'll give you a perfect definition of miscreants later. That should be easy … and we'll see whether you're on the list."

So while Elizabeth, head bowed, put on a tremendous show of enjoying her supper, Stuart told the story of the trip to the sea and how easy it had been to find themselves with no way back.

"We knew we were going the right way," he ended, "because we had worked out where South was … but it didn't help … once you're in there, all the paths seem the same."

He looked miserably at Mrs Bradley.

"We didn't mean …"

As Uncle Albert listened, his face grew more and more grave. He sat looking silently at the tablecloth. Eventually, he pushed his chair back, got up, and walked across to the edge of the lawn.

They saw him fumble first in one pocket and then another and finally find one of his little cigars. He stood with his back to them for a long time, staring at the dense wall of trees across the grass.

Elizabeth did not look up. Ian was about to say something but Mrs Bradley put her finger to her lips. She reached out and spooned a little food onto his plate. Laura was biting her lip and looking anxiously across the shade of the terrace.

The squawk of some night bird broke the silence, echoing back at them from the deep of the forest.

Uncle Albert came back and slumped down in his chair.

"It's all my fault. No one's to blame but me. I should have told you not to go wandering off down those paths. The way to the pigeon hide ..." he corrected himself, " ... I mean your tree house, that path is easy. But after that you need to be with someone who knows the way. Anyway, the sea is a good few miles. Too far to walk in this heat."

"It should have been downhill all the way to the sea," said Ian. "That's what Stuart said. But it wasn't."

Uncle Albert managed a faint smile.

"I suppose he's right. The problem is, there isn't a path that way at all. Those paths were all made by woodcutters and they had no call to go looking for the sea. If you don't know that place you end up going round and round for ever."

Stuart darted a glance at Elizabeth, but she was fumbling with her fork, her eyes fixed on her plate.

"The point is, the tracks aren't intended to go anywhere. They just mark where some chap years ago decided to chop a tree down." He stopped speaking and sat nervously rubbing at a patch of white paint on the back of his hand.

Poppy knew something was wrong. "But we were there this morning," she said. "It's only a wood. Even if you get a bit lost, it's not very far."

"It's a serious business getting lost in there," said Uncle Albert.

"Without water in this heat you soon find yourself in trouble." His voiced trailed away to silence. They saw him exchange looks with Mrs Bradley. "Really bad trouble ..." he mumbled.

"There aren't bandits or anything, are there?" asked Poppy.

"No, nothing like that … it's the heat … if you're not careful you can get heatstroke. And heatstroke's a terrible thing … no joke at all … that's something for the doctor … and you have to be mighty quick about it at that."

Mrs Bradley, who had been looking at him with a very severe expression, suddenly reached out and put an arm round Elizabeth's shoulders.

"Let's just say you were lucky to meet the cart. And that can be an end to the matter. It's a lesson learned." She managed a little laugh.

"Some people have a charmed life … and to think, I imagined you'd all come down the road as a welcome party."

Ian wished they would stop sounding so solemn.

"I saw the cart first," he said, "and what's that word mean? The one you stopped me asking."

But Uncle Albert had suddenly thought of something.

"There's one thing I can tell you, though. It was years ago. I'd forgotten all about it. One of the old men in the village once told me what the woodcutters do if they ever got lost."

Stuart looked up at Elizabeth. If real woodcutters could get lost in the forest, perhaps it could happen to anybody.

"What you do is find a rotten tree trunk, you know, the sort that are hollow pretty well all the way through … and hit it as hard as you can with a stick. A heavy stick. You bang away like this."

They fell silent as Uncle Albert tapped out a steady beat on the table with the handle of a fork. It echoed back from the edge of the woods.

"If you work at it, it makes a huge noise. And that's what you have to do - stay where you are and wait until somebody hears the bang, bang, bang … They usually do, because a noise like that travels miles."

"They come to see who's making the noise?" asked Ian.

"More likely they think somebody who shouldn't is chopping a tree down."

"It's a jolly good idea," said Stuart. "You could use it to send morse. I mean you could send a proper message."

"They were making that noise here long before Mr Morse was born. Thousands of years before, I shouldn't wonder ..."

"But what if nobody hears?" asked Ian.

"I mean, there isn't anybody there to hear, is there? It's completely empty."

Uncle Albert laughed.

"Don't you believe it. That place is full of people. It's just so big you don't get to see them. No, if you'd known how to do it, I'm pretty sure somebody would have heard ... not that they'd have been all that pleased to lose a day's work rounding you up."

"Is anyone going to eat?" asked Mrs Bradley, "I'm hungry."

*

The bowl Cook had left on the table was filled with what looked like soft white shells, sprinkled with parsley. Elizabeth had already eaten some. She spooned more onto the other plates.

"What are they?" Ian whispered. "Can you eat them?"

By way of answer she picked one off her plate, popped it into her mouth, and made a face at him.

"It's called pasta," she said. "Lovely. I've had it before. All creamy with bits of bacon and mushrooms and secret things in it. Go on, it's cooked this time!"

Ian spiked a little shell with his fork, "I don't think I like mushrooms," he said, then added, trying to be fair, "at least, I've never had one to eat, but I don't think I'd like one."

He nibbled tentatively, trying to see whether he had picked up anything dangerous then smiled and swallowed the little shell whole.

"Jolly good. But the mushrooms are too small to see, so that doesn't matter ... it tastes very nice."

"Well, one thing I'm sure of," said Uncle Albert, looking round the table, "you don't let the sun set on a quarrel."

He looked up at a sky flecked with little grey clouds, edged in pink. The setting sun, a huge red ball, no longer fiery, was dipping into the tops of the trees.

Elizabeth stayed gazing at her plate, idly chasing a single shell round and round with her fork. Laura gave her a little nudge.

"I think you'd better hurry. The sun's setting." She gave Uncle Albert a timid look and asked in a tiny voice, "Can I say something?"

He smiled.

"I'd say you've more right than anybody. I don't think you've said a single word. Not since you got here, and the fight was well underway by then. Go on, speak up, or the supper's ruined. Listen everybody, we'll let Laura knock some sense into us."

"I think it's the weather," she said, and paused to collect her thoughts. "When I'm at home ..." She shot a shy conspiratorial smile towards where Mrs Bradley was sitting.

"When I'm at home, I always get very sleepy if there's thunder in the air. It was like that this afternoon. Much hotter than at home, of course, but the same feeling. I think there's going to be a storm." She hesitated, looking up at him, "and it does something else as well. I don't know why ... but it puts people in a funny mood ..."

"Uncles in particular," Elizabeth interrupted, then, in spite of herself, started to laugh.

"I mean it makes people cross," said Laura.

"Perhaps it was that made my arm ache," said Stuart. "Storms do that. I read it somewhere."

Uncle Albert leaned back, gazing into the sky above the roof of the house, shading his eyes. "You're right about the thunder, anyway. Listen, you can hear it."

They sat in silence, straining to hear. Far away, a low grumble echoed across the sky.

"It's miles off, but there's a storm in the mountains right enough. It's the time of the year. It won't come here, but the heat might break for a while."

And almost as if he had ordered it, the trees beyond the lawn began to rustle slightly and a faint puff of cool air flapped at the tablecloth.

Elizabeth had been busily straightening the cutlery round her plate. She looked up.

"Well, I suppose he said he's sorry, so that's alright ..." She grinned at Laura. "Yes ... well ... I'm sorry ... I just got worked up ... cross you might say ... probably the heat."

Poppy stood up.

"Me too," she said in a very little voice then quickly sat down again.

"Handsomely put," said Uncle Albert, "so that's settled. And just in time too - I'd better light some lamps; it'll be dark soon. I know they bring the moths, but we do need the light."

He lit the lamps, muttering to himself, "I really can't think what we were thinking of, sitting squabbling with delicious food going cold."

He pulled a face at Elizabeth and stretched out a massive hand towards her across the table. She took it in both hands.

"Pax, niece – will that do?"

She tossed her head back, pumped his hand vigorously, and sat beaming contentedly into his face.

Stuart was more sure than ever that he would never understand Elizabeth. When he had a row with Laura it could go on for days, and usually exhaust itself with neither of them speaking. But Elizabeth ... she had been really angry, and now there she was smiling at everybody in the friendliest way possible.

At everybody except Poppy, perhaps, who sat silent and awkward leaning back a little in her chair, out of the lamplight.

Uncle Albert finished his plate of cold pasta shells and poured two glasses of wine. He picked up the jug of lemonade and passed it to Poppy.

As she stood, holding it in two hands to pour, he said, "Since they say it's good for the soul, I suppose we two should confess as well, Poppy. Don't you think?"

She threw him an anguished look, but he went on.

"We may as well admit it. We were planning some more painting ... just the two of us ... for tomorrow ..."

Ian jumped up.

"Oh, no! What for? You've done painting. You don't want to do it again. It's not the same without Poppy."

Uncle Albert hurried on, "… But we've changed our minds, haven't we Poppy?" She nodded, looking miserable. "We'll find another time."

Poppy nodded again then suddenly had an idea.

"Uncle Albert, what about really early? That wouldn't matter. I'm always up before everybody else. We could do the lessons before breakfast."

His expression changed and Elizabeth burst out laughing.

"That's a wonderful idea Poppy! You set your alarm and wake your teacher in really good time."

She looked innocently at him, trying not to grin too much as he shuffled uncomfortably in his chair. He held his hands up,

"I give in. Defeated on all sides." He lifted the lid from the china bowl.

"I'd better eat up if I'm going to be hearing the lark at first light. I've not heard one of those for many a year. I always thought the dawn chorus was over-rated."

"I don't think there are larks here," said Poppy earnestly, "the only birds you hear in the morning make a funny noise like a bell pinging. I think they're magpies."

Uncle Albert tapped the side of his glass with a fork. They all looked at him.

"Best fill your glasses," he said, looking round. "Pink lemonade or red wine, it's all the same. I am going to give you a toast." He stood up and pronounced in a voice loud enough to send the bats diving and swooping away over their heads.

"I give you tomorrow!" They all clinked glasses.

"What about tomorrow?" Ian whispered to Poppy. He was looking round the table, "And I don't see any toast at all. Where is it?"

CHAPTER XIII

SETTING OUT

STUART woke in the night from a restless sleep filled with dreams about being lost in the trees. He had been knocking louder and louder on a log when he sat up wide awake.

The shutter outside was banging against the window sill. He had closed the windows, apart from a little gap, but had left the shutters wide open and not bothered to fix the metal catch.

The wind had got up, echoing in the chimney. And there was something else: the sound of rain bouncing off the stonework outside. Huge flashes of violet light were fluttering across the sky behind the clouds.

He jumped out of bed and padded across to the window, peering out at masses of tossing leaves. Rain was drumming against something metal outside. It must be the old wheelbarrow by the studio door.

He pulled the window open and a great gust of wet air met his face and rushed into the room. Another flash of light filled the sky, large and slow. Not at all like the sharp lightening that forked down over the hills behind the cottage at home. The undersides of vast billowing clouds were lit up grey and blue.

Another flash; this time followed by a crack like the sound of breaking wood. The rain increased, pelting down in solid lines, bouncing noisily off the stone of the window sill. Little drops splashed against his face.

Then it stopped.

Suddenly everywhere was quiet, just the drip, drip, drip of water pattering down off tiles from somewhere high above his head.

He flinched as a jagged blade of light shot down the sky to the sound of something huge being ripped apart. For a startled second the reflection of his face stared wide-eyed back at him from the windowpane. Then all was dark again.

The room had filled with a delicious smell of wet earth mixed with the faint remains of scented flowers. He leaned out, taking deep breaths, hardly caring that his feet were standing in a little pool of water on the floor. Something heavy that had been pressing down on him all day had gone.

The sky lit up again, ripples of blue light running below the clouds, but there was no following sound.

He found his way back to bed and lay rubbing damp feet against the sheets, listening to grumbles of thunder from beyond far-away mountains. Cool air from the window had chased the stuffy heat from the room.

The house was silent. Poppy didn't like thunder, but she was not calling out. Everybody must be asleep. His bad arm, the one that had been aching all day, suddenly seemed more comfortable.

He lay in the dark thinking again about Elizabeth's quarrel. Laura was right – it must have been the storm.

*

Perhaps because he had lain awake in the night, Stuart was the last to come downstairs. He hurried across the hall and could already hear the chatter of breakfast talk.

As he came onto the terrace, Cook was putting a jug of hot chocolate on the table. She turned and smiled at him.

There was no sign at all of the rain in the night. The morning smelled fresh but the sun was as hot as ever on your face. He kneeled down and touched the brown grass at the edge of the lawn. It was dry.

He filled his bowl and took it with him across the grass to the studio door. Yes, the old wheelbarrow was still damp inside. There had been water there alright. It must have all leaked away through the rusty holes.

"No use looking for Poppy," shouted Elizabeth, "she's not in there. She's gone to change her dress. She was covered in paint."

"Green paint," said Ian, "a bit like a painted warrior. You know, painted with woad."

"Woad's not green, it's blue" said Elizabeth. "I know, because it doesn't come off … at least not easily … I tried it once on my face."

"She had blue as well. Paint everywhere."

"No one thought to pack an apron," said Laura.

Stuart strolled back to the table, taking little sips of his hot chocolate.

"I was just looking at that wheelbarrow. It rained in the night. I heard it. It simply poured down for a few minutes then stopped. It's pretty well dry now."

Uncle Albert came ambling out of the kitchen eating a piece of bread and trying to stop jam slipping down onto his chin.

"I suppose I should sit down," he said. He caught the escaping jam just in time and stood licking his fingers. "Before somebody says I'm as bad as the children."

"But you are!" said Elizabeth, "that's what we like about you." She stopped, giving him a very hard look. "At least, that was before. You're on probation now."

Uncle Albert pulled a chair out and sat down with a sigh. He prodded Stuart's good arm.

"Did you hear the thunder? I was working very late and wondered whether you'd hear it. We get storms at this time of the year. Five minutes of rain, then it's all gone. Not enough to wet a whistle."

"Why would you want to wet one anyway?" asked Ian.

Uncle Albert looked at him, started to say something, then sighed again and shook his head.

Ian was carefully piling more jam on his bread with a spoon. You could easily get used to breakfast here. If there was not going to be porridge, you could certainly manage very well with jam. At home, jam was at teatime, but it was just as nice in the morning.

He watched Uncle Albert tap a hard-boiled egg on the edge of the table then shell it and cut it into four neat pieces on his plate.

There was a bowl of eggs on the table. Ian reached out and picked one up, avoiding Laura's eye. She did so disapprove of fingers, but there really is no way of shelling an egg apart from fingers.

Uncle Albert pushed the bowl towards her. She shook her head, then changed her mind and timidly picked one out.

"That cart should be here by now," he said, "it belongs to some relative of Madame Berri. Have you got everything packed? There'll be no chance to come back if you've forgotten anything."

"Mother did the packing first thing this morning," said Elizabeth.

"She says she's not coming camping. She wants to sit in the garden. But she asked me to give you this."

She handed him a bag with a big grin.

"They're all the things you've forgotten ... and the cart's been here for ages. The man's waiting at the side of the house. He's had his coffee and he's talking to Cook. Mum says they're talking about a bicycle race."

"Who gets to ride in the cart?" Ian asked, pulling at Uncle Albert's arm.

"Well, not all of you. We have to think about the weight. You could take turns I suppose, but really those with the shortest legs should go in the cart."

"My legs are quite long ... long enough, anyway ... it's just me that's not very long."

*

It was decided in the end that Ian and Poppy were the lightest and could ride in the cart, lying on top of the pile of tents. The others had to walk alongside the donkey as she clopped down the path towards the iron gate where Stuart had rested the day they arrived.

But the cart did not turn up the road towards the station. Instead, the man tugged at the bridle and Uncle Albert pushed the donkey's head until they were on a narrow rutted path, barely more than a break in the trees, plunging steeply down into the woods.

Ian looked back at Laura and Elizabeth, trying their best to keep up.

"It's lovely up here," he shouted, trailing his hand through the leaves that bent down above his head.

Elizabeth, very stiff from yesterday's walk, tried to say something, but was too out of puff and just managed a scowl.

Stuart had fallen well behind, walking carefully so as not to jolt his arm.

"How far is it, do you think?" he shouted.

Elizabeth turned and stopped to wait for him.

"I've never been down here. This must be the way to the sea - we'd have never found it. Uncle said a couple of miles. That's not too bad."

He gave a rueful smile.

"It is when you get lost ... come on, don't let them out of sight."

They hurried on, keeping the little cart in view. Uncle Albert had picked Laura up and seated her on a narrow ledge at the back, her legs dangling down. She waved to them.

The dust kicked up by the donkey gradually changed from white to red and her hooves began to sink into little drifts of sand.

The path widened out, with tussocks of coarse grass on either side. The trees were thinner now and the light ahead brighter.

As the cart began to climb towards the crest of a little hill, Elizabeth and Stuart found they were catching up.

Uncle Albert came behind the cart and leaned his shoulder against it, his feet sinking into soft sand. Elizabeth joined in, pushing with both arms. Laura jumped down to help.

"If the load's too heavy," Elizabeth panted, "you could always toss a few more things overboard. Like a small explorer or two ... for the wolves, I mean. That would lighten things up a lot."

But Ian didn't hear. He was doing his best to see what was over the top of the hill, standing with his arms firmly round Poppy's head.

Stuart added his good arm to the back of the cart and found his feet sinking into hot sand. The man holding the bridle gave one last tug, willing the little donkey over the crest of the rise.

The cart creaked to a halt and they found themselves looking across sandy dunes falling down to a wide beach.

Ahead, stretching to the far horizon, was the soft swell of a dancing blue sea and an endless roar of breaking waves echoing across empty sand.

Out of the trees, the air was hot and clammy again and the glare of the sun almost too bright to bear. Uncle Albert stood for a moment, looking left and right and mopping his brow.

"The last lap … and the worst … not all that far … but not so easy with a cart on the beach."

He gave the donkey an encouraging slap but she was happy standing where she was in the dappled shade and simply looked at him, rolling her eyes and flicking her ears at the flies.

The man pulled at the bridle. For a moment the donkey looked mutinous then changed her mind and clopped forward a few steps. The cart rolled ahead, fell back as the donkey hesitated, then careered down the dunes onto the soft sand of the beach.

"It's sinking in. We'll have to lighten the load," said Uncle Albert. "See whether you two can jump down. It's a bit of a risk stopping – we might never get her to start again. Donkeys can be stubborn."

Poppy clambered up onto the seat at the front of the cart and looked down at him, wide-eyed.

"It's alright, I'll catch you."

She hesitated a second then launched herself into his waiting arms. Uncle Albert staggered back then sat down heavily. The cart trundled on.

Poppy brushed sand off her legs and ran to catch it up.

"Your turn, Ian," she shouted, "come on, jump! I'll catch."

"I don't want to be caught. Mind out, I'm coming."

He waited until they were next to a drift of soft sand and landed upright, burying his legs up to the knees.

"That's the way to do it," he said proudly, adding, "gosh, it's burning hot, this sand."

He pulled his legs out and started to dig for his sandals.

With its load less, the little cart made better progress towards a point where the trees ran out to a rocky outcrop, the sea almost lapping at its foot. There was just room to squeeze past, the wheels sinking into the damp remains of the last high tide.

Beyond the trees, a stone building with a battered wooden door came into view. There was not much else.

"Here we are then," said Uncle Albert. He was very red and panting to catch his breath. "Phew - next time I'll not choose a heatwave for the journey."

Elizabeth slumped down on the sand, rubbing her legs, still stiff from yesterday's walk. Past the little stone building a barren shoreline seemed to stretch out for ever. She exchanged looks with Stuart. This was not at all a promising place for a camp.

Laura stood looking back at the trees, thinking of wood for the fire. The camp site looked bare and baking hot. There was no shade at all – just flat white sand. What would they do for water? Perhaps Uncle Albert didn't know about camping.

Elizabeth was standing looking thoughtful. She glanced awkwardly across and Laura saw the look in her eyes. She would never have picked this place. None of them would. No shade, no water, and, what's more, nothing to do, apart from walk over miles of empty shore.

Stuart was idly scraping patterns in the sand. He was biting his lip.

"Is this the place?" Ian asked, looking round and trying his best not to sound too disappointed. "Is this where we camp? Shall we unpack the things?"

Uncle Albert was fanning his face with his hat, looking strangely pleased with himself. He grinned at Poppy, gave Ian a wink and turned with an elaborate sweep of his arm to shade his eyes. He was staring out to sea.

Ian followed his gaze. Across the dazzle of white-tipped waves there was a smudged shadow of something on the horizon.

"It's land," he said.

"It's an island!" said Elizabeth.

Stuart was standing up on his toes, straining to see.

"No, it's two islands I think." He pointed to one end of the low silhouette. "Look, one bit seems to be broken off from the rest. It's too bright. I wish I'd brought the telescope."

Elizabeth clambered up onto the cart.

"You can see better from here. It's two islands right enough, a big flat one and a little squat one." She pulled Laura up to join her.

"What's that?" said Laura, "a house or something."

She was pointing to a tiny black mark on the island. "Over there!"

Uncle Albert had been talking to the donkey man. He turned his head to look up at her.

"You've got sharp eyes. No, it's not a house. Certainly not a house. Come on you two, jump down or we'll never reach the port."

Ian laughed. "That's silly. There isn't a port here. Port's have to have ships in them."

"Quite right," said Uncle Albert.

"He's just pretending," said Poppy. "It's too small for a port. Anyway, there aren't any ships. So it can't be."

But Stuart had trotted on ahead of the cart to the crest of the rise. He found himself looking down past the building towards a stone pier jutting out into the sea.

"There's a jetty," he called. He jumped up and caught a glimpse of the top of a wooden mast.

"And a boat as well, I think. So I suppose it is a sort of port ... a very little one."

"A boat!" shouted Elizabeth. "What sort of a boat?"

"Never you mind what sort of boat," said Uncle Albert. "I suppose you want sails and all that. But this one will do very well. And if it wasn't there, we'd all be going back home. So thank goodness for small mercies ... and for the Mayor who brought it here."

"You don't mean we're going in a boat?" Poppy shouted, grasping his arm. "I just knew it was going to be something exciting."

Ian looked intently at Uncle Albert as he helped steer the donkey towards the jetty.

"It's the island, isn't it? I know where we're going to camp. It's on the island, isn't it? I'm right aren't I?"

But Uncle Albert seemed not to hear.

"IS THIS THE PLACE?"

CHAPTER XIV

THE VOYAGE

THE donkey man had turned the cart away from the sea onto a narrow strip of hard clay and the donkey, feeling something solid at last under her feet, broke into a trot.

The cart tottered down the path swaying wildly from side to side. Uncle Albert caught it up and pulled hard on a big wooden lever. They skidded to a halt.

The donkey had enjoyed running and looked very content, tossing her head and snapping her teeth, doing her best to untie the harness.

The man rummaged in the back of the cart and handed Poppy a little bag of oats, opening it so that she could see what was inside.

"She's not a horse," said Uncle Albert, "so watch her teeth. It's the thumb they go for. If I were you I'd just put some on the grass for her."

Poppy started to pour a little pile of oats out onto the ground but the man tapped her arm and shook his head. He dipped inside and held out a handful to the donkey, stretching his hand out flat.

She made short work of the food and stood waiting for more. Poppy held her hand out uncertainly and the man gently pushed her thumb down and poured more oats into her palm.

"She's a very messy eater. And I can feel her teeth. They tickle a bit. I suppose she's hungry after pulling her cart all this way."

"How many handfuls does she eat?" asked Ian, creeping as close as he could and looking at Laura. They all laughed.

"You can have a go if Laura says you can," said Uncle Albert. "Only do keep your thumb out of the way."

"I'd better see if it's safe first," said Laura.

The donkey didn't mind at all who fed her and showed no signs that she had eaten enough. So while the three of them took it in turns, Stuart and Elizabeth wandered across to join Uncle Albert standing on the edge of the little stone jetty.

Below them, bobbing on a gentle swell, was a neat little motor boat with a tiny cabin and an open stern. There was a stubby mast with a pennant drooping listlessly in the still air. Three hemp fenders hung down to spare the gloss of the varnish from the stone of the jetty.

"She's not very big," said Stuart, wondering how they would all get aboard.

"We'll make two trips of it," said Uncle Albert. "I'll take you lot across then I'll come back on my own for the things in the cart."

Stone steps and an iron ladder, scaly with rust, led down from the jetty. Where the tide had reached, everything was green and slimy with wet seaweed. A strong fishy smell, laced with salt, came off the water as it swilled up and down against the stones. An iron handrail was fixed to the wall. It must have been painted white years ago but was brown with rust now, encrusted with hundreds of tiny shells.

They watched Uncle Albert walk down the steps and hop across into the boat. He pulled the door to the cabin open, standing back for a while to let the heat inside escape. He moved a lever and leaned down to do something near his feet.

There was a coughing noise; spurts of water glugged out of a pipe in the side of the boat and the engine roared to life sending a plume of white smoke up the steps to curl round their legs with a strong smell of fuel.

At the sound of the motor boat, Laura, Poppy and Ian came running across. Uncle Albert leaned out of the little cabin and shouted to them above the throb of the engine.

"Ian and Poppy first. Hold on to the rail and watch your step. Sorry about the smoke – she's always like that when the tank's full."

Poppy trotted down the steps, hesitated a second, and jumped aboard. Ian followed, stopping to scrape away seaweed with his foot as he went down the steps. Uncle Albert stretched out and lifted him into the boat.

Stuart looked anxiously at Laura but she just handed him her hat to hold and skipped down, barely stopping until she stretched a foot out onto the rail of the little boat.

Ian was already exploring. The stern of the boat was open, with slatted wooden seats running along each side. There was a raised wooden box with brass handles in the centre of the boat. Laced to both sides of this with thick cord were lines of black and white lifebelts. The name *Luc* was stencilled in thick black letters at the top of each.

He was trying to work out how they came undone.

Uncle Albert leaned out of the cabin door and called out.

"You'll not be needing them today. Not in this weather. Squeeze up a bit and make room for two more."

Elizabeth and Stuart jumped aboard and felt their way round towards the stern.

"But what's *Luc*?" asked Ian.

"The boat's name, of course," said Poppy, "so that when they find the lifebelts floating in wild seas they'll know where they came from."

"But what's it mean?" he persisted.

"Just a name," shouted Uncle Albert, "every boat needs a name. It's 'Luke' in English. There's to be no lifebelts on this trip. And no wild seas either."

He counted everyone, pointing a finger as he went.

"I make it five. That's the lot then. Hold on tight."

The engine coughed a little then settled to a dull throaty throb. The boat seemed to come alive. He backwatered away from the jetty wall, paused for a second to wave goodbye to the donkey man, then spun the little wheel round.

Before they had time to look, they were running past the stone blocks of the jetty towards the open sea.

The sea had seemed quite flat and calm from the shore, but now they were moving, the little boat had to ride a steep swell. Her bows broke the top of each wave, leaving the surge of a thick green wake behind them.

As they passed the end of the jetty, *Luc* met a brisk salty breeze on the port bow. She lurched over and the passengers found themselves hanging on. Tiny flecks of foam began to blow across the bows.

"It tastes salty," shouted Ian, licking his lips. But only Poppy heard him above the beat of the engine.

The tiny boat was pitching and rolling in a most unexpected way. Laura gripped the underneath of the bench. If they were going to bucket about like this, it could easily make you feel sick.

She glanced towards the cabin. Uncle Albert was trying to light one of his little cigars, fighting to keep a match alive. He didn't seem to mind the sea at all. He gave her a cheery wave.

Poppy was looking at the line of lifebelts. If you had to take them off in a hurry – a real hurry – it was not very clear how you did it. She shuffled along the bench and grabbed Laura's hand. Laura gave it a little squeeze but went on looking straight ahead, swallowing hard as if she was drinking something.

Uncle Albert banged on the cabin window then made a tiny horn on the roof go poop-poop. They all turned to see.

He was signalling to Stuart and Elizabeth, pointing to the wheel as if to ask would you like to try.

Elizabeth leapt up, tottered back as the boat hit a wave, and tipped into Poppy's lap. She pushed herself up and stumbled towards the tiny cabin, Stuart following, hanging on as best he could. They crowded inside, pushing against the cabin wall to make room.

There was not very much to see: a black lever running down into the floor and a polished shelf with some brass switches on it. There was a wooden wheel that seemed almost too small for the boat and a compass set in the bulkhead under the window.

The cabin was very hot and filled with a strong smell of fuel. The floor beneath their feet throbbed to the sound of the engine. After the quiet outside, the noise was almost painful.

Uncle Albert pushed Elizabeth towards the wheel and stood behind her for a moment, his hands resting on top of hers. He pointed to the compass and made a chopping motion with his arm to show the course. Then he let go.

She peered down at the bleary glass of the compass, tossed the hair out of her eyes and grasped the wheel, risking a single excited glance back at Stuart. He managed a little grin, hanging on as they crested the top of the swell.

"Not such a bad uncle after all." She was shouting at the top of her voice. "Your turn next. We won't have long – we must be half way across. Gosh, this is wonderful!"

But Stuart was content to let Elizabeth steer their course. It would be hard with his sling. Anyway, she seemed so happy. After all, there might be another chance. It was enough to watch Uncle Albert calmly working the controls of the engine.

Dead ahead, the island, tipping and tilting, rose out of the sea. No longer a blurred shape on the horizon, it had a proper coast with shallow cliffs topped by stunted trees.

Their course was leading them towards a tiny finger of sandy red beach running down between low cliffs.

They were suddenly caught between land and open sea, bouncing violently in choppy water. Stuart pressed himself against the cabin wall, holding on to the edge of the door. He tried to see how the passengers were faring. Anybody could feel a little sick with a boat bouncing about like this.

Even as he thought about Laura, a strange tight feeling gripped his own throat. He tried not to think about it and peered through the splattered glass of the cabin window. The passengers were all on the starboard side, pointing.

Running out onto the beach ahead was a pier, perched on huge wooden piles. As the sea surged under it, streamers of thick green weed trailed through the waves. Creamy white water rushed past to break onto a sandy beach.

Stuart stood in the doorway, gulping in fresh air and swallowing hard. Uncle Albert tapped Elizabeth on the shoulder and she reluctantly stepped aside to let him take the wheel.

The sound of the engine slowed to a steady beating chug, chug. They had come round to port and were running beneath the cliffs. *Luc* ran quietly up alongside the pier, her fenders creaking as she gently bumped against the wood.

Ian had already squeezed past the cabin door and found a coiled line in the stern. He held it up and waved, ready for the signal.

Uncle Albert shouted, "Just hop ashore - she'll hold on that. But mind your step. We'll tie up here." He stopped the engine.

Suddenly there was nothing to hear but the slap of water and the creak of the boat against the wooden piles.

A gull flew down to look at them, calling as it swooped past.

One by one they disembarked, feeling the solid ground a little unsteady under their feet. They stood clustered together on the landing stage, looking down at the little boat.

"Stay where you are!" shouted Uncle Albert. "I'm not coming ashore. I won't be long. Keep a good eye out for me and don't go wandering off."

Once again, the engine roared into life.

CHAPTER XV

PITCHING CAMP

"DON'T go wandering off ..." Uncle Albert's voice was lost in the beat of the engine.

He leaned out of the little cabin and shouted something to Elizabeth, but nobody heard what he said. Stuart had thrown the stern line aboard and received a wave of a straw hat in return. *Luc* gently backed away from the pier and the sound of the engine increased.

They watched as she bounced her way back towards the mainland until all that was left was her wake, a line of white water on a dazzle of sparkling blue.

Suddenly, the landing stage seemed very quiet.

"No point standing here in the sun," said Elizabeth. It will be a good while before he gets back. Let's have a quick look round. We won't go far."

"I'll wait here," said Laura, sitting down and dangling her legs over the side of the landing stage. "We were rather bucketing about and I could do with a rest. There's some shade under here – I'll wait for you."

But Elizabeth was having none of it.

"You were just a bit seasick. So was Stuart ... I felt a bit green myself. But it wears off. Ignore it."

She ran along the bleached wooden planks and jumped the last couple of feet into the soft sand.

"Come on, it's a pity to waste a desert island when we've got it all to ourselves. We'll go up there and have a look."

Stuart looked at Laura.

"She's right, you know, you'd be better walking." He watched Elizabeth splash her way across the beach with Poppy and Ian trying to keep up.

"Anyway, we should keep together."

Laura hauled herself up and gave a little sigh.

"But he said we shouldn't go wandering off, you heard."

"It's only as far as that hill - that's not wandering. In fact, we'll see him coming back better from up there." Stuart was thinking hard how to persuade her. "Anyway, we've got to find somewhere to camp. You could look round ..."

Laura smiled. "Alright, you win. But not for long."

She looked across the beach to the sloping dunes. The air over the sand was shimmering.

"It's very dry everywhere. Where do we get water?"

"We'll have to look."

They followed the footprints of the others and began to climb the dunes. Away from the sea, there was no breeze and the heat fell on them like a blanket.

"A good job we've got sandals," Stuart panted, "this sand's too hot to touch."

Near the top, the soft sand ended and they were walking between clumps of grass and dry little shrubs covered with bright red flowers. He stopped, leaning forward to ease a stitch pain in his ribs and breathing hard. Laura leaned against him trying to catch her breath.

"You're almost there," called Elizabeth, "just a few more steps. It's quite a view ... you won't believe it!"

The others were taking in the scale of their new home from the shade of a clump of thirsty-looking trees.

The island was much bigger than they expected. They were standing at the edge of an expanse of brown grass that dropped gently down towards woods, already in deep shade.

Far away to their left, at the other end of the island and seeming to rise out of the trees, was a familiar shape - the top of a stone tower.

"It's our tower," said Laura, staring open mouthed.

"Poppy said just the same," shouted Ian, "but that's silly, it can't be, we're miles and miles from home. It couldn't have walked here."

"But it's the same shape. Look," she strained up to get a better view. "I think there's even a window at the top. It's just the same."

Stuart had been looking thoughtful. He shaded his eyes.

"I wish we had the telescope. But you're right about the shape ... it's much taller of course ..."

"That's because it's not fallen down," said Ian. "Ours has mostly fallen down."

"It must have been built by the same people."

"Or person ..." said Poppy. She stopped. "I wonder which one he did first?"

Elizabeth was standing silently next to Laura.

"We could see something dark from the tree house ... remember? When we found the sea."

"You saw it," said Laura. "I couldn't lean out that far."

"But you were there." She grabbed her arm. "Have we got time to look, do you think? There's no sign of the boat. It wouldn't take long."

Laura looked horrified. "But it's miles away. And we said we'd not go wandering off." She turned imploringly to Stuart.

He looked at his watch.

"There and back in this heat would take a long time. And remember – no water." He grinned cheerfully at her. "So off you go - we'll keep some supper for you."

Elizabeth shrugged, "Perhaps you're right. It does look like quite a trek ... but first thing tomorrow without fail ... our very first exploration. The trip to the tower."

"He's here!" Ian shouted.

They turned and looked back out to sea. A tiny brown boat was already changing course, heading towards the landing stage.

"Gosh," said Elizabeth, "that was quick. Come on ... we've got to be standing there when the boat comes in. She glowered ferociously at Ian. "As good as gold, mind you, and not out of breath at all."

She had already started off, half jumping and half running in a diagonal line across the face of the dunes, kicking up a spray of sand as she went.

*

Nonetheless, the crew that arrived only just in time to greet the motor boat was very red in the face and finding it difficult to breathe normally.

They waited as the motor boat came alongside. Uncle Albert grabbed the first of the canvas sacks and heaved them onto the landing stage.

"Hello you lot, what have you been up to? You look hot. Not exploring again. I'll have to find a way of roping you together."

"You only said don't go wandering off," said Elizabeth. "And we didn't wander at all. We just went up to the top of that hill over there."

"And back again," said Ian, remembering to add, as a way of excusing everything, "and Laura didn't want to go at all."

Uncle Albert started to say something, then changed his mind and burst out laughing.

"I'm sure that makes it alright. Good for Laura."

He handed Elizabeth another canvas bag and some parcels then hopped ashore with a sack slung behind his back.

"But you've still got to work for your supper. There's tents to pitch before the sun goes down or you'll be sleeping on the sand."

He saw Poppy looking anxiously at the growing pile of bags.

"Don't fret, the painting gear is in there somewhere – we'll find it later. We'll just take the tents for now. I'll bring this bag; it's got food in it. The rest we'll leave for the morning. Come on."

"Shouldn't you say 'Lucy'?" asked Ian, tugging at one of the sacks. "It's too heavy – I can't even pick it up."

Laura handed him a package to carry and went to look at the pile of luggage left on the landing stage.

"What if it rains?"

Uncle Albert pushed his hat back and wiped his brow.

"It won't."

She went on looking thoughtful. "Still, if you leave things here somebody might find them."

"They won't, because there isn't anybody. We have the place to ourselves."

Poppy jumped up and tugged at his arm.

"Really? Not all of it? The whole island? Really alone? That's wonderful – our own desert island." She paused. "But how do you know? Somebody might live here. Whose island is it?"

"Actually, it's mine. When I bought what you call the Pink House years ago I found that a bit of the shore went along with it. A bit of shore and a little island. I used to come here a lot when I was young. I don't come so often now … too much work to do ... and too old ... anyway you need a boat. There's only *Luc*, and she's only half mine."

"Are you really that old?"

Poppy saw Laura's warning look and looked away to hide her confusion, but Uncle Albert just shrugged and pulled her hat down over her eyes.

"Old enough, I'd say."

"Who's the other half of *Luc*?" asked Ian. "Does the other half live here?"

"Oh, that's the doctor in the village - the Mayor. You met him the other day. In fact, you'd have met him again at the breakwater back there if today had been Tuesday. He's always fishing there on a Tuesday afternoon. But no, he doesn't live here. There'd be a shortage of patients I would think."

Ian thought for a second. "What if somebody's poorly on a Tuesday?"

"I really don't know. I suppose they have to cough until Wednesday. I'll ask him if you like."

Elizabeth was getting impatient. "Where do we set up camp? Is it far? And what do we do for water?"

He pointed vaguely towards a line of trees showing over the top of the dunes. "There's a flattish bit of ground up there. No, it's not very far." He grinned at Ian.

"Come on Lucy; the big ones can manage two to a bag. Poppy and Ian, just bring what you can carry. Don't worry about water for the moment, there's plenty in here." He patted the bag over his shoulder. "There's a spring down by the woods somewhere - but we won't need it."

Laura was still looking puzzled.

"Look, I'll show you later ... we'll call it a secret for now."

Stuart and Elizabeth gave *Luc's* moorings a final check and picked up their sacks.

The sun was low in the sky now, shadows starting to fill the ridges criss-crossing the sand. Uncle Albert led the way, a canvas bag in each hand, walking towards the dunes.

He turned off before they reached the steep slope and followed a narrow clay path running parallel with the beach. They followed him, in single file.

After a few yards nobody felt like talking. The worst of the heat had gone and there was a little shade in the lee of the dunes, but it was dreadfully heavy work, nonetheless.

The path eventually veered off and began to meander up a slope. They trudged up towards the crest of a rise finding themselves looking down a steep slope towards a tiny level plateau surrounded on three sides by woods.

Uncle Albert dropped his sacks and sank to the ground, breathing hard.

"That was hot work. I don't spend my days running about like you lot." He looked up enquiringly at Laura, one eyebrow raised. "Well, what do you think?"

"It's perfect," said Poppy. "Like a secret bower - absolutely perfect."

Laura knew they were waiting for her to say something. She always decided about the best place to camp. She looked round. The ground was flat enough - that was one thing. It seemed perfect for tents. And there were trees; that meant firewood. What else? Her book said *check for dry water courses*. That was silly - everywhere here was parched dry, even the grass had gone brown.

"I can't think of a better spot," she said, beaming back at Stuart's anxious face, "so long as the water problem is solved, that is."

But Uncle Albert had not waited for the decision. He was pulling things out of the sack and had found a short mallet packed among a mass of poles and canvas. He stood looking at it thoughtfully.

"I'd completely forgotten about a hammer ... I told you I didn't know about camping ... of course, you need one to get the pegs in ... a good job the scouts packed it. I'll admit it now - I don't have the foggiest idea how tents work ... so I'll be the hired help. Just show me what to do ... but you really have to get a move on ... it gets dark fast here."

Elizabeth had started laying things out on the ground. She stepped back, eyeing the white canvas. "It's a bell tent I think. And a big one."

"We've never pitched one of those," said Stuart.

"I think I remember how it goes." She was threading the brass ends of two poles together. "Here, have one of these ... gosh, it's old-fashioned ... still, we'll manage."

Stuart pulled a square of wood out of the sack. Somebody had carved a shallow depression in the centre.

"What's this for?"

"It's for the centre pole. To stop it sinking in - it takes all the weight."

Ian was tugging at the stiff canvas.

"Why's it a bell tent? What's a bell got to do with it?"

"You'll see," said Elizabeth. She shook a thick sheet out onto the ground.

"Right, Stuart, grab an end. Start with the groundsheet ..."

*

Laura tried to help, but soon discovered they were getting on well enough without her.

"I think I'll make a start on the fireplace," she said, almost to herself, "there are some stones over there. A bit small, but they'll do." She looked round. "I need a volunteer to collect dry wood. There should be plenty over there."

Ian scampered off and she set about making the fireplace, feeling happier than she had for days.

"You're lucky this year," said Uncle Albert, holding onto a pole that Elizabeth had thrust into his hands. "We usually don't light fires in August. A few stray sparks is all it takes. But we're alright here."

Ian came running back, his arms full of sticks. He dropped them on the ground, stood for a moment panting like a dog with his tongue out, then set off for more.

Poppy watched the tent-builders, passing them pegs as they called for them. Ian came back proudly dragging a huge branch behind him.

"Enough for tonight." He was very out of breath. "It's so dry you can just snap it into bits."

"We'll have to organise a proper wood collection in the morning," said Laura, "along with the water."

"Uncle Albert, is the water in here?" Ian asked, prodding the wicker basket. "Is that why it's heavy? Can I have a drink of water, please? I'm thirsty."

"It's time we all had a drink. I'll break out some rations. Our supper's in there as well."

*

It was almost an hour before Elizabeth and Stuart could step back and admire their work. Two sturdy bell-tents, guy ropes neatly pegged out, were standing facing Laura's new fireplace.

"A bit antiquated, but none the worse for that," said Elizabeth. She rummaged in one of the sacks and started laying bundles of blankets out on the groundsheets. "Stuart and Ian can have this tent ... and the three of us can share the other. There's bags of room. We can spread ourselves out a bit ... from the numbers on the walls, I think they sleep six scouts."

Ian had crawled inside the first tent.

"They must be quite small scouts ... but there's masses of room for two."

Elizabeth started to pull at the laces on the last bag.

"Come on ... we've one more to do."

But Uncle Albert stopped her.

"It's a nice idea, but I really am too old to sleep on the floor, you know."

He fished in his pocket and pulled out a large brass key with a cardboard label tied to it and waved it at them.

"This is my last secret for the day. I've my own accommodation," he looked around uncertainly, "somewhere ... it's just a case of finding it. And that may not be so easy now it's getting dark. I'm going to take your hammer – I think I'll need it tomorrow. If we're to find water, that is ..."

Laura wanted to ask about the water again but he just winked at her. He put the hammer in the sack and started walking away from them across the field towards a break in the trees that sheltered the camp. He turned, wiping his brow.

"Well, don't you want to see?"

"See what?" Poppy whispered to Laura. "Where's he going?"

Then she saw Stuart and Ian already halfway across the field. "Wait for me, Iggie, I'm coming."

Elizabeth had been arranging blankets in the other tent. She crawled out backwards to find Laura waiting on her own looking a little cross.

"We'll never get settled at this rate. I was just going to light the fire and now they've all gone over there. It's a nuisance … something about a key."

Elizabeth had discovered that crouching down in a hot tent tugging at a stiff groundsheet with your knees in the way is frustrating and she emerged looking a little green. She stood up, filling her lungs with fresh air, swallowing hard.

"Much longer doing that and I would be seasick all over again."

The sound of shouts and laughter floated across the field towards them and she grabbed Laura's hand.

"Something's up! Come on! The fire will just have to wait."

*

When they got closer, they could see the woods on the other side of the field were no more than a few trees deep. The pale pink of an evening sky was breaking through the leaves.

They followed the sound of voices along a short path and suddenly found themselves looking at a most unexpected sight.

In a tiny hollow edged with thorny shrubs, stood a tall stone house surrounded by a low wall with a little iron gate. It was so like the gingerbread house in the fairy story that Laura blinked. Even the door and the shuttered windows were painted bright blue. A flagpole stuck out through the pantiled roof.

One of the downstairs shutters flew open and they were looking at a very flustered Uncle Albert, knocking ancient cobwebs off the window sill.

"Hello you two. Here's where I'm sleeping. It looks like I'll have a few spiders for company … and a mouse or two … but nothing worse." He turned back inside. "Now … where is it? There's a broom somewhere in here."

"I could sweep it out for you," said Laura, who was dying to look inside.

"That's very handsome of you, I must say. Don't stay out there. Come on in. The others weren't so shy – they're exploring upstairs, I think. We won't stay here long. I'll just take these few things of mine upstairs out of the way. That's where I'm sleeping. But I'm eating with you … if I'm invited, that is."

Poppy came skipping down the stairs and stood smiling up at him. "Of course you're invited. There's a big pole in the middle of one room. And a flap in the roof. What's it for?"

"Can't you guess?"

"I can," shouted Ian, clattering down behind her, "I can … I opened the shutters ..."

He looked at Laura and stopped a second to explain his duties in the Pink House to Uncle Albert. "I can do that now ..." he caught his breath, the words tumbling out, "… we're right on the sea. It's for sending signals to the ships."

"Yes, that's right. I'll tell you all about it over supper. And speaking of supper, you'd better let me get on. Off you go.

*

They left Uncle Albert setting out his things in the Signal House and hurried back to the camp. The sun had almost set. As they came out of the trees it caught them unawares, bathing them in a friendly red glow.

Across the field, the tents were just vague white shapes in a gathering gloom. They picked their way through the camp stepping over invisible guy ropes stretched out like snares.

Laura rushed across to her fireplace. She had scraped a deep hole in the sand and surrounded it with two rings of small stones then stamped two large ones opposite each other to take the kettle.

She kneeled down, struck a match, and held it to the dry tinder. It crackled and flared bright yellow in her eyes, throwing her shadow into the dark.

Suddenly, the air was filled with the smoky scent of autumn. As the larger wood caught, a dense white plume rose up. Ian held out a selection of sticks and she sorted through them, adding them one by one as the others caught. She topped it off with two stout logs and stayed for a moment, leaning back on her heels and watching the flames licking at the wood.

"It's all awfully dry. It burns in no time. We'll have to get lots more tomorrow."

"What's for supper?" asked Ian. "Shall I open the hamper?"

*

It was awkward picking among things in the hamper with no more than the firelight and Stuart's little torch to see by.

Elizabeth stretched out a groundsheet in front of the fire while Laura passed her little paper packets.

"We don't have to cook anything. That's a help. It's getting quite late."

Poppy opened the packets and arranged them so that everybody could reach - pieces of chicken, bread already broken into chunks, slices of sausage, five huge tomatoes, radishes in a dish with a knob of butter. She pulled a big bottle out of the hamper and some china beakers.

"Something to drink - pink lemonade, I think. Perfect, anyway."

Laura was sorting through the hamper, peering inside and feeling down to the bottom.

"Is there to be pudding afterwards?" Ian asked. "What else is in there?" But she pushed him back and handed him Stuart's torch.

"Trot across the field and signal that supper's ready. Mind you don't trip in the dark."

He jumped up and was about to set off when they all saw a lamp bobbing towards them. It was Uncle Albert, carefully picking his way across the grass. He took a long time to arrive and sank down on the ground, breathing hard.

"Too much manual labour for one day. Here's my contribution to the feast. A couple of old hurricane lamps – you'll need some light. They last a good while ..." he looked at Stuart. "But you know all about that. I'll leave one behind for you, but don't let it burn all night."

He watched Laura flipping the ends of burnt sticks back into the fire.

"I can see you've done that before. You're a useful person to have about. When I light a fire I always use a whole box of matches and even then end up on my knees blowing at it."

He lit the other oil lamp and perched both of them on top of little heaps of sand.

"Laura only ever needs one match," said Ian proudly, kneeling down to check that his logs were burning.

*

They had all been looking forward to this first meal round the campfire. But now they were eating it, something seemed to be missing. They were tired, but it was not altogether that.

Laura looked at Stuart's face in the flickering yellow light. He was watching Ian and Uncle Albert decide who was going to eat the last piece of chicken. It was lovely having Uncle Albert here - after all, without *Luc* they would not be here at all - but even the best of grown-ups was, after all, a grown-up. This was not going to be quite their own camp.

"Eat up Poppy," Elizabeth gave her a little push and Poppy straightened up with a start.

"Sorry. I think I was nodding off. I was up very early for my lesson." She rubbed her eyes and looked at Uncle Albert.

"What about tomorrow?"

"I won't let you down. You turn up at my little house and I'll be waiting. If the door's open, come in. If it's not, bang on it. Only let the lark or magpie or whatever it is sing for a bit. There's no hurry."

Laura looked at Poppy. "If you're falling asleep, we'd better think about bed. There's a bottle of water for teeth."

But Ian insisted on finishing whatever was in the hamper for pudding. He pulled the lid back and felt inside.

"I know what these are. They're coconut."

He passed round little sticky cakes, each wrapped in its own crinkly paper.

"Jolly nice ... but not very big."

"Teeth," said Stuart. "Then it's lights out."

*

Much later, when Uncle Albert had disappeared into the dark, calling out goodnight as his oil lamp bobbed into the distance, Stuart lay on his back in the tent.

It was not very comfortable at first with only a rug and a groundsheet between you and the sand. But if you wriggled hard, eventually you could press your shape into the earth and that was a nice feeling. Like a hibernating animal snuggled down in its burrow for the winter.

Ian was restless, trying to lie first on one side then on the other. A flash from his torch threw weird shadows across the stiff canvas and there was an urgent whispered voice from the other side of the tent.

"Stuart, are you there?"

"Of course, I'm here. Go to sleep. You'll wake the others."

"Can we have the flap open a bit? I don't like it being so dark."

Stuart rolled out of his blankets and stood up to untie the door of the tent and fold it back.

A silent sky encrusted with stars loomed out over his head. He could see the Plough, brighter and larger than at home. And much steadier. In fact none of the stars were shimmering like they did over the lake. Here they stared back at you, fixed and cold.

He stepped outside. There was no moon yet but it was strangely light everywhere. Above him a faint white band ran across the sky. He had read about the Milky Way, but never seen it like this.

A yellow light like a silent firework streaked across the sky and disappeared behind the black line of the trees. A shooting star. Even as he was working out where it would have landed, there was another in almost the same place.

From way across the dunes he could hear the splash of the sea flopping down onto the beach and a sighing sound as it drew back.

He had taken his sling off to sleep. He tried lifting his arm. Stiff perhaps, but that sharp jab through his shoulder had gone.

He tied the top of the door flap back, and crept inside the friendly warmth of the tent. Ian's torch had rolled from his hand

and lay on the ground. He picked it up and propped at the foot of the tent pole where he could reach it in the night if he needed it. He wriggled under the mound of blankets and quietly settled back into his burrow.

A tiny breeze blew the scent of the dying fire into the tent. A triangle of black sky filled with enormous stars, white, blue and yellow, looked in at him. He closed his eyes.

*

That first night under canvas, Laura lay awake for a long time. She was snug and warm and very tired but sleep would not come. She lay listening to the distant sound of breaking waves, sniffing the scent of woodsmoke in the air. Now and then from far away there was the echoing squeal of a hunting owl. She turned on her side and looked across at the white blur of Poppy's sleeping face. The little picture of the apple seemed to have changed something for Poppy - something that could not be taken back.

She remembered she was homesick. Only she wasn't, not anymore. She grinned to herself in the dark. It had gone away on its own. It was lovely here lying wide awake under a huge crystal sky. Far away over the dunes there was the endless swish of the sea. It would be lovely to stay here for ever.

Laura closed her eyes.

CHAPTER XVI

THE SIGNAL FROM THE WOOD

STUART woke with a start. Somebody was signalling, tapping a stick on a hollow log, the sound still echoing in his ears.

He lifted his head and looked round. The red light of a very early morning sun was flooding through the open flap of the door. The air smelled of wet grass, dead woodsmoke and canvas. Everywhere seemed very quiet.

He was sure he had heard something. He propped himself up on his good elbow to listen.

Then he heard it again. It hadn't been a dream. There were shoes rustling quietly across the groundsheet outside. The sound stopped; there was nothing to hear now, apart from the thump of his heart and the swish of the far-off sea echoing through the woods.

A bird started to make a tiny cheeping sound then stopped suddenly as somebody knocked into one of the metal water bottles and it fell over. Silence again.

Then a new sound, like a rough cloth rubbing against something.

Somebody was out there. He looked across the tent. Ian had rolled himself up like a sausage in his blankets and was fast asleep, one hand clutching his torch. Above his head a dull red shadow on the tent wall was moving restlessly up and down.

Stuart sat up, his heart drumming. Uncle Albert had said there was nobody at all on the island. *So who was it?*

He wriggled his hand from under the blankets as quietly as he could and pulled them back. Out of bed, the early morning air on your face was cool and sweet. He crawled onto the groundsheet.

Another clink outside as the bottle knocked against the stones of the fireplace.

He crept up to the crack in the tent door and peeped out.

Close enough to touch was a deer, ginger brown like an old leather saddle and not much bigger than a large dog. So close, he could hear it breathing. It was standing in a little pool of spilled water and seemed to be looking at him, huge rabbit ears twitching warily and bright black eyes staring out as if daring him to move.

Stuart froze, one hand hanging onto the tent flap, his knees aching with the strain. After an endless minute, the deer shook its head, bent down and went on licking the water, making the same odd rasping noise.

The deer shifted round almost out of sight. Stuart let go of the flap and gently lifted his arm; but that was more than enough.

The deer started up and backed nervously away, clattering across the stones of the fireplace. Then it was off, hooves barely touching the grass, bounding into the air as if jumping an invisible fence. In no time at all it had reached a tiny gap in the trees and disappeared.

He stayed kneeling a long time, scanning the edge of woods, but there was nothing to see. He crawled across and lay on his back on top of the blankets.

Should he wake Ian up and tell him about the deer? The bundle on the other side of the tent snorted and rolled itself over.

He watched the triangle of sunlight inch its way across the floor, wondering whether Elizabeth had ever been that close to a deer. He closed his eyes. He had just started to wonder in a drowsy sort of way whether the deer drank from the spring when he fell fast asleep.

*

Much later, Laura was lying on her back looking at Poppy's sleeping face. She had propped her precious drawing pad against the tent pole next to her head. She looked very peaceful.

Poppy opened her eyes. "Good morning," she said sleepily, "are you awake? It's stuffy in here. You look very hot."

Laura nodded across to the heap of blankets that was the sleeping Elizabeth and put a finger to her lips. The two of them gathered up their clothes and crept out of the tent into the heat of the morning.

"It was so hot in there," said Poppy, "you couldn't breathe. At least you can breathe out here, but it's hotter." She looked up to see where the sun was. "It must be getting late." She turned in a panic, looking round for her sketch pad. "Oh, I'm going to miss my lesson; he must be waiting ... I'll have to run."

"No. You can go after breakfast. It's alright, Stuart's not even up yet."

Poppy looked through the flap at the door of the other tent. Stuart was lying on top of his rumpled blankets, his mouth open and his face very red and shiny. Ian had pushed his blankets off altogether and was curled up on the groundsheet.

"They're both asleep." She giggled. "Ian's fallen out of bed, I think. Shall I wake them up?"

"They'll hear us soon enough ... phew, it will soon be too hot to do anything at all." Laura straightened out the crumpled groundsheet in front of the fire. "We seem to have made an awful mess last night. Somebody must have knocked a bottle over in the dark; there's water everywhere."

She crouched down over the fireplace, pushed two stones back where they had fallen over and poked a handful of leaves into the ashes.

"I'm going to get the fire going for breakfast."

She lit a match and invisible flames licked up round the curling leaves as she piled the last of yesterday's sticks on top. Dense white smoke swirled round them.

Poppy stepped back, rubbing her eyes. "I'll get dressed and get some more wood ... there's none left ... I won't be long."

There was a voice behind her.

"I'll go, it's my turn." Stuart was standing in the door of his tent, rubbing the sleep out of his eyes. "Good morning. I was up before everybody ... honestly ... very early ... but I went back to sleep. It's so hot, you can't help it."

He set off, walking a little unsteadily towards the woods.

"You've still got your pyjamas on," called Laura, but he just waved his hand as if to say don't fuss. "Well at least put something on your feet."

"It's not far, I'll be alright." But even as he spoke there was a squeak and they turned to see him wobbling on one leg, trying to pick something out of his foot. He hopped sheepishly back to the tent. "On second thoughts I'll put some sandals on ... thorns everywhere."

"Is that you, Laura?" It was Ian's voice. "What are you all doing? Is it time for breakfast?"

"Yes, it's me," said Laura. "Stuart's going to get some wood. Time you were up. You could help. Get dressed."

"Is Elizabeth up?"

"She is now," came a cheery shout from the other tent. "But I'm not getting dressed. Just bathers. I'm going to have a dip in the sea. It's hot enough to fry an egg in here. I need to cool down."

Stuart came hobbling back with a bundle of sticks under his good arm. "I didn't go far. We'll have to organise a proper wood collection." He looked at Elizabeth. "Did somebody say something about the sea?"

"She said an early morning swim in the sparkling sea," said Poppy. "It sounds too good to be true."

"A swim's a good idea," said Laura. "Breakfast can wait today ..." She laughed, "And the sea can't be any colder than the Pink House shower." She looked at Poppy's eager face. "Although I'm not so sure about the 'early morning' bit. It's getting late. We must have overslept."

*

A few minutes later they were all creeping as quietly as they could past the Signal House down to the little beach beyond. The shutters were closed and there was no sign at all of Uncle Albert. Ian looked wistfully across.

"Shall I go and knock on the door? It won't take a second. He told Poppy to bang on the door. I can do that."

"Best not," said Laura. "He's probably having a bit of extra sleep."

Elizabeth ran across the sand and started to wade into the sea.

"Uncle said you can swim on this side of the island any time. It's perfectly safe. The only problem is it doesn't get very deep."

She pushed on until the water was up to her waist, then flopped forward and dog-paddled round and round.

"Come on Stuart," she shouted, "what does this remind you of?"

"When we got *Fairway* out of your boathouse," he shouted cheerfully. "And you pulled a bit too hard on that rope!"

Ian stood looking down through clear water at ripples of sand. He was shivering slightly.

"Go on!" Laura shouted, "try and swim properly. You won't drown."

"I'm waiting for the waves to stop a bit, the water gets up your nose."

He had never swum in the sea before. It was not at all like the swimming baths at home. He hesitated a long time, making up his mind, while tiny waves rushed past, surging against his legs. He would just count to three and then let go.

He closed his eyes and fell with a splash against a rising wave. Salty water filled his nose. There was a moment's panic as his legs floated up then he felt his fingers slice into soft sand.

He pulled himself along like a crab, keeping one eye closed and his mouth tight shut. He was about to call, 'Both feet off,' when a wave slopped against his face and he tipped over to find himself kneeling down in warm shallow water.

He looked round to see whether anybody was watching. But the others were all further out, swimming happily round.

He stood up and shouted, "It's not really deep enough to swim."

Stuart shouted back, "Don't come out this far until you're sure."

"I'll try scooting along the bottom again. It's more fun than swimming."

Poppy swam over and dog-paddled round, watching him.

"I invented it," he spluttered. "You pull yourself along like a crab. If you work at it you can go quite fast. You try. It's better than swimming."

The two crabs finished their first race and stood panting in the shallow water.

"That was a draw," he said. He looked at the other seals swimming around and turned to Poppy.

"Are you really going to be painting every day?"

"It's not painting, it's drawing. Uncle A says you can't rush painting. So I'm drawing things."

"But you do that anyway."

"Yes, but I have to get better."

Ian was puzzled, but there was a look in Poppy's face.

"I'll race you back to that rock."

There was so much sand churned up that they couldn't decide who won and were about to start another race when a familiar voice boomed across the water. Uncle Albert was standing on the beach waving his hat.

"Do you lot ever eat anything? I was thinking about breakfast ..."

*

It was a very merry party that finally managed to eat a late breakfast. Uncle Albert had arrived with a frying pan from the Signal House and Laura made a mountain of scrambled eggs using the butter before it melted away altogether.

Elizabeth rummaged inside the hamper and found some tin plates. She rattled them together like a dinner gong.

"Come on! Grub's up! Spoon it out Laura, while it's still hot."

They took turns with a big spoon dipping into the pan and fishing for scrambled eggs. There were chunks of cheese and apples to follow and some of the little coconut cakes. Beakers of pink lemonade washed it all down.

It was an untidy breakfast but a very happy one. It was a real camp now they were eating their own cooking.

"What about the Signal House?" asked Ian. "You said you'd tell us about it last night, but you didn't."

"Well, my audience was half asleep - altogether asleep, some of them."

"We're awake now," said Poppy, "and we'd like to hear the story ... I mean to say if it's a proper story."

"It's a story right enough."

Uncle Albert fished in his pocket and found one of his little cigars. It was slightly bent, but he lit it all the same. He finished his bowl of coffee and leaned forward towards them.

"I'll have to go back a bit. When I was a young artist – a bit older than Poppy here, but young enough – a very rich man bought a lot of my paintings. I didn't really know what to do with the money, so I bought the Pink House and its island and came and lived here."

He reached across with his foot and prodded Elizabeth.

"That's before you were even born. Years and years ago.

You'll have to imagine a very thin me. I could run about just like you lot then …   although of course I had to watch out for dinosaurs …"

"That's just pretend," said Ian, laughing. "Dinosaurs were before there were any people at all. Ages and ages before."

Uncle Albert winked at Stuart.

"You could be right … shall I go on?" Ian nodded vigorously.

"Well, when I got here, I met a young chap and we became friends. You've met him yourselves. He's a doctor now although those days he was just a student. And the two of us bought a little motor boat …"

"I know … I know … it was *Luc*," shouted Poppy, tugging his arm.

"More like the grandfather of *Luc*," I'd say, "but pretty much the same sort of little boat … they've all been called *Luc* because somebody told us Saint Luke looks after artists and doctors … and he did, I suppose, come to think of it …" Uncle Albert fell silent, gazing into the distance and running his hand through the white sand. He was remembering something, thought Laura: just like Mrs Bradley and the toys she left behind.

He shook his head. "Sorry: I was miles away … right, where was I? Here's the point of the story. One day, we decided we'd take a trip right round the island. It's further than you think, and by the time we were halfway round it was getting a bit dark. There's a tower off the end of the point over there – it marks where that little bit of the island seems to have broken off." He waved his cigar vaguely in the air.

"But you'll find out about that when you go and have a look. We thought we knew enough about the tower. What we didn't know was there's a monster rock out there. There's a big tide here. The rock is safe enough at high water – a good eight feet deep. The trouble is, it's barely under water when the tide is low. You can't see it, but it can take the bottom out of a boat before you can say knife."

Ian was listening intently. He was not sure why anybody would want to say knife, but was too interested to stop and ask.

"And it was low tide?" he said.

Uncle Albert nodded gravely and sat silently looking at his shoes for a long time. Then he looked up.

"That's right, you've got the idea. A big rock, a fading light, a little boat and two sailors who should have known better. Is that a good enough story?"

"What happened?" asked Poppy. "You didn't drown, because you're here. And the doctor as well. So what happened? Hurry up and tell us the end."

"You've forgotten about the Signal House," said Uncle Albert. "That was the last day for the man in the Signal House, but he did his stuff. As we were running past he hoisted a checkered flag. Red and white."

"I know that one," said Stuart. "Daddy told me. It means 'you are standing in danger' doesn't it?"

"Yes, we knew that much, but if you think about it, it just made things worse. We had no idea what the danger was and no way of turning back. There's no safe landing this side of the island and it was getting dark – we just had to go on, feeling our way ahead. So that's what we did … that is, until we heard a bell. There's a buoy chained to that rock now, but in those days there was just a sort of floating bell. It disappeared years ago in a storm, but that night it saved us. That, and the chap who hoisted the flag. Even so, we ended up a lot closer than we should. But hearing that clanging come at you out of the dark … well, I won't say it was a panic, but I can tell you, we came about in pretty short order."

He smiled back at Poppy's anxious face.

"Don't you worry … we learned our lesson …" he chuckled to himself, "anyway, nobody's going sailing on this trip."

For a moment, silence fell on the group round the fire, everybody thinking about Uncle Albert and the doctor all those years ago. Before Elizabeth had been born.

*

Stuart looked round. Nobody was in hurry to get up. They had eaten all they could and were leaning back finding patches of shade.

Uncle Albert was looking across the field with one eye closed making little sketches with his finger in the sand.

"I saw a deer this morning," said Stuart, "right next to the tent. It was looking for water."

"Ah, so that's what knocked the bottle over," said Laura, "I wondered."

"The woods over there are full of them," said Uncle Albert, "they've been here as long as I've known."

"But how did they get here," asked Poppy. "Can deer swim? It's a long way."

"A mystery. I think they used to hunt them. Perhaps the hunters brought them over."

Ian looked up at Laura and she smiled back in an encouraging sort of way. "It's called venison," she said, then seeing Poppy's face, quickly added, "but I wouldn't like it myself."

"Uncle Albert - you were going to tell us about the water," said Stuart, to change the subject. "You said it was a secret."

"It can be if you like. There's water in the Signal House, if you know where to find it."

"You mean you've got a tap in your little house?" asked Ian.

"Not a tap. It's a pump. And it's not inside, either. It's by the gate when you come in. I managed to get it going this morning. It just needed priming and a bit of a whack with the hammer. You waste a fair bit of water priming it, but now the thing works, we'll have as much fresh water as we want ... good sweet water at that."

"We've got a pump like that in the garden at the cottage," said Laura, "a thing with a big spout and a handle that goes up and down."

"That's it."

"And you have to pour water in the top to get it going."

"Not every time ... only when it dries out. It was dried out this morning. It hadn't been used for months."

"The plan for today," said Elizabeth, who was thinking how time was slipping away. "An expedition to the tower."

Uncle Albert looked doubtful.

"You really want to do that? It's right at the other end of the island. A long walk for a hot day."

"We'll take something to drink this time," said Elizabeth.

"There's something you'll have to promise. No more scrapes. You're not to go doing anything stupid."

"We don't ..."

"And if I say forest walks in the midday sun?"

She scowled at him, "That was almost your fault."

"Well, 'almost' never got the boat home. And what about people hopping up ladders without asking?"

"Alright, we promise." She glanced nervously at Stuart, "Don't we?"

He nodded, feeling very awkward.

"Actually, I already promised Mother. But sometimes things just happen."

"Well that's settled then," said Elizabeth, standing up. "We'd better be making tracks. Time's getting on."

But Laura was shaking her head.

"We can't. Not yet, anyway. There's hardly any wood. What Stuart fetched has gone already. It's no good putting it off, we simply must have a decent pile for tonight. And you've forgotten something - we left all the supplies down at the landing stage. We have to go and get them. If we don't, there'll be nothing to eat at all."

"I think there are still some coconut cakes," said Ian, but Laura just looked at him.

Uncle Albert pushed himself up with a groan.

"My joints are not made for sitting on the ground, you know. But Laura's quite right - the hamper's pretty well empty. There's supplies for three or four days down at the landing stage. We have to go and get them."

Elizabeth was trying hard to hide her disappointment.

"I suppose if we ran like mad, we could manage both. The wood collecting and the landing stage."

But nobody was going to be running; it was almost too hot to think, let alone run. She settled back down on the groundsheet looking miserable.

"That's that then," she mumbled. "There won't be much of the day left by the time we've done everything."

"I'll tell you what," said Uncle Albert, "you lot go and hunt for wood. And while you're doing that I'll hop down and fetch the bags from the landing stage." He looked at Laura.

"What do you think? There's no point in all of you coming. So long as you promise to be here when I get back."

"We promise ... I was thinking ... if you can get the food I could make something to take with us ... that would solve everything. We can take sandwiches and eat our dinner on the way."

Elizabeth was suddenly much more cheerful.

"A real trek with our own supplies ... and eating on the go ... to the tower and back. Perfect!" She grinned at Uncle Albert. "And don't worry, we'll be back in time for supper, that's a promise." She jumped up.

"Well, what are we waiting for? The wood won't collect itself."

"Can I go with Uncle Albert?" asked Poppy. "I'm not much use with wood and we can talk about painting."

"I'd appreciate the company," said Uncle Albert.

*

Collecting firewood on a hot day is thirsty work and the walk from the camp to the woods and back seemed to grow longer each trip.

Once the edge of the woods had been cleared of dry sticks, there was very little left to collect. They were forced deeper and deeper into the trees, dragging fallen branches out of cocoons of clinging brambles. Even then, those too big to break by jumping on them had to be reluctantly abandoned.

After the third trip back to the camp they collapsed on the ground and sat surveying scratched arms and legs. Laura served a round of beakers of lukewarm lemonade. Elizabeth was eyeing their rather feeble pile of wood.

"Perhaps that's enough. After all, we only need the fire for cooking."

"We'll need a good bit more than that," said Laura. "This dry stuff burns up in no time at all. If only we could find some proper logs."

"How many more trips?" asked Ian who was getting very bored. "Poppy will be back soon. Perhaps somebody should stay and wait here for them."

"I'll wait if you like," said Stuart, then laughed when he saw Ian's face.

"Cheer up Iggie. One more trip - the last, I promise."

He led the way across the parched grass towards the break in the trees where the deer disappeared.

He scoured the ground for tracks. Everywhere was baked hard and the morning deer had left no trace. But the walk was worth it, nonetheless. Only a few yards along the track, a neat pile of cut logs was lying half-buried in undergrowth.

"Just what we need," shouted Elizabeth trying to pull a log out from under a cloak of dragging weeds.

"I don't think anybody wants them now, they must have been abandoned," said Stuart.

Laura looked uncertain.

"Do you think we should? Somebody must have cut them. They're not really ours."

But Elizabeth was not going to give up her prize that easily.

"Look, they've been here for years and years. They're pretty well buried in weeds. If we don't use them, the beetles will. Anyway, they must be Uncle's logs - it's his island."

She pushed a tangle of brambles to one side with her foot and pulled out two logs.

"And you said yourself we needed some proper wood. This is proper wood ... and there's enough for weeks."

*

But logs are heavier than they look, and another thirsty half hour had passed before there was anything like a proper woodpile in the camp.

After his first heroic effort to carry two logs, Ian managed only one at a time.

At last, Laura declared the pile big enough and he sank exhausted onto the ground.

"Stuart said just one more trip," he complained, "and it was lots ... anyway my arms ache." He paused, sitting up and looking round the camp with a frown.

"Where's Poppy?"

Stuart looked at his watch then remembered he had forgotten to wind it up. He glanced at Laura. She was anxiously scanning the edge of the field where Poppy and Uncle Albert had set off down the path to the landing stage.

"I thought they'd be here waiting after that last trip," she mumbled. "I wonder where they've got to?"

"Probably stopped to draw something," said Ian. "Just like Poppy." But he went on looking across the field.

"Just sitting down having a good rest I shouldn't wonder," said Elizabeth, "it's stifling. The hottest day yet. Haven't you noticed? Even the birds have stopped tweeting."

She was right. A curious silence had fallen over the island, as if it was waiting for something to happen, hardly daring to breathe. She reached inside the hamper and pulled out the bottle of lemonade.

"Who's for a drink while we wait?"

Stuart mopped his forehead. That same odd feeling was creeping back, as if something heavy was pressing on his head. The sky was a deep cloudless blue, filled with a fierce sun, painful to look at. The day was restlessly gathering itself for another of those summer storms.

He fumbled to find his beaker and held it out to Elizabeth. She filled it up.

"We might as well finish it all before it boils. After all, there's plenty more on the way ... when they get here."

Laura sprang up. ""I'm going to look ... it's too bad of them, worrying us like this ... they should have been here ages ago."

They watched her hurry up to the edge of the field and peer down the steep slope of the path, shading her eyes. She turned towards them and shook her head despairingly, dropping her arms at her sides.

She stayed a moment longer staring into the distance then walked slowly back towards them. Stuart saw her face and felt his heart turn over.

"Not even Poppy could get lost on that path," said Ian. "You just follow your nose. I know what they're doing - they're looking at the boat."

"Of course they're not!" Laura rounded on him and shouted with impatience.

"Oh, I'm sorry Iggie, I was just upset. Yes, it's an idea, but they wouldn't do that would they? They know we're waiting. Poppy knows. I'm sure something's gone wrong."

She turned to Stuart and he saw the concern in her eyes.

"We should have gone with her. Oh, Stuart, where on earth are they? What are we going to do?"

He glanced at Elizabeth. She was looking thoughtful, her head bowed, tapping her fingers on the sandy soil. The trip to the tower didn't seem all that important any more.

He watched her face and knew she was thinking the same. She raised her head and caught his look.

"You're right," she said in a very quiet voice. "Something's up. We'd better go and see. No point just sitting here wondering."

"I'll wait here for you," said Ian, "you're only going to come right back."

"Don't be silly, Ian." Laura took his hand and pulled him up. She was looking very severe.

"One of you lost is quite enough. You're coming with us."

He was about to protest that nobody was lost when he stopped. Echoing through the woods beyond the slope of the path, there was a thin clear sound. The steady beat of wood on wood.

Laura stared wide-eyed and caught at Stuart's arm.

"It's a signal. But what's it mean?"

CHAPTER XVII

TAMING *LUC*

THE strange signal had stopped. The only sound now was the rhythmical chirp of hundreds of cicadas in the midday sun. The heat was stifling.

"It sounded quite close," said Stuart. "It was probably Poppy just testing whether we can hear."

But that was the sort of thing Elizabeth would do, or Ian, but not Poppy. Laura heard the doubt in his voice. He was biting his lip. He set off, almost running.

"I'm going to look."

"We'll all come," said Laura. "Something's wrong, I'm sure."

Ian had been sorting through the woodpile looking for the sort of stick that would do as a hammer. He found one and was testing it on one of the new logs.

"We can signal back, only this log's no good ... I'll have to find a hollow one ..."

He looked up to find he was alone. The others were already halfway to the little ridge. Laura was running but she turned and waved urgently for him to follow. He dropped his stick and ran after them.

"Wait for me ... I'm coming."

As they reached the point where the path turned down the steep slope, the signal started again. It seemed very close, a clack clack sound, harder and faster than before, as if the mysterious signaller was making one last desperate effort.

"It's coming from the woods down there," said Elizabeth. "It can't be far – come on."

"You shouldn't run, remember ..." Stuart shouted. "We're supposed to walk ... it's too hot to run."

But she seemed not to hear him and they watched her hurtle down the slope, skidding and sliding to keep her balance.

Where the path turned to the right, along the edge of the little wood, she disappeared. The knocking sound stopped. Then Poppy's voice came echoing through the trees.

"Elizabeth! Elizabeth! I'm here. Hurry! Do hurry!"

Laura stared at Stuart, her eyes wide with alarm. All thoughts of walking were forgotten. She grabbed Stuart's hand and the two of them raced down the hill.

Ian stood for a second then broke into a trot. It wasn't exactly running, he thought; but it wasn't walking either.

*

Poppy was standing in the middle of the path, looking impatiently up the slope towards them. Canvas sacks were scattered on the ground, left where they had fallen at the side of the path.

Stretched out, his back propped against a tree, was Uncle Albert. His hat lay at his side and his head was lolling forward against his chest. He managed to look up as they approached and they could see he was trying to say something, but although his lips moved, no words came out.

Poppy ran up the path to meet them.

"I couldn't think of anything else to do." Her voice was trembling.

"I just had to hope you would hear ... I've been doing it for ages ... I was about to give up ... but I couldn't leave him ..."

Laura held her arm. The relief at seeing her safe was draining away, to be replaced by something else. She looked across at Uncle Albert. He gave a little grunt, tried to lift himself up, and fell back awkwardly against the tree.

"What on earth happened? Did he fall?" Laura looked at the path. It seemed impossible - the ground here was quite level.

"No, it wasn't that ... it was awfully hot on the beach by the landing stage. We found the bags with the food inside ... only three of them, but they were so heavy. Uncle Albert gave me this little sack to carry ..." She poked with her foot against one of the bags.

"He wouldn't let me carry anything else ... I couldn't really ... it was so hot ... he couldn't manage ..."

Poppy had fixed her gaze on the outstretched form of Uncle Albert while the words tumbled out breathlessly. She tugged her arm away from Laura's grip and made to go over to him.

"We got this far … and he just said … 'I'm too hot,' and sat down … I thought it was to take a little rest. He sat down … and … and …"

Tears welled up in her eyes and she pulled away to kneel by his side.

"And he sort of went to sleep … except I couldn't wake him up … I prodded him … and …" she stopped, stifling a sob. "What's the matter with him? I think he's really poorly … that's when I thought of the signal … it was all I could think of."

"You're alright now," said Laura, looking for a handkerchief.

"We're here … do stop … you know that won't help."

"You did the right thing," said Stuart, squeezing her shoulder and trying to smile. "It was exactly the right thing to do. Come on … crying doesn't help."

Elizabeth was crouching down over Uncle Albert, mopping the sweat off his forehead. He opened his eyes a fraction and managed a little smile.

"Hello niece … 'fraid this heat's got to me …" His voice was hoarse, almost a whisper.

"Trying to carry a bit too much … my fault."

He tried to push himself up a little higher against the tree, but fell back breathing heavily.

"Can't seem to catch my breath … I'll need some help to get back up there …" His eyes wandered round, uneasily scanning the trees. "I was asleep … I'm not sure where I am … is it very far do you know? I don't remember."

Elizabeth and Stuart exchanged frightened glances.

"Not very," she said, "and you can lean on us … we'll have to manage." She held out a hand. "Do you think you can get up?"

"I'll try," he croaked, "but don't you go pulling at me … see whether you can get on either side."

*

Uncle Albert struggled to his feet and stood blinking and swaying, one hand leaning against a tree trunk.

Poppy opened the sack with the water inside and Laura held the bottle while he drank a little.

At last, he managed to push himself forward and totter for a few steps, leaning heavily on Elizabeth. She was buckling under the weight. Stuart rushed round to the other side and held him up.

Step by step, the three of them stumbled painfully up the slope. The awful heat, aching arms and weary legs – all were forgotten.

Laura was walking ahead, half-dragging the heavy food bag, Poppy and Ian following behind, carrying one of the sacks between them. The rest were left by the side of the path.

"What's the matter with him, do you think?" whispered Ian.

"I think he was trying to carry too much. We'd forgotten how many sacks there were. I helped a little bit, but Uncle Albert had most of them. That's why it took so long ... he could only manage a few yards and we had to stop."

She drew closer and whispered, "And then we reached the bit where the path gets really steep." She looked at the little party ahead, inching its way up the hill.

"He couldn't manage it ... we should have left the things and come back ... it's not his fault ... he kept saying we had to get back ... it's just too hot everywhere. It's what he said the other night - after you three got lost in the woods. I think he's caught whatever it is the sun does to you. I've forgotten the name. Something to do with heat ..." Her voice broke.

"But I remember he said it was very bad ... I do remember that."

She dropped her end of the load. Ian let her walk on ahead, pulling a handkerchief out of her pocket. He stood by the canvas sack. Best leave her alone for a bit - Poppy was like that. He dragged the sack to the side of the path.

"Let's leave all the bags here. We'll come back for them later. We know where they are ... anyway, you can't miss them. Let's go and help Laura."

As they ran past Uncle Albert he tried to say something to them and Poppy stopped. The whole of his head was bright red and his mouth seemed strangely swollen. He managed a sort of hoarse whisper, just loud enough for her to hear.

"Go ahead and run some water, there's a good girl."

She looked at him, puzzled. He tried again, "Tell Laura ..." but his voice failed.

"I know what he means," said Ian, "it's the pump at the little house. Come on, we'll find it."

Uncle Albert opened his eyes wide and stared. It was only a look, but it was enough for Ian; he was sure he had guessed right.

They were not far from the top of the slope now. Uncle Albert had slumped down on a fallen tree trunk to rest. Elizabeth was mopping his face. It looked as it would be a long time before he got up again.

Ian called to Poppy and they ran down the field as far as the camp.

Their woodpile was still there. He paused to look at it. It looked different now. Everything looked different.

Poppy had not stopped. She ran ahead and reached the iron gate of the Signal House. Her heart was thumping as if it would burst and she had a stitch pain in her side.

She hung onto the metal rail, panting to catch her breath. Uncle Albert had said the pump was next to the gate. The pump at their cottage was set into the wall, with a metal trough underneath it to catch the water, but there was nothing like that here. She ran along the wall peering at gaps in the stones. No sign at all of a pump. She was about to shout in frustration when she heard Ian's voice.

He had run past her through the gate into the tiny garden. "Why are you looking at the wall? It's here ... it's absolutely enormous ... taller than me."

Poppy rushed across. Ian was standing next to a tall iron pump with a spout. The tent peg hammer was perched on a little metal shelf half-way up.

She grabbed the handle, hanging on to it with relief. "Oh, well done Iggie! You've found it!"

"It wan't hidden really ... and uncle A must have got it going. He's left the hammer here."

He waited for her to let go then reached out and took hold of a big S-shaped handle.

"It's like the one at the cottage only lots bigger. Shall I have a go?"

"I'll get a bowl."

She dashed inside the little house and came running out with a bucket.

"This will do. See whether it works."

The handle was very stiff and squeaked in protest, but as he raised it the inside of the pump gave a throaty sucking noise. He pulled it down as hard as he could. There was a slopping glugging sound inside; nothing came out of the spout.

He tried again, up and down. The same glugging noise, as if the water was trying its best. On the next go, water spurted into the bucket. Only a little, but it was a start. He pushed the handle up as far as it would go and pulled it down. A steady flow of clear water, as wide as the ancient spout, fell splashing into the bucket.

*

They had just carried the water into the house when a sad little knot of people came into sight inching its way slowly across the parched grass past the two tents of the camp.

"There they are!" shouted Poppy, letting water slop over the side as she dumped the bucket down. She ran to the gate to wait for them.

Elizabeth's knees were buckling. She looked as if she could not hang on much longer. Laura, holding the straw hat in her hand, had joined Stuart on the other side of Uncle Albert. He was leaning so heavily against them it was hard to move forward.

As they drew closer, Elizabeth stumbled and for a moment all four of them stood swaying. Then with one last effort they reached the gate.

Uncle Albert, his face bright red, was gasping noisily for breath. A deep line cut into his swollen forehead where his hat had been.

"Get the door open, somebody," Elizabeth panted.

Poppy ran and pushed at the door. The shutters inside were closed and the little room was dark and airless. But it was mercifully cooler out of the sun.

Uncle Albert, half-carried and half-pushed, stumbled into the room and pitched onto the couch, breathing hard. His eyes were closed.

Laura took charge. The pain in her side from running was subsiding.

"Quick, Poppy, find a beaker, he'll want a drink."

Elizabeth had slumped down onto the floor breathing hard. Her face was scarlet.

Laura poured water into the beaker and held it to Uncle Albert's lips. He drank a little but did not open his eyes. She hesitated then reached down and lifted his legs up onto the couch.

Elizabeth heaved herself off the floor, unlaced his shoes, and tugged to get them off. She looked grimly at Laura.

"They won't come off. His feet are all swollen."

Slowly, they managed to prise his shoes off. Uncle Albert gave a little grunt and half-opened his eyes.

"Better ..." he croaked, "much better ... feet hurt ..." He closed his eyes, murmuring, "Dreadful headache ... head hurts."

Laura put the beaker of water to his lips again. He gulped it down and leaned back, panting heavily.

"He looks awfully hot," said Ian. "Is that why he's gone red? He's red all over."

Stuart was still standing by the door. He pushed it to behind him, plunging the room into darkness.

"Look here, Poppy, can you take Ian outside for a bit? We need some space in here ... it's only making the place hot, us all crowding round."

Poppy looked at him.

"You want to talk on your own, don't you? That's alright, we'll fill another bucket. Come on Iggie, you know how to work the pump."

*

The dark little room fell silent. The three of them stood looking down at Uncle Albert stretched out on the couch. He was breathing quietly now but somehow this seemed more frightening than before. Instead of the dreadful gasping noise all they could hear was a fast little catch in his throat, hardly a breath at all. He seemed to have fallen asleep.

Laura dipped a towel in the bucket of water and sponged his face. Water dribbled down onto his neck. She gently dabbed at it.

He opened his eyes, just for a second and they heard a low hoarse mumble that might have been, "Thanks ..."

Elizabeth pulled the two of them across to the other side of the room. There was a desperate look in her eyes.

"He's caught the sun really badly," she whispered. "I'm sure of it ... that's what's the matter ... if it's heatstroke, he needs the doctor. Remember what he said."

Laura stared back, her eyes wide with alarm.

"But there isn't one ... there's nobody here ... just us ... what are we to do?"

"We'll have to get the doctor," said Elizabeth rushing on before Stuart could speak. "We know who he is ... we've met him ... half of *Luc* belongs to him ... we only have to find out where he lives. There's the boat. It got us here. It can get us back."

She saw Laura's eyes but grabbed her arm before she could speak.

"No ... seriously ... I think we could do it ... we have to try anyway." She looked at Stuart, "It wasn't that hard to steer across and it's no distance. I'll need some help, of course."

Stuart looked down. He didn't know what to say. Elizabeth was already tugging at his arm.

"We don't know where the doctor lives," he mumbled in a low flat voice. "Even if we got across we'd never be able to walk all that way. It's impossible."

He looked at Laura and she saw the frustration and disappointment in his face.

"I think you're wrong, you know" she said, adding quietly, "what day is it?" He stared wildly back at her. "No, what day is it?"

Elizabeth suddenly grabbed Laura's arm.

"You're right!" she shouted. "Good for you, Laura!"

She glanced down at Uncle Albert and lowered her voice.

"Of course! He's there! The doctor's there right now. Tuesday is his fishing day."

She looked at Stuart, adding triumphantly, "And today's Tuesday!"

Laura went over to Uncle Albert.

"He doesn't sound so bad. He's stopped panting."

She prodded his arm. Then, when he did not open his eyes, she gently shook his shoulder.

"Stuart!" she cried, "he won't wake up. I don't think he's better at all."

Elizabeth picked her hat up from where it had fallen on the floor.

"I'm going. Will you help?"

Stuart turned to Laura, "I can't see what else we can do. We'll be as quick as we can. Poppy can help you here. I'll tell Ian to stay outside."

Laura had dipped the towel into the water and was holding it, looking at Uncle Albert's face. Drips splashed down onto the boards at her feet.

"When you go, tell Ian not to go wandering off. I'll call him if I need him." She started to sponge Uncle Albert's face again.

"And tell Poppy I need her." She dared not look up. "Just be as quick as you can … and take care."

She heard the door close, shutting out the sun.

*

Stuart chased after Elizabeth. Outside, Poppy was sitting on a pile of stones.

"No questions," he called, "tell Ian to stay within earshot. Go inside and help Laura."

He looked across the field. Elizabeth was already halfway to the camp. "I must go …"

He dashed out of the gate and sprinted over the dry grass. Poppy stood and watched the two of them disappear behind the tents on the other side of the field.

Elizabeth had darted inside her tent. She emerged waving something at him.

"It's the key to the boat. Uncle asked me to keep it safe; he's always losing things."

The two of them ran down the grassy slope, hugging the side of the path for a little shade, and hurried past the sacks abandoned by the side of the path.

It was cooler for a few precious seconds in the little wood, but beyond the trees there was no shade at all and the air seemed almost too thick to breathe.

Across the beach, they could see the wooden landing stage wavering unsteadily. It was madness to be running like this. Elizabeth stumbled onto the sand, dizzy with the heat.

As they came onto the beach, Stuart pitched over, losing his sandal. Elizabeth did not stop, but turned for a moment and tried to say something. He saw her desperate red face, sweat dripping onto her shirt.

He pulled his foot out of the scorching sand and fastened his sandal then walked as fast as he could to the looming wooden posts of the landing stage.

Elizabeth had already unhitched the forward line and thrown it aboard the boat. As he hauled himself onto the planks she unwound the stern line and pulled the boat close in.

"You jump aboard," she croaked. "I'll throw you the line and jump."

Stuart could barely speak. He managed to whisper, "If you do that, she'll be adrift."

"Not when we get her started."

He was about to protest, but it was too late. She pushed him aboard, the boat bobbing under his feet.

A second later, a line flew over his head and Elizabeth landed heavily alongside him. She swayed a little on one leg, righted herself, and made for the cabin.

Luc, freed from her moorings, drifted gently away from the wooden piers.

*

They stood in the stifling cabin. Through the window on the starboard side the sea was flat and calm, twinkling with oily rainbow colours. They had lost contact with the landing stage and were slowly drifting parallel with the beach.

Elizabeth pulled the key out of her pocket and pushed it into a keyhole inside a brass ring.

She turned to Stuart and managed a grim little smile. "It's alright. It can't be that hard. We just have to try. Here goes!" She turned the key.

Nothing happened.

"I think you have to press something. I think I saw him press something."

"It must be this," said Elizabeth pointing to a little push-button set into the bench. She stretched out her hand.

"Wait!" said Stuart. "We have to see she's not in gear; I'm sure of that."

There was a long lever coming up out of the floor. It had been left pulled back as far as it would go.

"I saw him put it in the middle. I think that's right. Alright, try now!"

"What's this for?" Elizabeth was pointing to a little wooden handle under the window.

"It can't be anything. It's to open the window I think. Have a go with the button."

Elizabeth turned the key and pressed the button. She jumped back as something juddered briefly under their feet. There was a faint wheezing noise and then silence. She looked at him desperately.

"Something happened. I'll try again - there's nothing else we can do."

He looked at the controls. There was only one knob left on the ledge. "Wait, we don't know what this knob does."

Elizabeth reached out and pressed it.

"It doesn't do anything."

"I don't think you press it; you pull it out."

Then he remembered. When they had gone into the cabin with Uncle Albert this little knob had been pulled out. He pulled at it, gently at first, then as hard as he could, until it was standing up on a little stalk of wire.

"Now try the button again." Elizabeth pressed. The engine sluggishly turned and gave a single loud chugging sound. White smoke puffed out of the hull from somewhere on the starboard side and drifted in through the cabin window.

She pressed again, this time holding the button down. The engine turned and turned until it coughed briefly into life. It spluttered feebly for a second or two then stopped, leaving a tiny cloud of smoke hanging over the water.

Elizabeth stared wildly at him.

"Isn't there anything else? You can tell she's trying. Why won't she start? Think!"

Stuart shook his head.

"I am thinking. It's hopeless. I don't know what to do. I never saw him start the engine; I only remember what he did when we tied up." He suddenly stared out of the window.

"Quick – do something! She's running aground."

All the time they had been working, *Luc* had been drifting closer and closer to the shore. He pushed past Elizabeth, ran out of the cabin, and looked over the side.

Although they were still well out, you could see rippled sand through the shallow water. Little foamy waves had started to break against the hull.

They had both felt the first touch of the keel on the sand. Now they felt it again. *Luc* leaned over slightly, righted herself, and stopped drifting.

CHAPTER XVIII

THE LITTLE DINOSAUR

WHEN Stuart dashed out of the Signal House, Laura had busied herself with the soaking towel, sponging Uncle Albert's face. She hoped he had not noticed her hands were trembling because then he might not have gone at all. She was very frightened.

She leaned down and dipped the towel into the water then squeezed it out. The bucket at her feet was almost empty. With Stuart gone, the room was dreadfully quiet: just drips splashing onto the bare floorboards and the sound of Uncle Albert breathing. She stared down at him, willing him to wake up. If only he could tell her what to do.

The door opened, briefly flooding the room with sunlight. Poppy tottered in, carrying a bucket.

"This is the next one. If that one's empty, I'll take it to Ian."

Laura passed her the empty bucket and she took it outside. There was the faint sound of the two of them talking quietly, then Poppy came back in.

"Ian will fill it. He likes working the pump. I've told him to sit in the shade when he's finished. It's getting dreadfully hot."

"I think he's best out there. I don't want him upset."

Poppy looked down at Uncle Albert.

"How is he? Is he any better?"

"I don't think so ... I don't know."

They could hear the squeak of the pump outside. Uncle Albert seemed to be trying to catch his breath, making fast little clicking sounds in his throat. Laura looked at Poppy.

"There's nothing to worry about, but if you want to go out with Ian ...?"

Poppy shook her head and wiped her eyes with the back of her hand. She pointed at the floor.

"It's getting very wet. There's water everywhere. He's going to be cross ..." Her voice trailed away.

"I tried to stop it dripping at first, but it's impossible. It doesn't matter anyway."

Water had run down his neck and soaked into his shirt. Water had soaked into the couch. A slender black line had broken away from the pool of standing water on the boards and was slowly snaking its way towards the door.

"I did think he was getting a bit cooler before you came in, but the sun blinded me. It's hard to see."

Poppy bent over and looked closely at his face.

"He doesn't seem so red." She rested her hand gently on his forehead then took it away looking thoughtful. His head was fiery hot. They could hear his breathing, fast and faint. His chest was barely moving at all. Tears welled up into her eyes.

"Do you think he's going to die?" But before Laura could reply, Poppy stood up and rushed to the other side of the room, tugging to find her handkerchief. She had never seen anybody really ill before. But people died of really serious things - surely you couldn't die of the sun?

Laura went on sponging Uncle Albert's face. "Look Poppy, all I know is we've got to do our best. We've got to try and make him better. This is all I can think of." She tried to smile.

"Would you be better outside with Ian? I won't mind."

"No, I'm alright ... what can I do?"

"I've been thinking. You're good at making things - do you think you can make a fan? He's so hot - I can go on with the water but it would be better if we could fan him. Have a look round. Anything would do."

Poppy gazed helplessly round the empty room. Apart from Uncle Albert's table, there was nothing at all.

"You could make something out of his sketch book," said Laura. "I used to know how to fold a fan – it's not hard."

"I can make a fan. But he'll be awfully cross about the book. You can't touch his sketch book. He doesn't let anybody even look at it."

"Just use the blank pages. Don't worry, I'll explain it was all my idea. He won't blame you."

Poppy picked up the precious book and turned it face down. It was almost full, just a few blank pages at the back. She gave one last anguished look at Uncle Albert stretched out on the couch and tore a page out from the back as carefully as she could.

She folded it into a fan, thinking of the last time she did this, when she was to be Aladdin in the school play and had caught chickenpox instead. She held the fan out to Laura.

"It's not very good, but it might work."

"I have to go on with the water. You stand the other side and fan him. We can take turns if you like."

Poppy edged round the couch and started to fan Uncle Albert's face, a welcome puff of cool air catching the back of Laura's hand.

"That's right. Don't go too fast, you'll tire yourself out. We don't know how long ..." Laura stopped, holding the dripping towel in her hand. She was right. Neither of them knew how long they must go on.

It's hard work waving a fan up and down, particularly when none of the cool air comes your way. Poppy changed to her other hand but that got tired even faster. Finally, she settled to both hands at once, standing a little back and making long slow sweeps over Uncle Albert's face.

*

There was a timid knock at the door and Ian's voice calling.

"Shall I bring it in? I've filled another bucket."

Laura draped the wet towel over her arm and went to the door. The handle felt hot in her hands.

She pulled the door open and stepped back, dizzy in the glare of the sun. It seemed unbearably hot out there. She took the water from him.

"Go and sit in the shade Iggie. I'll get the next bucket for you, but there's no need to hurry with it."

As she rushed over to the couch, Ian peered into the dark of the room. Poppy was waving something over the sleeping form of Uncle Albert, fanning him with a piece of paper using two hands. Something about the fierce strained look on her face stopped him calling out to her. It should have looked funny but when he saw Poppy's face his stomach turned over.

He took the bucket and backed away. Laura closed the door.

"This fan's wearing out. It's starting to go floppy."

"You'll have to make another. Try it with a double sheet of paper."

"There aren't many blank ones left."

"That doesn't matter … I think the fan is helping. You'll just have to tear some of the other pages out." Poppy stood hesitating. "Go on … he won't mind … only hurry."

Laura dropped the towel into the bucket, jumped up, and reached for the book off the table.

"No … I'll do it. Give it me." Poppy took the book and tore out the remaining blank pages at the end.

"I'll fold them double; it will last longer."

They worked on in a kind of frantic silence, Laura mechanically dipping into the bucket and Poppy waving the fan. Her arms hurt so much that tears started into her eyes.

"It's dreadfully hot in here. My arms ache."

"I'll have a go, if you like. You try sponging. Don't worry about the drips – there's water everywhere. It doesn't matter."

"I'll have to stop fanning anyway. This one's gone floppy as well. It was no better double – it only wastes paper. I'll make another."

Poppy went across to the little work table. There was just enough light to see. She turned the book over and opened it looking for blank pages.

The first page stared up at her. It was filled with drawings. She bent down to look at them and was instantly transfixed. Every inch was covered with exquisite tiny faces. She leafed through the book. All the pages seemed filled with drawings.

She paused at a bit of a railway line. It was at the station. Next to it was the edge of the platform with a tree bending over the wall; and a tiny little drawing of Ian, standing on one leg looking at his mantis.

The next page was washed over with colours – green and yellow and little spots of red. It was a clump of weeds in a crack between paving stones.

Poppy pushed the book across the table into a shaft of dusty sunlight from a crack in the shutter and turned the page. She put her hand to her mouth to stifle a little cry.

Laura looked across impatiently. Poppy was leaning down, her face almost touching the page, running her fingers over the paper.

These drawings seemed more careful - he had gone over the pencil with ink, etching out the figures in black. There was a smear of colour across some of them.

They were jumbled together, even on top of each other: Stuart and Laura standing together, the same little drawing over and over again; drawings of herself; drawings of Ian.

"What's the matter, Poppy?"

"There aren't any blank pages."

"Just take the used ones. He won't mind."

Poppy gently tore out the drawing of weeds with washes of colour.

"Hurry!"

She folded the drawing into a green and yellow fan and took up her place over the sleeping face.

"It was practice for the surprise," she whispered. "Pages and pages of pictures. They're lovely. That's how he put you and Stuart in his painting; he was practising ... and now they'll be spoiled." She looked despairingly at Laura.

"Nothing's happening, is it? The fan's not working, I know it's not ... he's no better." Her voice was trembling. "I wish somebody would come."

Laura barely heard. She just went on slopping the end of the towel into the bucket and sponging Uncle Albert's head. Water splashed down onto her feet.

She looked across at Poppy solemnly beating the air with her fan. She pushed the hair back out of her eyes.

"It will be alright, Poppy. The doctor will be here soon. They'll all be here any minute, I dare say. We just have to keep going."

*

Ian didn't take long to finish filling the bucket. It would be ages before they needed it. He looked at his hand. There was a sore bit, just the start of a blister. It was hard work, pumping. Thirsty work, as well. Uncle A had said it was alright to drink it.

Good sweet water was what he said, although water wasn't really sweet. Not unless you put something in it.

He pushed the handle up and hurried to hold his hands under the last of the gush of water from the spout. It ran deliciously cold over his fingers. He lapped at the little pool in his palm as it drained away.

This was a good way to drink, if you got it right – a bit like a dog, although he couldn't get his tongue to work the same way.

He pumped out another handful, working faster this time, burying his mouth in the water.

He straightened up, wiping the cool water from his face. He would carry the bucket round to the side of the house and sit in the shade. You could hear Laura from there.

*

There was a pile of cut stones at the shaded side of the house. As if somebody had decided to build something, then changed their mind and just abandoned them. They looked as if they had been there for years.

A pair of lizards scuttled for shelter as Ian sat down. One thing he'd learned, there was no need at all to be frightened of lizards. They did look a bit strange, but it was the lizards who were frightened. Well, they needn't be frightened of him; he wasn't going to hurt them. It was only buzzards they should worry about.

He looked up. An empty sky, the sort of blue you never saw at home, stretched out above him, a fierce blue; and a little shrunken sun high up and so bright you didn't dare look anywhere near it.

It was always the same. When something important happened nobody ever explained. You were told to go and play. It was the same now. Laura didn't want to explain, he could see that. She just wanted him safe outside here.

He pulled his legs in as the sun moved across his feet. *What was the matter with Uncle Albert?* Why would nobody ever tell him what was going on? Perhaps he was going to die. He hadn't meant to think that – the thought just slipped out.

Uncle Albert had been there with them this morning, Laura saying he shouldn't be sitting on the grass and him rolling over, and saying that rule was for wet grass. And now he was in there, with Poppy looking a way he'd never seen before. And Laura with that special voice she had when she thought you didn't know she was scared.

Ian got up. He'd be better walking about. He'd never been round this side of the Signal House. You could see the beach where they had been swimming.

A mountain of sand banked up by wind and storms towered above him. He tried to climb it but it was too soft and he fell back, sinking up to his knees.

Then he saw it.

High up in the sand, half-buried, was a line of curved ribs, for all the world like some long-lost prehistoric beast. It was a dinosaur perhaps, although quite a small one.

He clambered up the bank of sand to get a better look. The ribs were a pale yellow, bleached by years of sun. They ran round like a barrel. He pulled at one, trying to shake it loose. It was stuck fast. But they weren't the bones of anything; they were made of wood.

He started digging with his hands, scraping the dry sand away. The wooden ribs ran down for a long way, but it was easy enough to scoop. The thing was hollow. He shaded his eyes and peered inside through a gap between the ribs. It just seemed black.

He stood up, bracing his feet unsteadily on the slipping sand and grasped the top of the buried wood, shaking it as hard as he could. The whole thing seemed to rock against him.

You could feel it was too heavy to lift, but you could rock it and as you did this, sand trickled out from the bottom. More and more of the strange wooden beast emerged.

It was a sort of ribbed cage. There had once been something on top of it, but all that was left of that was a metal plate with a ring of holes in it. Now the sand had gone, you could see more of it. Half way down was a band of rusty metal. The ribs must have been fastened to this once - some of them were still fastened, with the remains of little rivets dangling out. But mostly there were just holes.

He scooped more sand away then gripped the top and shook it again. Something seemed to slip inside, as if a giant pendulum had moved. The ribbed cage rocked over towards him and he fell back into the sand. He could still hear something moving inside. It went on moving for a long time.

As he stood there panting, he heard Laura shouting for him. He picked up the bucket of water and scampered across as quickly as he could. She was waiting impatiently, the door half open.

"You won't go wandering off, will you? I don't have time to come looking. And what have you done to your knees?"

He brushed the sand off.

"It's just sand. I've been discovering things. I found ..."

But Ian never got a chance to explain about the mysterious ribs. Laura thrust the empty bucket into his arms and turned to listen to something Poppy was saying.

"Tell me about it later ... I have to get back." She saw his face and paused.

"I'm really sorry Iggie, there's no time." She patted his shoulder. "Remember, stay out of the sun."

And then she was gone.

He stood for a moment looking at the closed door, then shrugged and carried the bucket over to the pump. He worked the handle until cold water splashed over his sandals then tottered back towards the little house with his bucket, brimful and slopping onto the ground.

*

Digging out the sand was easier than he thought. It was very powdery and dry and very little of it had got inside through the ribs. He scraped it back, making a little circular wall. Slowly, the top of a huge wicker basket emerged. He dug down alongside the nearest rib until he reached the bottom.

There was a big slab of something like wood in the way. Like wood, but not quite hard enough. He managed to brush enough of the sand away to look.

It was cork. A huge piece of cork, bigger than he was; bigger even than Stuart. He tried it with a finger nail. Yes, a circle of cork, like a giant bottle-stopper.

He stood up and tried shaking the whole thing again. It leaned forward and slithered a little down the bank of sand. He pushed and found his feet pressing against a length of rope as thick as his arm, dry and bristly to touch. He tugged at it and a line of sand heaved up like a snake. He took it in both hands and pulled, to find himself looking at a big iron ring spliced into the rope.

Well, he had found one end. It must be fastened to the cork at the other end. All he had to do was pull.

As it toppled out of the sand it was like nothing he had ever seen before. A sort of wicker basket mounted on top of a massive circle of cork with thick rope tied to a metal loop at the bottom. Wooden ribs, hooped round with rusty iron bands, passed through a wooden block at the top. It must have been painted once. There were flakes of rusty red lodged in the cracks of the wood.

Now he had pulled most of it out, he could see inside. It was not empty at all. A brass bell, green with age and sea water, hung down from a hook at the top.

Ian had been dreadfully thirsty for some time but had ignored it while he dug. Now, sitting back on his haunches and grinning with triumph, thirst overtook him. Just one last thing, though.

He pushed his arm between two of the ribs and reached out to the bell. It would be splendid to hear it. His own bell. He grabbed the bottom of the brass and pulled it towards him until it was touching the wicker, then let go. The whole thing rocked violently as the bell swung across, but there was no sound. Nothing but the creak of the swinging bell.

He kneeled down and looked inside. The metal shell was empty. There was nothing there. Nothing to make the bell ring.

It was a disappointment after all that digging. He walked slowly back to the pump, brushing sand off his legs and trying to shake it out of his hair. It was a pity, but still, he had found it. Nothing would change that. The others didn't even know about it. That was something.

He pulled the pump handle down and washed his hands under the rush of water then splashed more onto the heat of his face. Then he was a dog for a long time, lapping greedily at pools of water in his hands.

It had been a long time since Laura had called. He sat down on the pile of stones looking across at the door. The scouts' hammer was still perched on top of the pump. He jumped up and grabbed it, running back to kneel down alongside the giant cage. Yes, it went in easily. He reached through, lifted the hammer, and let it fall.

Chapter XIX

ABOARD *LUC*

ELIZABETH was leaning over the side of the boat, staring into bubbling white water curdling round the hull. The tide was coming in and with each wave *Luc* sluggishly lifted up, only to slip further into the sand.

"She's well and truly beached ... I could hop over and push ... but it's going to be awful pulling her."

"No!" Stuart hadn't meant to shout. He saw the misery in her face and suddenly felt ashamed. She had an urgent hunted look in her eyes, scanning round the cabin.

"I think I've done something to my arm again. If you go jumping overboard I'll never be able to pull you in. Just wait a minute, I've got to think."

"There's nothing to think about, it's no go." She was beating the rail with her fist in frustration. "Isn't there anything else? We've got to get the doctor ... we've simply got to ... if we don't ..." she left the sentence hanging in the air.

Stuart looked at his watch. It had stopped.

Elizabeth watched him turn and run his eyes over at the wooden ledge again, checking the controls.

"We tried them all," she said. "There's nothing. I can't think what else to do ... and it's all my fault she's going aground ... I should have left a line until we got her going."

She slumped wearily down on the slatted bench and stared at her feet. The shadow of the cabin tipped across her face as *Luc* idly listed over.

Stuart went back inside, aimlessly checking the controls one by one.

A bigger wave lifted the boat and he felt the jolt as she dug further into the sand. Elizabeth jumped up in alarm.

"If she goes on this way, we'll be aground for good. I'll see whether I can pole her off. Try and think of something. Try the engine just one more time. You never know."

Stuart turned the key and pressed the little button again. The engine coughed into life. Elizabeth's eyes lit up. "She's going! She's going!"

She ran inside the cabin grabbing his arm in excitement. There was a spluttering noise and it fell silent again. "No, it's no good – it's just like last time. She won't go."

She stumbled past him and stood outside staring silently towards the distant mainland. A tiny puff of white smoke swirled over the water. He saw her rub a hand against her cheek, then throw her head back to breathe.

He looked away, turning hopelessly to the controls on the wooden bench. A seagull landed on the bows, looked at them, gave a single melancholy cry, and took off. *Luc*, listing gently, drifted side-on towards the beach.

*

There was a thin pole fixed against the inside of the hull, held with white canvas tiers. It had a metal hook at one end and was almost as long as the boat.

Elizabeth undid it and managed to hold it wavering unsteadily high above her head. She ran to the bows and let it fall with a splash into the water. It was an ungainly way of going about it, but with every wave the boat was cutting deeper into the sand.

She let the pole sink until it found a solid bottom then waited, straining to look over her shoulder until she saw a decent wave. Finally, one came swelling towards them, surging under the boat.

As *Luc* lifted slightly, Elizabeth pushed with all her weight, feeling the pole flex in her hands. She staggered forward as the bows slipped into clear water.

A huge tug to free the pole from the clinging sand and she was running past the cabin, trailing it behind her in the water. Another heave and the stern broke loose.

"I can keep her afloat, I think," she shouted, leaning for a second on the rail to catch her breath, "for a while, anyway. The tide must be coming in. That's a help."

*

Stuart had heard a muffled shout and seen Elizabeth running along the boat. But he hardly noticed. For the hundredth time he scanned the little wooden bench.

He looked up as the shadow of an extremely red-faced Elizabeth struggled past the cabin, dragging a huge pole behind her. She shouted in through the open door.

"Perhaps she doesn't have any petrol."

"No, I thought of that. He said she was full. It's not that ..." She had already gone, rushing towards the bows with her pole. She looked exhausted.

He ran his hand over the ledge - the key, the starter button, the little knob on a stork, the two little dials that sprang to life whenever you turned the key, and the compass. He rested his hand on the handle for opening the window.

That was very odd ... the handle moved, but the slats of the window stayed still. He pushed the handle up and down. It didn't seem to do anything at all.

He kneeled down on the scorching wood of the floor to get a closer look. It was a little brown handle made of polished wood sticking out of the ledge under the window. He stood up, giddy with the heat, and shouted to Elizabeth through the open window.

"I've found something. Come and see." She looked up, hearing the excitement in his voice, gave one last push and hauled the dripping pole aboard.

"I'm coming! Hang on!"

She ran down to join him in the cabin. *Luc* was just about afloat. They could feel the gentle scrunch of sand under her keel.

"It's this," he said, pointing to the handle. "We thought it was for the window, but it's not. Look at that."

He touched the little knob on its stalk and at the same time wiggled the handle up and down. The tiny stalk gave an imperceptible shiver.

"You're right," she shouted "it must be something to do with the engine."

"It was all the way up before. I'm going to press it down a bit and try again."

He pushed the handle half way down, turned the key and pressed the button on the ledge. The engine pulsed for a few deep throaty beats, then died. He glanced at Elizabeth. Her face was bright with excitement.

"Go on! A bit more! Hurry! It's lots better."

He pushed the handle down further and pressed again.

There was a noisy explosion and black smoke belched out from somewhere outside. Water started to squirt from a pipe in the hull. The cabin was filled with a screaming roar as the boards drummed against their feet. A rich smell of fuel filled the cabin.

Stuart held on to the handle for dear life managing a tiny smile as he turned to Elizabeth. The cabin was filled with a glorious fog of dense smoke.

"Oh, well done, Stuart! We'll make it yet. Wait though - I'll have to pole her off again."

She looked out of the starboard window. For a miraculous second Luc's stern was floating free. If they could only move now, perhaps there was no need for the pole. She grabbed his arm.

"Quick! Make her go backwards ... I mean hard astern."

He pulled the gear lever back. The whole boat juddered and the sound of the engine dropped almost to a stop. But Stuart was ready this time. He pushed the wooden handle down as far as it would go. The engine hesitated, skipped a beat, almost stopped, then fluttered back to life.

Luc was free, chugging stern-first away from the shore into a gentle swell.

*

"You take the wheel. You've done it before," said Stuart. "Do you remember the course?"

"It was more or less due South-East coming, apart from the last bit. I'll steer North-West. But we can't go wrong - you can see that building by the jetty."

All they had been thinking about was how to get the boat to go. Now that the voyage had started, the triumph of a few moments ago seemed to evaporate. Stuart stared vacantly over

Elizabeth's shoulder at the narrow stretch of water, the engine drumming in his ears.

Away from the shore, *Luc* began to pitch forward, smashing through the swell. At first, spray broke away and whipped against the cabin window. Then, as she crashed down, huge lumps of white water broke over the bows and surged along the bottom boards. Elizabeth glanced back at Stuart.

"It's because we're riding in with the tide," he shouted.

"And there's a bit of a breeze behind us ... Daddy says you're not supposed to do that in a heavy sea. It can tip you over ... it's alright though ... this isn't a heavy sea ..."

But even as he spoke, *Luc*'s bows lifted right up and for a giddy second all they could see was bright blue sky. She crashed down. Water poured over the bows, surging along the boat and slopping over their feet. They were rolling now, running down the side of the swell.

"You can come off a bit if you like," he shouted. "We don't need a course really ... there's the jetty dead ahead."

Elizabeth seemed not to hear. *Luc* plunged forward, climbing across the mounting swell, carving out huge slices of green-white water. The knuckles of her hands were white where she gripped the little wheel and her mouth was set. The quickest way was straight across and she had set her course.

*

The sea was much calmer at the little jetty. Stuart pulled the handle up until the engine was chugging gently. They inched towards the steps.

"It's got to be this side," Elizabeth muttered to herself, "because of the fenders."

She brought *Luc* alongside and nodded for Stuart to pull the gear lever back. They were barely making way now, just bobbing quietly towards the wall.

Stuart scrambled out of the cabin, ran along the deck and pulled the line out of a pool of water resting in the bows.

"Pull the handle right up when you're ready – that should stop her. I'll see to the mooring."

As *Luc* drew alongside he jumped onto a stone step, thick with seaweed. The engine stopped as the thick hemp fenders crushed against the wall.

He stood waiting to catch the bow line feeling a little dizzy, the noise of the engine still ringing in his ears. Elizabeth landed next to him holding a line in one hand. She tied it to a rusty iron post and started to climb the steps.

*

Nothing was there to greet them apart from a flock of gulls squabbling for something to eat. The gulls decided that two people climbing the steps, even small people, was two too many, and rose in a cloud of wings, circling and crying, finally settling a wary distance away, near the old stone building. A lonely call of gulls echoed everywhere.

Stuart shaded his eyes. You could see for miles along the beach. The place was deserted. Certainly, there was no sign of a doctor fishing. There was nobody at all. Just empty sand for as far as you could see.

Elizabeth started to hurry across to the little hill where they had stopped to feed the donkey.

"Come on, he must be over there. We'll see better from up the hill."

The two of them walked as fast as they could up the path. They could still see the tracks the little cart had left the day they arrived. There were hoof marks in the sand where the donkey had stood.

Elizabeth reached the top and anxiously peered round. Nothing but white waves gently turning over at the margin of a deserted shore.

They looked back to the jetty and both saw it at the same time. A little car, drawn up in the shade of the stone building.

Even as they watched, the flock of gulls rose up, wheeled round and made for the open sea, calling out in protest. Somebody was pushing the wooden door open.

A figure came out of the building, clutching a fishing basket. He walked across and started to clamber into the car.

"It's him!" shouted Elizabeth. "It's the doctor. And he's going. Come on or we'll miss him!"

She hurtled back down the slope kicking up a spray of sand and ran full tilt beyond the jetty frantically waving her arms.

The little car moved a few yards then stopped as a flying Elizabeth, all arms and legs, came to rest with her hands pressed against the bonnet.

Stuart watched the doctor get out and walk round towards her; she was bent double, coughing to get her breath.

*

She was already in mid-flow, as Stuart arrived, but she could barely gasp out the words.

"Come … quick … it's uncle …"

The doctor looked very puzzled, turned to Stuart with a friendly sort of smile. "You're the children I met the other day, aren't you?" He seemed happy to speak English.

He put his hand under Elizabeth's chin, gently lifting her head up. She was still panting.

"Don't try and talk. Come in here a minute, both of you."

They meekly followed him back to the wooden door. He pulled it open and beckoned them inside.

It was quite dark, just a tiny window at the back throwing a patch of light across the floor. It was a single room, packed with fish boxes, lobster pots, tins of paint, coils of rope and fishing nets. After the heat outside, it was deliciously cool and damp. There was a faint smell of cigar smoke.

Stuart sank down on a wooden box and wiped his brow. His legs ached.

Elizabeth, still purple-faced with running, tried to sit down but sprang up at once, as if she could only breathe standing up.

The doctor had been fumbling with the straps of a leather bag. He took out a bottle of water and handed it to her with a gentle smile, then snatched the bottle back as she gulped at it, saying, "Slowly, slowly."

There was another bottle perched on top of a lobster pot and he gave it to Stuart. It was half empty. The water was warm and tasted vaguely of tar, but Stuart drank it greedily.

The doctor peered through the open door, frowning as if he expected someone else. Finally, he turned to look at them.

"Right. First tell me how you got here?"

Stuart pointed towards the jetty.

"We came in the boat. In *Luc*."

"Yes, so I imagine. But where is Albert?"

He said the name in a funny way then said it again, turning to Elizabeth.

"You couldn't have come on your own. Where is your uncle?"

"But we did. On our own I mean." She saw his smile vanish, but pressed on.

"Please, can we talk about that later? Uncle's not here because he's ill. He's at the camp; in the Signal House. But he's really poorly ... I mean ill."

The doctor muttered something to himself and turned to Stuart.

"Alright, we'll talk about the boat another time. What do you mean ill? Take your time. Tell me about it."

Stuart did his best.

"He went off to collect the supplies. We'd left them on the landing stage. We weren't with him, but Poppy - that's my sister – Poppy was. She said it was the heat. He was in the sun for a long time and it was too hot. Anyway, he was on the ground when we got there ... lying down. So he must have fainted."

"He's asleep now," Elizabeth interrupted, "only he won't wake up..."

The doctor's face changed. He suddenly looked very grave.

"He won't wake up. You are sure? Now tell me ... this is very important ... when did all this happen? I mean, how long ago?"

Stuart desperately tried to think. "At least an hour ... no ... it must be more than that ... I forgot how long it took to get him back to the house ... that took ages. Two hours, maybe ... anyway, lots more than an hour."

The doctor stared at Stuart for a long time then turned away frowning. He was walking round, pushing his way past nets and fish boxes muttering to himself in French.

Eventually, he stopped and looked at them. Elizabeth put the water bottle down and started to say something. She saw the look in his face and fell silent.

"You are correct," he said. "He is ill ... very ill."

He turned to Elizabeth. There was a strange expression in his eyes. "How long did you say?"

"Quite a long time. We had to get the boat to start. Much more than an hour. Can you come and see him?"

"Yes ... of course ... I will come with you ... but ..."

He seemed to make up his mind, walking quickly past them out into the sun.

"I need some things. You must come with me. It won't take long."

Stuart followed in silence, thinking of that grim little word 'but.' He glanced at Elizabeth. Her face was set. A single line of tears had run down one side of her cheek. She did look at him.

As the doctor shepherded them into the seats at the back of the car and was closing the door, he asked her again, more urgently this time.

"He was asleep you say, but not just asleep. You could not wake him up?"

Then he saw her face and did not wait for an answer.

CHAPTER XX

TO THE SIGNAL HOUSE

THE doctor's little car bumped over rutted sandy paths through the woods. For a while they ran parallel with the beach and brilliant flashes of a sparkling sea broke through the leaves. Stuart felt the cold leather seat on his legs. Something tight seemed to have gripped his stomach.

They turned at last into a long alley of tall trees and drove up to the front of a house with green shutters. The car stopped and the doctor turned to them.

"Come inside for a while. I'll find you something to drink."

They followed him into the house and stood in the cool of a shuttered hall. He called out and they heard hurried footsteps clattering across the tiled floor.

The doctor's wife came running to greet him carrying a straw basket filled with roses. She must have been cutting flowers. She woman hesitated when she saw them and stood there with a puzzled look on her face.

The doctor took her by the arm and led her across to the other side of the hall talking all the time in a low voice. Once or twice he heard the name 'Albert' - again not quite the way they said it, but clear enough. At one point the doctor's wife gave a little cry and looked at them, her eyes wide with alarm.

When the doctor had finished talking, she came across to them. She was finding it hard to smile.

She said something to Elizabeth, speaking French. Elizabeth raised a tear-stained face but did not speak. The doctor's wife gave a shake of her head and walked away, but not before Stuart had seen tears in her own eyes.

She went into another room and they heard the sound of a tap running. The doctor followed her and came back with two glasses of water. He stood for a second lost in thought then pointed to long bench set next to a polished wooden door with a little brass plaque on it.

"Sit there, please. I won't be long."

He opened the door and a shaft of sunlight sprang out across the tiled floor of the hall. There was a faint smell of disinfectant.

Stuart could see a big desk and a leather chair. There was a white cabinet with glass shelves filled with rows of little bottles and strange instruments.

They heard the doctor shuffling about putting things down on a table, talking to himself to make sure he had everything he needed. Then rapid footsteps hurried across the floor and he came out carrying a leather bag.

"Good - you've finished? We must hurry." He suddenly remembered something.

"Have you brought the key to the motor boat?"

Stuart glanced at Elizabeth.

Elizabeth was still looking at the floor, rocking one foot against the other. "It's on the boat," she said, in a small flat voice that Stuart barely recognised.

Suddenly, she lifted her head, catching the doctor unawares before he could look away.

"Uncle Albert? Is he going to be alright?"

The doctor stood looking at her for a long time.

"We'll do the best we can."

He looked at his watch and rushed across to a doorway at the back of the hall, calling out again. The doctor's wife hurried out and shook hands, first with Elizabeth then with Stuart.

She followed them into the heat of the afternoon and stood watching long after the little car had disappeared into the trees; long after the sound of the engine had faded into silence.

*

When they reached the jetty, *Luc* was straining at the single line to her bows. She had drifted away from the wall.

The doctor handed Stuart his leather bag and hurried down the steps to haul the boat in. He helped them aboard then freed the mooring line and followed them.

He stood looking round for a second to get his bearings then went into the cabin. Almost at once, the engine burst into life. Stuart and Elizabeth exchanged bitter glances.

Luc pulled away, her wake bouncing back from the stone blocks of the jetty. Churned water creamed in a long wake behind them. You could not see the jetty now. In a minute or two they would be there.

*

The heat of the deserted shoreline was waiting. The engine stopped, leaving *Luc* bumping against the planks of the landing stage. It was suddenly very quiet; just the creak of the fenders, the sigh of breaking waves and the far-off call of gulls.

Stuart hardly noticed Elizabeth uncoiling the stern line. She was standing, silently waiting for a signal from the doctor. He waved and she jumped ashore to make fast. She caught the bow line as he threw it and looped it round a post.

The doctor went back into the cabin and pulled the key out of the little brass ring in the bench. Stuart watched him stand for a moment looking at it; then shake his head and put it back. He took the bag from Stuart and jumped down onto the sand.

He suddenly cocked his head in the air.

"What was that? I thought I heard a bell."

The three of them stood listening. There was nothing but the sounds of the sea shore.

"I thought I heard something," said Stuart. "It was probably a gull."

The doctor shrugged his shoulders.

"You'll have to show me the way. I've not been on the island for a very long time. I only come as far as this landing place," he tried to smile, "to fish."

Neither of them could think of anything to say. The doctor saw Elizabeth's anxious face and put his hand gently on her shoulder.

"You show me the way. I'll do the best I can." She continued looking at him.

"It's all I can do," he said, as if he was answering a question.

The silent little procession made its way along the narrow clay path skirting the shore. Elizabeth led the way, setting a good pace at first, but slowing as the heat fell on them. As they approached the grassy slope she stopped and turned to the doctor.

"Here's where Uncle had to sit down."

A heap of hurriedly abandoned sacks was piled by the side of the path, but the doctor only glanced at them and hurried on, shouting, "I think I know where I am now. The house is across a field, isn't it?" He sounded out of breath.

"We were camping up there," Stuart shouted.

The doctor turned, waiting for them to catch up.

"There's something I must explain … when we get there … "

But they were never to hear what he had to explain. A huge buzzard suddenly heaved itself into the air over their heads and clouds of smaller birds rose up from the trees chattering and screaming in alarm.

From somewhere not far away, beyond the top of the slope, a bell rang out. Not even a very sweet bell, but a monstrous sound, a huge discordant clang. They stood stock still, straining to hear the echo from inside the woods. Then complete silence.

The doctor was staring up the grassy slope with an air of disbelief. He turned to them and started to say something in French, then said, "That was the old bell in the narrow approach. I know it well. There isn't another like it."

He looked back up the slope, straining his head to listen.

"But it's impossible. The approach is miles away – at the other end of the island. You couldn't hear it from here."

He rubbed his ears as if he hardly believed them and looked at Elizabeth. "You heard it as well?"

She nodded.

"Yes, of course," he went on. "We all heard it. But the bell is not there anymore … the bell disappeared many years ago … it must … "

He never finished his sentence. The bell rang out again. A single clang but louder than the last, leaving an echo buzzing in their ears. As the sound died, the doctor stood shaking his head then set off almost at a run, gesturing for them to follow.

"I have something more important to do. The bell is not important."

*

Alone with Poppy in the Signal House, Laura had lost all track of time. The minutes now were measured in buckets of water from the pump. Sponging took all her strength; there was hardly time for thoughts.

Ian hadn't been waiting at the door when she went to get the next bucket. That was the trouble with Ian - he did wander off. When she called him she could see he wanted to tell her about something, but hot air was pouring into the house through the open door. She grabbed the bucket and rushed back inside shouting, "Tell me about it later … I have to get back. Stay out of the sun."

She heard his footsteps scuttle away as he ran round to the side of the house.

The handle of the bucket was almost too hot to touch. It must have been standing there a long time in the sun. She carried it wearily across to the couch and looked for the sodden towel. It was lying on his chest. She gently lifted it off and squeezed it out onto the floor.

They had long since stopped worrying about the mess and all the water everywhere. Crumpled paper fans were lying in sodden piles all about them. Wet footprints were everywhere.

The thin line of water running across the boards to the door had changed itself into a dark stain covering half the room.

Poppy was standing at the table carefully tearing out another page from the precious book.

"What did Ian want? He sounded very excited."

"He wanted to tell me something. I didn't have time. I had to close the door. It's so dreadfully hot out there."

"He could go and keep a look out for the doctor. They've been an awfully long time."

"Best leave him where he is. I heard him run round the side of the house. I think he's playing with something he's found. It's alright – there's some shade there."

Poppy lifted up Uncle Albert's book and held it out to Laura.

"I'm lots more than halfway through. What do we do when there's no more?"

"Don't worry, they'll be back long before then." She started mopping his face again. He seemed to be breathing more quietly.

Poppy took up her station on the other side of the couch, holding the new fan with two hands and beating the air with long slow sweeps.

The pain in her arms wasn't getting any worse; it had settled down to a dull ache. They worked on in silence, only the splash of water now and then breaking the quiet in the dark little room.

"This water won't do. It's warm. It must have been standing in the sun. I'll ask Ian to get some more." Laura laid the towel on the back of the couch and placed her hand on Uncle Albert's forehead.

"He's not as hot as he was before." She leaned over him. "And he's hardly red at all. Just a bit sunburnt."

Poppy stopped fanning and put a hand timidly on his shoulder. She shook him gently. He gave the smallest of tiny snorts and moved his head a little. She tried again.

"But he still won't wake up ... and that's what matters isn't it?"

She threw a despairing look at Laura.

"It's getting to be a long time. Why don't they come?"

"There's nothing to worry about. It's a long way. And they have to find him first, remember. We'll just have to wait. I'll call Ian."

She was about to pick up the bucket when Poppy dropped her fan and gave a startled cry. From somewhere outside there was the clang of a gigantic bell, so close that the door rattled.

Laura jumped up, staring wide-eyed around the room. A colossal sound had left their ears singing.

Uncle Albert sat bolt upright.

"We're too close," he shouted. "Bring the boat about! Come about!"

He sank back onto the couch with a little sigh, staring eyes darting nervously round the room. He patted his soaking shirt, and looked down, mumbling.

"What's all this? What's all this?"

Poppy rushed across, kneeled down in the puddle of water at his side and held on to his arm.

"You're awake! You're awake! We've been so worried."

He took her hand and squeezed it.

"So it's you Poppy. I've been thinking about you. You missed your lesson."

He tried to push himself up the couch a little but fell back, breathing heavily.

"You know what? I've a terrible thirst. Can you find me something to drink?"

Laura dashed to the table and poured a beaker of water, trembling hands letting it splash all over the floor. She was about to hold it to his lips but he took it from her and gulped it down.

"Hello Laura ... it looks like I've caused a bit of a stir." He sat for a moment staring into space.

"I remember now - it was trying to lift all that gear. Altogether too hot."

He gave her a crooked smile and held the beaker out.

"You couldn't find another one of those, could you? I could drink the sea dry."

As Laura was pouring the water, a crack of sunlight fell across the floor and Ian's face appeared, peering into the darkened room. The form on the couch pushed itself up a little.

"Is that Ian there? Come in where I can see you."

Ian pushed the door wide and came inside.

He walked rather awkwardly up to the couch and looked at Uncle Albert.

"Your shirt's all wet."

Uncle Albert started to chuckle, but it turned into a cough. He took the beaker from Laura, drank it down in one go, and handed it back for more. He ran his hands over his shirt.

"You're right about that Ian, I'm wet through. Laura's work I dare say." He turned his head to look at her.

"It looks like you saved my bacon, young woman."

"It wasn't just me," said Laura. "Poppy did the fanning. You were so hot. We tried to make you cold."

Ian looked on in amazement. Tears were running down Poppy's face. She was doing nothing at all about them. And Poppy never cried. Why on earth was she crying now? He watched as she gathered up a bit of soggy paper from the floor.

"I'm so sorry," she said in a choked sort of voice, "I had to use your drawing book ... there was nothing else." She pressed the crumpled page of folded paper into his hand. He looked down at it.

"Oh, that ... don't you go fretting about a sketch ... nothing to cry about ... it was probably pretty awful anyway ... that's why I keep that book to myself." He was looking at the paper in his hand.

"So you made a fan out of it." He spread it out. "I wonder why you picked that one? Not that it matters."

"I didn't pick them. We used lots and lots."

Uncle Albert stared at her with a puzzled look on his face.

"Lots, you say? What do you mean, lots? How's that?"

He struggled up a little higher on the couch and gazed round at the carpet of paper fans strewn over the floor. He sat looking at them for a long time, picking at a button on his shirt.

Ian thought he should explain about the pump. After all he'd been the one filling the buckets.

"You've been asleep for ages, you know. When Elizabeth and Stuart went, there was shade round the side of the house and it's all in the sun now. But you'll never guess what's round there ..."

Ian was about to explain about the great discovery, but Uncle Albert was looking at him in such a strange way, that words failed him.

"What do you mean, ages? And who went where? Where have they gone to?"

"They went to fetch the doctor," said Poppy. "It's Tuesday today and you said that was his fishing day. They've gone in *Luc*."

"But they can't have done that on their own ..."

His voice was very quiet; almost a whisper. Then he saw Laura's face and checked himself, sinking back on the couch.

"No ... I'm not cross ... to tell the truth, I don't know what I am ... I have to rest for a bit."

But as he closed his eyes Poppy grabbed his shoulder and shook him hard.

"I'm sorry," she said, "I thought you were ... it's when you close your eyes ... it makes me scared."

"Can I go and see whether they're coming?" Ian asked.

Laura poured a beaker of water and held it out to him.

"Alright, but drink this first. And you mustn't go far."

"No thanks, I drink straight from the pump. I worked out how. It's easy. And it's lots colder."

He stood by Uncle Albert's couch and looked down at him.

"Did you hear my bell?"

"So it was your bell ... I thought it was a dream."

"I found it," Ian added proudly.

"Of course we heard it," said Poppy. "It was worse than the dinner gong. Lots worse."

"If it's what I was dreaming about," said Uncle Albert, "there's quite a story to tell ... but I'm not sure ... was I really dreaming?"

"It woke you up," said Laura quietly then added in a very small voice, "just when we thought you'd never wake up."

"I'll ring it again for you, if you like," said Ian. "I use the little hammer – the one for the tents. The thing inside the bell that makes it ring has fallen off, but the tent hammer's just as good. I'll do it again so you can hear it properly. You can't do it much because it hurts your ears."

He started to trot towards the door, then stopped and came back.

"I'm jolly glad you're better."

There was a sudden wave of hot air in the room and a bright splash of yellow light then he was gone. Laura looked at the sodden wreckage everywhere.

"They must be here soon. I think I'll tidy up a bit before they get here."

*

Although the sun had started to sink, it was as hot as ever outside. Ian stood blinking in the glare. He looked round to find where he'd put the little hammer. It was resting on top of the lizards' stones. He picked it up and made his way round to the side of the house.

The sunken bell was waiting for him, hanging inside its huge wicker cage. He kneeled down and poked the hammer through the ribs.

Little flakes of green had fallen off where he'd hit it the first time. You could see the beginnings of shiny brass underneath. It would be nice to get it out somehow and clean it properly. Uncle Albert would know how. He pushed the hammer underneath the bell and turned his head away.

It really did make the most tremendous noise. He steadied himself and struck the metal as hard as he could, letting go of the hammer and falling back onto the sand to plug his ears with both hands.

It was like being under water, your head swimming with sound. He scrabbled back up the sand and reached into the wooden cage to fish the hammer out. He pushed his arm through, holding the hammer as high as it would go, then crashed it down with all his might. The bell swung violently back, throwing out a tremendously satisfying clang.

It was not at all like a church bell; in fact it was like no bell he had ever heard - an odd fractured sound that stayed singing in your head long afterwards. He backed away, his hands pressed hard against his ears.

*

After Ian had happily lapped his thirst away at the pump he filled a metal water bottle and went across to the iron gate. Through the trees you could see the tents of the camp. He'd said he would not go far, but, after all, you could see the camp and that wasn't far. What's more, the hamper was still in the camp. He gave a guilty look at the closed door of the Signal House, quietly opened the gate, and ran down through the trees.

The camp looked exactly the same: the silent tents, the groundsheet in front of Laura's fireplace, things scattered about where they'd been left, the little woodpile. And the wicker hamper.

He sat down next to it, disturbing a cicada hiding in a fold of the groundsheet. It took a few clumsy steps then jumped into the grass to join its friends. There must be hundreds of them, filling the air with their chirping.

He swung back the lid of the hamper. A wave of heat rose up and rather an odd smell. The bag of coconut cakes was still there with a satisfying bulge in it. Cakes didn't go off, he was sure of that. After all, you had to bake them in an oven just to make them.

He fished the bag out. There were still cakes inside, all stuck together. He broke off two. He let the lid of the hamper fall back and perched himself on top of it to eat his trophies. They were warm and sticky, but tasted as nice as ever.

There was a sound of slow footsteps scrunching up the path behind. He jumped up and saw the figure of a man struggling over the brow of the slope. A sad-looking man with a large moustache, carrying a leather bag. He was breathing heavily and looked extremely hot. Behind him in single file, strangely silent, came Stuart and Elizabeth looking very solemn.

Ian gave them a friendly wave and sank back down onto the hamper, grinning broadly. Stuart saw him and hurried on. He arrived first, hot and panting, followed shortly by Elizabeth. They stared silently down at him. Both had very grim looks. Ian managed his friendliest smile.

"It's alright, Laura said I could go outside so long as I didn't go far. And this isn't far really ... and I'm not wandering off."

Nobody said anything at all; they just went on staring at him.

"I ate two of the cakes ... there's some left ... I was a bit peckish."

The man with the moustache was staring at him now. Ian started to feel very uncomfortable. After all, it wasn't such a terrible thing to eat a few cakes. He tried again.

"Laura would say it's better somebody eats them up ... before they go off." He had saved his best argument till last.

"Anyway, Uncle Albert said I could ring the bell for him."

He looked accusingly at Elizabeth.

"You were away for ages and ages you know. And he was asleep all that time. He must have been jolly tired ..."

He stopped. He could think of nothing else to say. There was a stunned silence.

CHAPTER XXI

THE RESCUE PARTY

STUART kneeled down next to the hamper and put his arm round Ian's shoulders.

"You shouldn't be down here on your own - you know that. Does Laura know you're here?" He was talking in such a funny voice, Ian stared at him. "There's nothing for you to worry about, you know. You're alright now, we'll stay with you."

"You don't need to stay with me. And I'm not worried. It was Laura and Poppy who were worried. But they're alright now Uncle Albert isn't asleep anymore."

He wriggled round from under Stuart's arm.

"Do you know what was the matter with him? Laura says it was my bell that woke him up. She was scared – she didn't want you to see, but I know she was … and Poppy."

He turned defiantly to Elizabeth standing over him with a bewildered expression on her face. "I was a bit scared as well. Where did you go all this time?"

Nobody was speaking and they were both looking at him in such an odd way he began to feel very awkward.

"I've been thinking – we ought to get the sacks or we won't have anything to eat. You must have walked right past them."

Stuart started to answer when he realised the doctor was speaking. It was in French, and almost to himself, but he looked from one to another with a puzzled frown on his face, as if he half-hoped somebody would understand him. He saw Ian looking at him and started again in faltering English.

"What did you say then about your uncle? You said something about your Uncle Albert and a bell."

Ian had been waiting all afternoon to tell somebody about his great discovery. It was enough for him that he heard the word bell.

"That's right – Laura says it was the bell woke him up. It was me that found it. That was outside the little house of course. Then when I went inside, Uncle Albert asked if I'd ring it again. He'd been dreaming, you see." He settled back on his wicker seat and gathered his thoughts together. "I'd better start with when I first saw it." He swivelled round on the hamper and grinned at Stuart.

"You've not been round the side of the Signal House. There's a big pile of sand, you see ... a really big pile."

There was a sound of footsteps behind him and Ian turned to see the doctor hurrying away across the field towards the Signal House clutching the leather bag to his chest. He shouted back to them over his shoulder.

"Please stay here."

Ian shrugged. "Oh, he's gone. And I hadn't started."

Elizabeth was looking hard at Ian. She crouched down and took him by the shoulders. "Look – start again. We can hear about the bell another time. When did he wake up? Is he really alright? Are you sure?"

He shook her off.

"I know one thing, he was wet all over. Laura had been mopping him with water for ages. There's water all over the place. It was me got the water for them - buckets and buckets of it. Poppy helped with the pump at first, but then it was just me."

He held his hand up and showed her the sore spot.

Elizabeth slumped down on the ground and sat clutching her knees. If Ian had not known that this was Elizabeth, and so it was impossible, her eyes seemed suddenly to be swimming. She sat grinning to herself for a long time, rocking back and forth, then threw him such a cheerful smile that he smiled back.

It was Ian who eventually broke the silence.

"I think Poppy was fanning him with something. I'm not sure. I didn't go inside much. You can ask her."

"And you say he just woke up?" said Stuart. A wave of tiredness swept over him. He sat down on the groundsheet next to Elizabeth. Neither of them spoke. Ian handed him the water bottle. He took it, picked up two beakers from where they had been lying since breakfast, and filled them.

"I don't know where Poppy got the fan from," Ian continued, "but that's what she was doing ... fanning. So I filled the buckets and carried them to the house ... then there was the bell ... shall I tell you about the bell?"

Ian was about to begin when he saw two rather bedraggled sisters making their way across the field. Stuart recognised the doctor's water bottle in Poppy's hand.

"The doctor sent us out," said Laura. "He wanted to talk to Uncle Albert on his own." She looked at the two figures sitting silently hunched together in front of the dead camp fire.

"He had that thing for listening to your chest," added Poppy, "and he mixed up something in a big glass. Fizzy stuff full of bubbles. Then he told us to come and bring you something to drink."

Laura filled the beakers and passed them round. She saw Stuart looking at her hands. They seemed to tremble all on their own. There was nothing she could do about them.

"You were a long time coming back," she said. "Were you looking for the doctor?"

"He's very nice," said Poppy. "He sat down next to Uncle Albert and held his wrist. You know, the way doctors do. Then he noticed how wet it was everywhere and found he was sitting in a great big puddle of water. But he didn't even get up. He just smiled."

"And he made a little speech in French," said Laura. "He knew we couldn't understand, but I think he wanted to say it in French because it sounded better that way. It sounded very grand. Uncle knew what he was saying because he nodded."

Poppy wanted to finish the story. "Then the doctor shooed us out," she said. "But he looked very pleased, all the same."

Laura collected some sticks together and crouched down over the fireplace.

"I'll get the fire going. It's been such a terrible time, I'd forgotten we've not had anything to eat. We'll have to get those sacks up from where we left them."

"I didn't forget," said Ian. "About eating, I mean. I ate some of the little cakes. Shall I go and get one of the sacks? It's not far."

Elizabeth rubbed her face then looked at her hands.

"No, I'll go. I don't know what's the matter with me. I'm half asleep. I need to put my head under that pump of yours. But I'll scout around for the food first. Although I can't promise to be very quick about it."

"I can help," said Ian. "If you only bring one sack, I can hold the end. I can tell you about the bell on the way."

She got up stiffly and stretched her back.

"No, you stay here. I'll be quicker on my own."

*

For the first time ever, Laura took several matches to start the fire. She watched as the little bundle of moss smoked itself out, leaving a faint bitter smell hanging in the air. Ian kneeled down to help, but she waved him away impatiently.

"You're standing in my light. I can't see with your shadow everywhere."

Stuart gave him a look as if to say 'leave her alone'. He walked across to the tents and tugged at the guy ropes.

"They could do with being a bit tighter. Come and give me a hand Ian."

When they were working behind the first tent he leaned over to whisper.

"I think she's awfully tired. Poppy as well."

"They used up buckets and buckets. I'm tired as well ... we'll be better when we've eaten something. Breakfast was ages and ages ago and all I've had is two little cakes."

"Run and see whether you can give Elizabeth a hand. She'll be here in a minute. Then we can all eat something."

Ian signalled to Poppy, but she shook her head and stayed slumped on the grass looking a little dazed.

He shrugged and set off trotting towards the top of the slope just as Elizabeth appeared with a sack slung over her back. He took up station behind her, taking a little of the weight, and the two of them tottered into the camp. She dumped the sack on the ground.

"I looked inside. This one's the most likely. There's bottles of soup. And a giant loaf of bread ... and there's some tin bowls. I could get another sack if you like ... now I'm up and about I feel a bit better."

"This will do," said Laura. "We can use the frying pan. It's not exactly clean, but I wiped it out. I'll put it on the fire for a while – that should do. We'll heat up the soup. We'll have to eat soon, it's getting dark."

Elizabeth pulled the neck of the sack open and fished out a large glass bottle with a metal ring at the top. There were white beans and bits of meat floating inside. She tried to twist the lid off but eventually shook her head and passed it to Stuart.

He wrapped his handkerchief round the jar and they watched him strain until he was red in the face. As he was about to abandon it, the top suddenly came off in his hand and they were surrounded by the delicious smell of rich soup.

Laura perched the frying pan on the stones and checked it was steady. She carefully emptied the bottle out, pouring until the pan was brimful.

"There's some left in the bottle. We can heat it up while we're finishing the first lot."

She spread the bowls out and unwrapped the bread, snapping a little piece off and tasting it.

"It's a bit hard but it's not really stale." She smelled it, "I think it's fine. It'll go with the soup anyway."

She looked across to where Poppy was sprawled out, her back against the wicker basket. Her eyes were closed.

"I think she's gone to sleep," said Ian. "Shall I wake her up?"

"I'm not asleep … well not really … I could hear you all talking. It was just easier listening with my eyes closed a bit." She sat up and sniffed the air. "Something smells lovely. I'm awfully hungry. I don't think I've had anything at all since breakfast."

*

The handle of the frying pan was much too hot to touch, so Laura spooned the soup out into the bowls. Then she emptied what was left in the bottle into the pan for seconds. She snapped the bread into chunks and handed it round, remembering how Uncle Albert said hands came first.

Nobody spoke for a long time as they drank their soup, capturing little bits of meat with chunks of bread. When the second helping started to bubble Laura spooned it round using her handkerchief to lift the pan off the fire. Ian dipped his bread into the hot pan, mopping up the last of the soup. He went over to the sack and looked inside.

"There's some apples in here. Shall we have them for afters?"

Laura nodded. The soup had been very tasty but one bottle was hardly enough for five of them.

She had just decided to look inside the sack for more soup when there was the noise of footsteps and she looked up to see the doctor standing next to the first tent. He was carrying another bottle of water in one hand.

He walked across to them with a curious expression on his face. He seemed very pleased and a little shy at the same time. He put the bottle on the ground and cleared his throat.

"Are Elizabeth and Stuart here?" He was peering round in the fading light, looking from face to face. Eventually, he spotted Elizabeth and smiled.

"I came to tell you your uncle is well. He is a little tired but he is quite well. I will stay with him tonight. I suggest you visit him in the morning ... it is too late now and he must sleep." He hesitated again and they could see he was thinking how best to say something.

"I wanted to say ... what you did with the boat ... it was necessary ... it was right you came for me ... it was the right thing to do ..." He seemed to be struggling again to find the words, "... foolish perhaps, but you did the right thing."

He put a hand on Elizabeth's shoulder, "One might say foolish ... but very brave. Both of you ... very brave."

The fire seemed to be burning brighter now, sending yellow shadows dancing across the grass. Night was drawing in round them. They could no longer see his face very clearly.

"Is Uncle really alright?" Elizabeth's voice out of the darkness spoke for all of them. Poppy was the closest and she looked into his face, her heart thumping in her throat.

"Perfectly. He is perfectly well. It is astonishing. I did not expect it ... he is perfectly well. But we can talk about that in the morning."

He gave a formal little bow, then he was gone. They heard retreating footsteps and watched his figure blend into the shadowed field and finally disappear.

It was as if something tight holding them all together had suddenly snapped. Laura looked at Elizabeth.

"If you light a lamp, I'll look for another bottle of that soup."

"You're right. The soup was nice but there wasn't enough of it. We should crack open a few more of the stores. No point going to bed hungry. It isn't as if there's any hurry. We're at home, after all."

*

As the second bottle of soup started to bubble, a little breeze got up. The comforting swish of leaves in the darkness surrounded the little camp. Laura spooned out helpings into each bowl by the light of the oil lamp, the tents no more than vague pale shapes on the edge of the darkness.

Poppy prodded Ian awake and he ate the last of his bread, mopping up soup from the pan.

They sat in silence, staring up into a black sky filling with huge stars. An owl screeched from somewhere above their heads.

Not even Laura could find the strength to stand up. She let waves of sleep sweep over her and closed her eyes, only to wake with a start as her head fell forward. She could see Elizabeth lying across the hamper, her head buried in both arms. It looked very uncomfortable, but she was fast asleep.

Stuart had let Ian lean against him and now the two of them were breathing quietly together. There was a moment of panic when Poppy was nowhere to be seen, then Laura saw her, curled up in a little ball on the edge of the groundsheet.

This would never do. She shook her head and struggled up, prodding Stuart with her foot. He woke with a start, grabbing hold of Ian. Poppy sat up and said, "What's that?" then nestled down again.

Laura shook Elizabeth's shoulder.

"Wake up! You must wake up! We can't lie out here all night. We've got to go to bed properly. No teeth, just for this once. It's too dark anyway. But everybody into bed. Come on, I'll hold the lamp for you."

She hauled Poppy up by the arm and handed the oil lamp to Stuart.

"Go on, you take it. And hold on to Ian, he's falling over. It's alright, we can see the way. Good night ... good night."

"Good old Laura," said Elizabeth. "Glad to see you're back to knocking us into shape." And Laura knew she was smiling. "I want to see that uncle of mine in the morning. He's got a lot of explaining to do."

CHAPTER XXII

THE BROKEN BELL

STUART wriggled into his hollow in the sand and fell asleep before he had time to pull the blanket round his shoulders. But it was not to last. A storm roaring across the sea in his dream eventually woke him to the sound of wind creaking at the canvas of the tent. The pole near his head was straining against the roof and shifting slightly on its wooden block. Outside, branches were tossing and shaking.

He sat up to listen. The noise of the wind was everywhere. Bits of branch and old acorns were bouncing off the tent and hitting the groundsheet. A water bottle left by the fire went bowling away, clattering into the night.

He risked a flash of the torch. Ian was lying peacefully with the blankets pulled tight around his head in case of bats.

The flap at the door had been tugged half open and a cool breeze was streaming into the tent. The weather had broken. The sticky heat had gone. The air on his face was night air, sweet and fresh, almost chilly sitting up, but worth it just to breathe.

A distant rumble of thunder seemed to shake the earth. But it was far away, well beyond the mountains. He nestled down again into the hollow, remembering how Uncle Albert had visited the cottage that night - so long ago he'd almost forgotten about it. He said it hardly ever rained here.

He closed his eyes and fell back into a restless dream. He was trying to reach something in a motor boat but had forgotten what it was. An uncomfortable sort of dream that seemed to go on aimlessly drumming in his ears. Then the engine in the boat stopped and the sudden silence woke him to sunlight and broad day.

He stared at canvas walls, bright with a strange morning sun, and wondered what had happened to the door, struggling to remember where he was.

As he rolled over to see whether Ian was awake, there was the crack of a branch outside. The wind of the night before had dropped and everywhere was very still. Just a few birds starting their morning twitter.

There was no doubt about it, somebody had stepped on a branch. It must be that deer again, looking for water. He smiled as soft feet shuffled on the edge of the groundsheet, waiting for a hoof-clink against the water bottle. But none came. Then, as he was pulling the blanket round his ears, there was a cough. A very human cough.

Stuart rolled out of his blanket and crawled towards the flap in the door. This wasn't a deer. These steps were human steps and they were getting closer. A kind of soft tramping noise behind the tent. There must be lots of them, whoever they were.

A single shadow like a puppet show passed across the canvas wall, then another, then another. A whole line of people walking through the camp. People wearing tall round hats with little peaks.

Suddenly, two shadows in the puppet show faltered and the whole tent twitched violently. For a second the shape of a hand pressed against the canvas. There was a soft grunt and a rustle of bodies stumbling about. Somebody had tripped over a guy rope.

A deep voice said 'shush", but loud enough to wake the whole island. If they were trying to be quiet, this particular herd of elephants was making a poor job of it. They thumped through the camp, breathing heavily, and out into the field beyond.

Stuart pulled the flap back and stepped outside in time to see a procession of men lumbering slowly across the grass. They were wearing dark blue uniforms and big gold and black helmets. They must have decided they were out of earshot because they were talking quietly to each other now.

One of them had stopped and was looking at a map. He pointed and they all set off, making for the trees and the Signal House beyond.

Two of the smaller elephants at the back struggled with some long poles, bound round with canvas. They shared the load between them and tottered doggedly across the field.

Poppy and Elizabeth must have heard the noise and were standing outside their tent looking across towards the Signal House, shading their eyes against the low sun. Poppy was dressed. She had combed her hair and was holding her sketch book. A very tousled Elizabeth was still in pyjamas.

"Good morning," whispered Poppy. "Isn't it a lovely day? Sunny, but not so hot anymore. Is Ian still asleep? I thought I'd go for my lesson. I'm not hungry yet – I won't be very long."

She saw Stuart looking doubtful and pressed on.

"No, it's alright, it was the very first thing he said when he woke up. He asked about my lesson ... anyway, if he doesn't feel like it, I can just say hello and come right back."

And she was off, trotting briskly across the field before he had time to say anything.

Stuart turned to Elizabeth and shook his head.

"It's no use trying to stop her, honestly. Best let her go." He pointed towards the Signal House.

"Who were all those men? They looked like firemen."

"That's what you do in France when you want an ambulance. Uncle told me. You call the fire brigade. The doctor must have arranged it."

"But how did they get here?"

"Another motor boat. I heard it. It arrived at first light. They must have been hanging about for ages. Looking for the landing place I suppose. The engine woke me up. I was dreaming about motor boats all night."

"So was I," said Stuart, then he laughed. "I wonder why?"

Elizabeth went back into her tent.

"I'll get dressed then we can go and see what's going on. Lesson or no lesson, I want to see how he is."

"Breakfast first!" It was Laura's voice. A very cheerful Laura hurriedly pulling clothes on and giggling as she tripped over Elizabeth who was trying to do the same thing. "This won't do – I overslept again. I'll find us something to eat. Ian and Poppy were eating at all hours yesterday."

She called out again.

"Is Ian up yet? Tell Poppy to stay here – she's not to go running off until she's eaten something."

"Too late," said Stuart, "she's already gone." He laughed.

"She said she didn't want to eat. She must have got up at dawn to be ready for her lesson. I'd better get dressed – I won't be a minute." He went back into the tent to wake Ian up.

*

Poppy missed a splendid breakfast. Elizabeth found another set of tin plates in the sack and laid them out neatly on the groundsheet while Laura sorted out the food.

"It'll have to be cold things. I'm not starting the fire. But there's lots of fruit here. Pears and figs ... and this ..." She had buried both hands in the sack and was heaving out a huge melon. "We could cut it up ... if we had a knife."

Stuart ran and got his penknife from the tent and began work, hacking at the melon.

"It's all very well, but they don't eat what you could call a proper breakfast in France," said Elizabeth. She was squinting at the label on a squat little bottle.

"It's in French - it would be. And handwriting, what's more!"

"I know what that is," said Ian emerging blinking in the morning sun.

"It's jam. Jolly nice. Breakfast jam ... although I suppose you could have it any time."

Laura unwrapped last night's bread.

"There's lots left. We may as well eat it up - it will only go stale. No butter, of course. But we'll manage."

She used the last of the water to wash out the beakers that had been left standing all night then stood a huge bottle of pink lemonade in the centre of the groundsheet for everybody to help themselves. She lifted the lid of the hamper.

"That's the last of the coconut cakes - unless there's some more in the other sacks. We'll have to look."

"Save a couple," said Elizabeth. "I've had an idea. We'll take something to Uncle. For breakfast. He'll probably be hungry by now."

They sat down on the grass eating and talking, and looking about as the new day woke the birds in the woods around them.

Laura sliced two thick pieces of bread and made a huge sandwich of jam. She flattened out the coconut cake packet and popped it inside, murmuring, "That'll do very well ... he'll like that ... we've no distance to go."

She saw Stuart watching her and grinned at him. "Cooks talk to themselves, remember?"

Elizabeth cut out a very piratical chunk of melon and balanced it on a tin plate. She added a few figs and a peach. "I'll just carry it like this."

"It's a pity we can't make him coffee," said Laura. "We don't have any."

"He's got a little stove in the Signal House," said Ian. "He makes coffee on that."

Elizabeth suddenly grabbed the paper packet from her hand.

"You were going to drop that - a penny for your thoughts. You've been standing there for ages. Come on! It's no use waiting for Poppy, she's not coming back. We'll take her something for breakfast. And an apple. She can eat it, if she doesn't want to paint it."

*

They heard the sound of voices long before they reached the Signal House. Lots of voices, laughing and shouting. The little garden round the pump seemed to be full of men. When the men in uniform had filed past the tents they had all seemed very solemn, but that had changed.

Somebody had carried chairs outside and they were sitting in a circle by the door, talking and drinking coffee. One of the men poured something into his coffee and passed a little silver flask to his neighbour. They all seemed very merry.

The two tall poles wrapped round with canvas had been abandoned and were propped up against the wall.

As the four of them reached the little iron gate, the smell of tobacco and coffee was overpowering. Somebody spotted Laura pushing at the gate and they all stopped talking. There was a great scraping of chairs and shuffling of feet and everybody stood up.

Laura hesitated for a moment then stepped forward, carrying Uncle Albert's breakfast parcel in both hands.

It was a bit scary walking past a silent herd of elephants, but as she neared the door they began to stamp their feet and clap.

Then one of them lifted off his peaked helmet and waved it, shouting something she didn't understand.

Laura threw a desperate look back at the others, but as Stuart and Elizabeth plucked up courage and walked down to join her, the noise of laughing and clapping and whistling grew even louder. One of the older elephants came forward and shook Stuart's hand then turned and grinned broadly at the rest.

The noise kept Ian hesitating at the gate for a long time, but finally he made up his mind and stepped onto the little path. He got as far as the pump when the group fell silent again and a man in a splendid uniform stepped forward. Ian would have said he was one of the bigger elephants, although they all seemed enormous.

He stood towering above him, then solemnly lifted off his helmet and held it out. It was made of shiny black metal with a big gold crest across the front. The man looked very serious but when he saw Ian's anxious face looking up, a tiny smile crinkled the corner of his mouth.

Ian had no idea what to do. There was a burst of applause and he found himself inside the dark of the metal, the top of his head pressed hard against leather webbing. It was surprisingly heavy; so heavy, it tipped forward and the whole world suddenly went black.

Dimly echoing outside there was the sound of people clapping. He pushed the helmet up and found himself looking at a line of cheerful faces. Even Stuart and Laura were clapping and Elizabeth, grinning from ear to ear, was rattling her hands on the tin plate.

The man in the uniform stepped back and composed his face into a serious expression. The laughter fell away and the little garden in front of the Signal House became very still and quiet.

It was a short speech and Ian had no idea what it meant. But when it ended, the tall man straightened his back and saluted. Then he broke into the friendliest of smiles and seized Ian's hand, shaking it so vigorously the helmet slid down and had to be rescued and solemnly placed back in his arms.

Then everybody went on sipping their coffee and talking together.

"I think he means it's yours to keep," laughed Elizabeth, tapping the hard metal of the helmet. "It looks like they've made you a fireman."

The doctor appeared in the doorway to see what the noise was all about. He shook hands with all of them in turn.

"Yes, it's the fire brigade. I asked them to come. I expected I would find someone here very ill. Someone in need of the hospital. Or worse ..."

He stopped speaking, looking thoughtfully out over the crowd milling about. "Yes, or worse ... but I was wrong."

He smiled as he saw Ian struggling to fit his head under the peak of the brass helmet.

"Ah, the young man with the bell. Yes ... they have all heard your story. And they are very pleased." He beckoned them inside.

*

The shutters in the Signal House had been flung back and the window was open. The room was filled with sunlight. Two bowls of coffee stood on the table, steam drifting up in a soft breeze.

The floor was dry and swept clean. There was no sign of Poppy's fans. No sign of anything, in fact, to remind them of the endless hours of yesterday. Nothing, that is, apart from a familiar form sprawled out on the couch. A smiling Uncle Albert, Poppy seated at his side. He had been drawing something in a sketch pad. He folded it closed and looked at Elizabeth.

"Hello niece. Now, before you go saying anything, let's agree not to. Not now. Later. It's one thing for me to owe you lot a boat. But now I owe you ... well, just look here ... we'll have to talk about it later."

He reached out and pulled her arm down.

"What's on the plate? Something to eat, with luck. One thing I'll say about doctors – they seem to forget people have to eat."

"It's breakfast." Elizabeth was still awkwardly clutching the plate. "Nothing much really."

"Laura made you a jam sandwich as well," said Ian. "A really big one."

"That's handsome of her, I must say. I forget when I last had anything to eat. Let's have a look."

As he peered into the paper package, he caught Laura looking at his face. He took her hand and patted the couch at his side for her to sit down.

"Hello, Laura. Well, I hear you do more than scamper up ladders. I saw you checking whether my old head had been polished enough with all that sponging. When the doctor here rushed you away yesterday, I had no idea what you had been up to." He turned and looked at Poppy.

"This one, too. What am I to say?"

The doctor heard his name and came across to stand next to them. Uncle Albert pointed at him.

"I can't stop him talking about it. Not that I want to. If he has his way, you'll be famous. He wants to call it 'Laura's and Poppy's Cure.' I told him it's a bit of a mouthful, even in French, but you never know."

The doctor had been listening intently. He held out a little notebook.

"I have already written down what you did with the water and with the fan. You have made a remarkable discovery, believe me. Remarkable."

"I fetched the water ... the pump was my job," said Ian.

"Yes, of course. You fetched the water. And it was you that rang the bell. I thought no one would ever hear that bell again. When I heard it last I was with your uncle. At sea. You could say we were in difficulty..." He saw Uncle Albert's face and checked himself.

"Perhaps he will tell you that story himself. But to hear that bell in the middle of a wood! I could not believe my ears."

"You can believe that bell alright," said Uncle Albert. "If it hadn't been for that, I would be still asleep now." He turned to Poppy.

"You'll have to wait for your lesson until we get back, young lady. Up you get – no time now."

Poppy jumped down, folding her sketch book closed.

"Get back where?"

"The doctor says I have to go back to the Pink House so that he can prod me a bit more. I'll go in the boat with those chaps outside. You can come with me if you like. I must say they were so relieved when he told them they didn't have to carry me all the way to the landing stage, they've been celebrating ever since."

Ian suddenly thought of something.

"What about us? Are we going to stay on the island on our own?"

"No, you're coming as well." He saw Ian's face.

"Don't fret, you can come back ... if you want to, that is. Anyway Cook knows we're coming and she'll certainly be fretting. I'll ask her to make us something special." He chuckled. "What would you say to tomato soup?"

*

In a little while the shutters had been closed and the Signal House locked up. They made their way down to the camp site, Uncle Albert walking a little unsteadily hand in hand with Poppy. The elephants kept them company until they reached the camp then they lumbered off to get their boat ready.

Uncle Albert sat patiently on the grass while Elizabeth and Laura packed up their few things and fastened the flaps to the tents. Ian sat down next to Uncle Albert.

"We're really coming back, aren't we? You're not just saying that?"

"If the doctor lets me. And he can't find anything wrong with me, so I don't see why not. Oh, and if your mother says yes. She'll be here soon now. That's two ifs, but you never know. Anyway, do you want to come back?"

As he asked the question he lifted his head and looked hard at Laura. "Island life has its problems, you know."

You could see Laura was about to say something but she changed her mind and gave Uncle Albert a special smile, as if they were sharing a secret.

"Come on, Elizabeth," she said, "I think we're ready."

*

At the landing stage, a huge motor boat painted bright red and with its own boarding plank was tied up alongside *Luc*.

Uncle Albert shook hands with the doctor and the tall fireman without a helmet helped him aboard. Poppy turned to look at the others, hesitating for a second, then made up her mind and followed him across the plank.

"You won't be long behind us, I dare say," shouted Uncle Albert as they pulled away.

"But we'll be home first. We'll save you some lemonade."

*

But *Luc* was a much smaller boat and much slower and it was a long time before they arrived at the Pink House. No sooner had they disembarked at the jetty when the doctor decided he had to drive first to his own house. So they bumped their way through the woods to the house with green shutters, to be greeted by the doctor's wife.

When she had heard their story she would not dream of letting them go until they had sat down to cake and lemonade.

Then the doctor asked Stuart whether he would like to see the room where the patients came. Stuart glanced at the door with the brass plaque. It was very tempting, but Elizabeth was itching to go.

He was trying to think of a polite way of saying no when Ian decided matters by shouting, 'Yes please'. Then more time was lost persuading Ian to leave his precious helmet on the bench outside.

Although they had no idea what she was saying, and Elizabeth and Laura were in an agony of impatience, a smiling doctor's wife led them out into the garden and sat them on swinging chairs while she pointed at the roses.

Then Elizabeth remembered Cook's way of tapping at her wrist and the doctor's wife burst out laughing and led them out into the hall to rap on the door with the brass plaque.

*

The doctor left the four of them at the end of the clay path that led down to the terrace of the Pink House and drove away, promising to come back later to see Uncle Albert. They waved him goodbye.

The house stood waiting for them, surrounded as ever by the sound of pigeons talking to each other and the familiar scent of sweet blossom.

As they crossed the terrace, they heard Poppy's voice asking endless questions and Uncle Albert's occasional chuckle as he tried to answer.

Mrs Bradley was sitting at one end of the table, talking to Cook. She broke off and waved to them then turned and started to pour out beakers of lemonade.

Poppy's lesson was in full swing. She was sitting alongside Uncle Albert, her sketch pad open on her lap. He was pointing to Cook.

"Go on, draw Pia – I mean Cook ... she won't mind at all. It's no use me doing it; you have to."

Poppy looked across as Cook turned to the kitchen door.

"But it's too late. She's moving."

"Just hurry up. That's what people do. They jump about. That's what they're for. No use asking them to stand still. Have a go before she goes altogether. Go on. Honestly, you don't want her standing still. You've had a good look at her lots of times – just do it."

He tapped Poppy's arm with his pencil.

"I'll tell you what. I'll let you have six lines." He chuckled, "Alright, I'm joking. But not many. As few as you can get away with."

Poppy still hesitated and he grabbed the sketch book impatiently from her, jabbing at it with a pencil.

"There. Like that. And I said I wouldn't do it for you."

She looked down at the book and shook her head. "I don't know how you do that, I really don't."

"Oh yes you do. You just don't know you do. Go on. Have a go."

Poppy turned the page and sat staring at it. She glanced up briefly as Cook opened the kitchen door then attacked the little paper pad. It was all over in a few seconds.

Uncle Albert took it from her and sat holding it up in the sunlight. He didn't speak for a long time.

"That's right. You've got her." He pointed at the pad with his pencil.

"This here - you can see that's wrong ... but it's pretty well right." He sat tapping the paper. "Ten lines, I think."

He gave a mock sigh and shook his head, handing her the little book.

"You know, it took me a year to get that right ... it's not going to take you that long."

He looked up as the others stood watching.

"That's the lesson over for today. Off you go, all of you. Showers all round. But be quick about it. I have a day's food to catch up."

*

Ian won the race to be first with the shower. The water did get a little colder the more you used, but nobody froze and in much less than an hour it would have been hard to recognise the well-scrubbed crowd sitting round the terrace table as travel-worn explorers fresh from their camp.

Laura persuaded Ian that he would not be able to eat anything at all wearing his helmet, so it was placed carefully under his chair with a promise that Uncle Albert would do a special drawing called 'The New Fireman' first thing in the morning.

Uncle Albert tapped the side of his glass and stood up.

"No, I'm not making a speech ... well, I might, but that's for later. While we're waiting for Cook I thought you might like to hear a story. It's a story about a bell. Not the one about two young men all at sea in a little boat in the dark. You already heard that one.

No, this is the story of a broken bell you might say, because no one's heard it ring for many a year. And it's a story for Ian to tell." Uncle Albert sat down and beamed round the table.

"Come on Ian, remember to start at the beginning."

Ian looked across at Laura and Poppy. He wondered whether he should stand up then decided it would be nicer sitting down. That way if he forgot bits, he could get them to help out. He collected his thoughts.

Where should he start?

THE END

I agree - it's not nice at all to turn a page and find yourself reading "THE END" when you know perfectly well this can't really be the end. So what happened next? You will have to read *The Pink House* to find out.

Meanwhile, if you don't know already, and you want to find out more about the great storm and the rescue of Uncle Albert's old boat, you must read *The Boat in the Bay*.

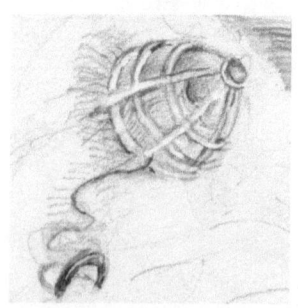